9

Books by Dan O'Brien

THE INDIAN AGENT
BUFFALO FOR THE BROKEN HEART
THE CONTRACT SURGEON
EQUINOX
BRENDAN PRAIRIE
IN THE CENTER OF THE NATION
THE RITES OF AUTUMN
SPIRIT OF THE HILLS
EMINENT DOMAIN

DAN O'BRIEN

THE INDIAN AGENT

HarperTorch
An Imprint of HarperCollinsPublishers

❦

HARPERTORCH
An Imprint of HarperCollins*Publishers*
10 East 53rd Street
New York, New York 10022-5299

Copyright © 2004 by Dan O'Brien
ISBN-13: 978-0-06-082381-8
ISBN-10: 0-06-082381-X

First HarperTorch paperback printing: January 2006

HarperCollins®, HarperTorch™, and ❦ ™ are trademarks of HarperCollins Publishers Inc.

Printed in the United States of America

Visit HarperTorch on the World Wide Web at www.harpercollins.com

10 9 8 7 6 5 4 3 2 1

This book's for Jill

Author's Note

This is the story of two strong men forced together by events so large that even their considerable egos were dwarfed. They did the best they could with what they had. And what they had were the tools that their very different cultures gave them—McGillycuddy from a protestant, Irish, immigrant family, and Red Cloud from the Oglala sub-band of the Lakota division of Sioux Nation. In many ways their goals were similar, but their respective cultures cast them as adversaries, even as the realities of conquest threatened to crush them along with the entire Great Plains of North America.

Though this is a fictional version of the events at Pine Ridge during the tenure of Agent Valentine T. McGillycuddy, most of the events depicted actually took place—most of the characters lived. But the events and characters that make up the history of the early days of the Pine Ridge Reservation are sometimes muddled by the passage of time and according to whoever is supplying the account. I chose the accounts that best lent themselves to the telling of the story. On occasion I blended minor characters to give the reader a better picture of the type of men and women who surrounded

McGillycuddy and Red Cloud. The serious historian will notice that events are left out. This was done to save the more casual reader from the tedium that was the hallmark of nineteenth-century Indian policy. For those who relish this sort of detail, I recommend the thousands of government documents on the subject and have included the following partial bibliography:

Ambrose, Stephen E. *Crazy Horse and Custer: The Parallel Lives of Two American Warriors*. Garden City: Doubleday and Company, 1975.

Andrist, Ralph K. *The Long Death: The Last Days of the Plains*. New York: Collier Books, 1993.

Bourke, John G. *On the Border with Crook*. Lincoln: The University of Nebraska Press, 1971.

Brown, Dee. *Bury My Heart at Wounded Knee*. New York: Henry Holt and Co., 2001.

Clark, Robert A., ed. *The Killing of Crazy Horse*. Lincoln: The University of Nebraska Press, 1988.

Connell, Evan S. *The Son of the Morning Star: Custer and the Little Bighorn*. New York: Harper Trade, 1991.

Driving Hawk Sneve, Virginia. *They Led a Nation: The Sioux Chiefs*. Sioux Falls, South Dakota: Brevet Press, 1975.

Eastman, Charles Alexander. *The Soul of the Indian: An Interpretation*. Lincoln: The University of Nebraska Press, 1980.

Hyde, George. *Red Cloud's Folk: A History of the*

Oglala Sioux Indians. Norman: The University of Oklahoma Press, 1937.

McGillycuddy, Julia B. *Blood on the Moon: Valentine McGillycuddy and the Sioux.* Lincoln: The University of Nebraska Press, 1990.

Neihardt, John G., and Black Elk. *Black Elk Speaks.* Lincoln: The University of Nebraska Press, 1988.

Olson, James C. *Red Cloud and the Sioux Problem.* Lincoln: The University of Nebraska Press, 1975.

Powers, William K. *Oglala Religion.* Lincoln: The University of Nebraska Press, 1982.

Robinson, Charles M., III. *A Good Year to Die: The Story of the Great Sioux War.* New York: Random House, 1995.

Sandoz, Mari. *Cheyenne Autumn.* New York: Hastings House, 1975.

Smith, Rex Allen. *Moon of Popping Trees.* Lincoln: University of Nebraska Press, 1981.

Starita, Joe. *The Dull Knives of Pine Ridge: A Lakota Odyssey.* New York: Harper Collins, 1995.

Walker, James R., and Elaine A. Jahner, eds. *Lakota Myth.* Lincoln: The University of Nebraska Press, 1983.

Chronology of Events

1822—Red Cloud is born into a small band of Oglala Sioux known as the Bad Faces.

1841 Autumn—After several years of distinguishing himself in raiding parties against other plains Indian tribes, Red Cloud solidifies his reputation as a warrior by killing Bull Bear, the chief of a band of Sioux feuding with the Bad Faces.

1841–1849—Red Cloud leads many successful raiding parties against other Great Plains tribes.

1849 February 14—Valentine Trant McGillycuddy is born in Racine, Wisconsin. Soon after, his immigrant Irish Presbyterian family moves to Detroit, Michigan.

1850—Red Cloud concocts a mixture of cedar needles and bark, which is believed to cure cholera. He becomes known as a medicine man.

1865 April—End of the American Civil War. Rebels surrender at Appomattox Court House, freeing the world's largest army to pacify the western frontier.

1866—Gold fields in Montana open. Red Cloud opposes the use of the Bozeman Trail to service the gold field. He advocates war and the United States decides to protect the trail by building and maintaining a series of forts across what is now northeastern Wyoming. The conflict is soon designated as Red Cloud's War.

September—Valentine McGillycuddy enters medical school at the Marine Hospital in Detroit, at age seventeen.

December 21—The Sioux, possibly acting under Red Cloud's order and led by Crazy Horse, decoy Captain William J. Fetterman and eighty men. They are massacred to a man.

1867—Bozeman Trail is effectively closed by Red Cloud's warriors who lay siege to the forts and maintain a steady harassment of all attempts at travel.

1868 April 29—Fort Laramie Treaty (also known as the treaty of 1868) is signed, ending Red Cloud's War. The treaty calls for the cessation of hostilities, punishment by the United States government for persons committing crimes against the Sioux, the surrender of any Sioux committing crimes against U.S. citizens, and the opening of any roads deemed necessary by the U.S. (except the Bozeman Trail). The treaty provides for annuities to be paid to the Sioux in return for peace. Indian children are to be educated by the U.S., and farmable land and farming implements provided. A reservation, made up of all lands in the present state of South Dakota west of the Missouri River, is established. The reservation includes the Black Hills and the treaty provides that no white man "shall ever be permitted to pass over, settle upon, or reside in the territory." Red Cloud and many other leaders sign the treaty but Crazy

Horse and Sitting Bull retreat to the north and continue resistance.

June—Valentine McGillycuddy graduates from medical school and joins the faculty at the Detroit Marine Hospital.

November 27—General George Armstrong Custer destroys Chief Black Kettle's Cheyennes on the Washita River in present-day Oklahoma. The village is attacked without reconnaissance, at dawn while Indians slept. Over one hundred men, women, and children are killed as they awake. Custer becomes known as Son of the Morning Star.

1870—Red Cloud makes his first trip to Washington to meet with the president of the United States.

1871—McGillycuddy joins Great Lakes Survey and directs a crew that resurveys Chicago after the Great Fire of 1871. He begins courting Fanny Hoyt.

1872—Red Cloud visits Washington to argue against the plan to settle his people on the Missouri River.

1873—McGillycuddy accepts position as topographer and surgeon with the international survey of the boundary between the United States and British America. It is his first contact with the Sioux and their way of life.

1874—Red Cloud finally agrees to be settled on the White River in present-day Nebraska under Indian Agent J. J. Saville.

1875 April—Red Cloud goes to Washington to complain about Agent Saville but is met by pressure to support selling the Black Hills.

June—McGillycuddy, as a member of the Newton-Jennings Survey, enters the Black Hills for the first time. He is the first white man to climb Harney Peak, the highest point in the Black Hills and holy site for the Lakota Sioux.

Autumn—McGillycuddy and Fanny Hoyt marry in Detroit, Michigan.

Autumn and Winter—White miners stream into the Black Hills, a blatant violation of the treaty of 1868, and conflicts between the Indians and whites increase.

December—Indians not on reservations in accord with the treaty of 1868 are declared hostile and advised to move to the reservations or face military action.

1876 January 31—The deadline for all northern Sioux to be on Dakota reservations. Few have complied.

February 1—Driven by rumors of an imminent attack on the miners in the Black Hills, Indian affairs are turned over to the War Department. Agents are replaced by military men, and war is declared on non-reservation Indians concentrated in what is now Montana.

March 17—Colonel Joseph J. Reynolds attacks and destroys Cheyenne Village on the Powder River, marking the beginning of the Yellowstone campaign by driving survivors out into the subzero winter.

April—Armies of Terry, Crook, and Gibbon begin to converge on the Sioux in the Powder River country.

June 25—General Custer is totally defeated at Little Bighorn Creek by the bands of Crazy Horse, Sitting Bull, and others.

Autumn and Winter—Revenge for the Custer defeat is extracted over the next six months and all hostiles are eventually killed or driven to the reservations. Red Cloud sits the war out but talks alliance with both sides.

1877–1878—Red Cloud is forced to move to the hated Missouri River but he remains recalcitrant and finally wins a new location for his agency—the newly named Pine Ridge Reservation—located on the south side of Dakota Territory.

1879 January 29—Valentine Trant McGillycuddy is appointed first Indian Agent at the newly named Pine Ridge Reservation.

1886—McGillycuddy is relieved of his duties as agent. He moves to Rapid City, South Dakota, where he is elected mayor and serves as dean of the South Dakota School of Mines.

1890 December 29—A band of renegade Sioux under Big Foot surrenders near Wounded Knee Creek on the Pine Ridge Reservation. The surrender is bungled. Two hundred Sioux men, women, and children are killed along with sixty soldiers. Many wounded are forced into subzero weather.

1897—Fanny Hoyt McGillycuddy dies of a second stroke at her home in Rapid City.

1898–1912—McGillycuddy serves as the Montana and Pacific Coast medical inspector for Mutual Life Insurance Company. In his travels he re-meets Julia Blanchard. They marry and together raise a daughter.

1909 December 10—Red Cloud dies and is buried on his reservation with full rites of the Catholic Church.

1915–1917—McGillycuddy is reactivated as a military surgeon during the worldwide flu epidemic. He serves in California mining camps and with the Aleut Indians in Alaska.

1939 June 6—Valentine Trant McGillycuddy dies in his final post—house doctor for the Claremont Hotel in Berkeley, California.

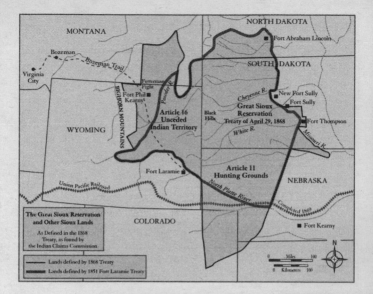

The Great Sioux Reservation and Other Sioux Lands

As Defined in the 1868 Treaty, as found by the Indian Claims Commission

Lands defined by 1868 Treaty
Lands defined by 1851 Fort Laramie Treaty

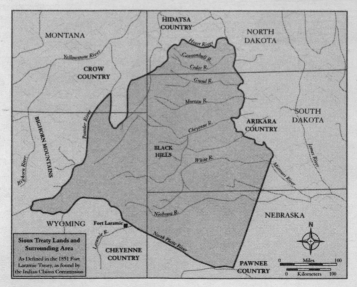

Sioux Treaty Lands and Surrounding Area

As Defined in the 1851 Fort Laramie Treaty, as found by the Indian Claims Commission

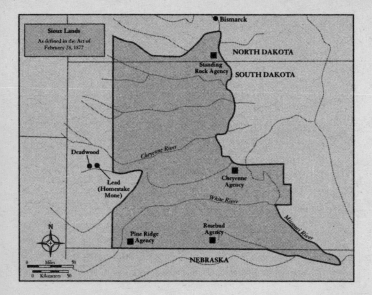

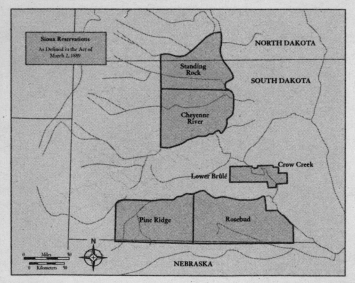

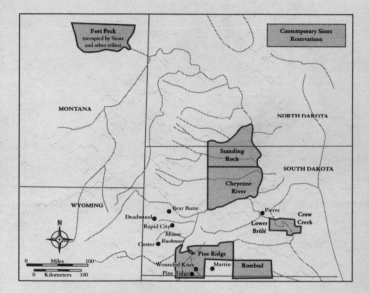

Fort Peck
(occupied by Sioux
and other tribes)

Contemporary Sioux
Reservations

MONTANA

NORTH DAKOTA

Standing
Rock

SOUTH DAKOTA

Cheyenne
River

WYOMING

Bear Butte

Deadwood

Pierre

Crow
Creek

Rapid City

Lower
Brûlé

Custer

*Mount
Rushmore*

N

Pine Ridge

0   Miles   100

Wounded Knee

Martin

Rosebud

0   Kilometers   100

Pine Ridge

Part One

The Capital

WINTER 1878–1879

I

McGillycuddy had come to Washington from Dakota Territory to apply for admission to the Army Medical Corps. He had been a contract surgeon to the army for the last three years and admission to the regular army was very important to his career and to his life. But two days after his arrival in the capital and before he could speak to the board of medical examiners, he was called to the office of the commissioner of Indian affairs. It was a bit irregular because the Bureau of Indian Affairs and the army were at odds and McGillycuddy did not know the commissioner. If the commissioner knew him, it was only by reputation.

Dealing with civilian stuffed shirts was not the way McGillycuddy wanted to spend his morning. He was more interested in trying to enjoy his time with Fanny and in arranging his examination for admittance to the army as an officer and a physician. But once he was ushered into Commissioner Hayt's office and asked about the situation on Red Cloud's agency, he jumped into a description of the tension on the reservation—what seemed to McGillycuddy an odd relationship between Red Cloud and the agent, Irwin. But Commissioner

Hayt didn't want to hear about that yet. "The Cheyennes," he said. "What about the Cheyennes?"

McGillycuddy was only thirty years old but had a natural military bearing and confidence born of years of independence on the frontier. He was tall with close-cropped red hair and sported a handlebar mustache common in the West. Part of his response to Hayt's question was to sit up poker straight and look directly into the little pudgy man's eyes. "I imagine they're dead," he said evenly. "Very likely they are all dead."

Hayt shook his head gravely. "No," he said. "Not quite. I received a telegram this morning. They're still fighting in the hills northwest of the fort."

McGillycuddy nodded. *Horse Creek. The willows are thick on Horse Creek. Excellent cover to fire from, a little shelter from the elements.* "Of course, they've been heading for the Powder River country since they left Indian territory four months ago."

"Four months and a couple dozen murders ago, I'm afraid."

McGillycuddy knew the conditions the Cheyennes had endured in Oklahoma. Disease, starvation, and, worst of all, heartsickness. And he knew that Hayt knew it too, though he might not admit it. "If they're still fighting it's only a handful," McGillycuddy said. "A tribute to their skill and bravery. I'd guess a couple hundred Cheyennes have been killed on that outing so far."

"Indeed." Hayt shook his head and McGillycuddy saw that he was bewildered. "They had a choice. After the break out from Oklahoma Territory they were held at Fort Robinson for a month. All they had to do was agree to return."

"Dull Knife, Tangle Hair, and likely every man, woman, and child in that barracks they used to confine them had no intention of going back to Indian territory." McGillycuddy spoke clearly. He was quite aware that Hayt had been instrumental in ordering the Cheyennes to be returned to the land they hated. It would have been a decision of little consequence to allow them to remain with their old friends, Red Cloud's people. "They were bound and determined to go back to the land of their birth, the Powder River country, but simple permission to remain with Red Cloud's Oglalas was the only thing that could have stopped them."

"And death."

McGillycuddy nodded his head. "And death." *But I wonder if even that would have stopped them.* He gazed calmly at the commissioner—ready for a confrontation if that was what Hayt wanted.

But Hayt did not want a confrontation and McGillycuddy felt sudden sympathy for this public servant whose military comrades and superiors derided so freely. "And you were there," Hayt said.

"At the beginning. A few hours. During the heavy shooting at the initial outbreak. I was scheduled to come here in the morning. The skirmish had moved miles into the breaks by then. No one had heard a shot for an hour or so."

Hayt leaned across his desk and his eyes went distant the way McGillycuddy had noticed other people's eyes go when they wanted the lurid details of battles with Indians. "So what did you see?"

McGillycuddy sat stock-still and considered how much to give this man. He did not seem like an evil man. A silly man perhaps but sincere in his desire to understand. *Well, all right then.* "The doors of the barracks were boarded up and the Cheyennes had received

no food for four days and no water for three. As you
know." Hayt nodded his head but looked tired and
ashamed. "A window was broken and the Dog Soldiers
poured out like mountain lions."

"Dog Soldiers?"

*He knows nothing. A decent man maybe, but igno-
rant of the people he is charged with protecting.* "The
warriors whose responsibility it is to protect the
women, children, and elderly. There were ten of them.
They managed to kill a few guards and get their Spring-
fields and ammunition to the main group. Nearly a hundred fifty souls, who were streaming past their fighting
shield and into the darkness."

"And Dull Knife?"

"In charge of the main body. He was long gone by the
time I got there. But I was there to see the last of the
Dog Soldiers die. They held off the army until their people had escaped. They fought like demons and died like
saints. They died bravely for the people—fought to the
last man. Killed in close combat."

Now Hayt was on his feet pacing. There was a large
window at the end of his office and he stood in front of
it and gazed at the national capital in its winter dress.
The trees were bare, black branches, but there was no
snow. No wind. Nothing that could freeze off the fingers of a man or kill a child. It seemed impossible that
this city outside the window was a part of the same
country as the cruel plains McGillycuddy had come to
know so well.

Know so well and love? He wasn't sure. He only
knew that the plains with all their cruelty were ever in
his mind and that he was constantly aware of the sting
of life out there. He knew also that the sting was what
Hayt was probing for. McGillycuddy could not see

Hayt's face as he stood at the window but he saw a hand come up to rub the bearded chin. "And you left the next morning."

"Yes, about the time some of the wounded women and children were coming into the clinic. About the time Red Cloud volunteered his men to hunt down the rest of the Cheyennes."

At this Hayt turned and looked earnestly at the younger man. "Red Cloud went out to hunt down his friends?" McGillycuddy did not respond. "Great God, what is going on out there on that reservation?"

McGillycuddy's diplomacy went only so far. "Are you asking my opinion, sir?"

Hayt moved back to his desk and sat down and leaned toward McGillycuddy. His forearms and hands rested resolutely on the desk like exhausted animals. "Yes. Tell me what you think, Doctor."

So McGillycuddy told the commissioner that the administration of the reservation was confused and divided. The civilian Indian commission did not understand the mind of the northern Indians. The military knew the Indian mind but lacked the compassion and the mandate for bringing the newly surrendered tribes to civility. No firm course had been set for succeeding in making the Sioux productive citizens. The agent, Irwin, was not strict enough. Red Cloud was more in charge than the agent was.

Hayt listened attentively. "The agent," he said. He pushed a telegram across the desk as if he wanted McGillycuddy to read it. But he didn't give McGillycuddy a chance. "The agent has resigned."

Irwin's resignation was the latest example of the chaos that had ruled the Great Plains since McGillycuddy first set foot on them ten years before. He had been with the Department of Geological Survey when the land of the Sioux was first surveyed and it was then that he met Crazy Horse. From his first chance meeting with the greatest war chief of all, their vectors continued to meet and cross. First as enemies when McGillycuddy rode with General George Crook but finally they had been thrown together at Fort Robinson. The young charismatic chief was the first true Sioux friend McGillycuddy had acquired. And the young charismatic doctor was perhaps the only white friend that Crazy Horse ever knew.

The general belief was that once the war was over, and Crazy Horse surrendered, the Sioux on all the reservations would step into the harness of civilization and begin to pull. But Crazy Horse was betrayed by his own people and murdered by McGillycuddy's. It was the lowest ebb of behavior on both sides and the plains reignited.

McGillycuddy was with his friend in the capacity of fort doctor on the night that the last free Lakota life leaked from the bayonet wound in the chief's side. The night was long and they relived the war that had brought McGillycuddy to the army and Crazy Horse to international prominence as a heathen general. They fought on opposite sides, of course, but McGillycuddy had come to believe that they craved the same equitable outcome. He was never clear in his mind what that outcome could be in such a hopeless clash of cultures but he knew that when Crazy Horse died and his people took his body and ran that there would be no equity, that the whites would not relent.

After the murder most of the Indians broke away from the reservation and McGillycuddy and Fanny were left at the fort wondering what would happen next. They were sitting on their porch in the cooling autumn air talking about their future when Johnny Provost, McGillycuddy's half-Lakota assistant and translator, appeared from around the corner of the house. The events of the last month had brought out the Indian side of Johnny and he refused to approach the porch. Both McGillycuddy and Fanny stood and moved to the porch rail. "For goodness sakes," Fanny said. She would have said more, but when she saw his face she retreated. She backed away and let her husband descend the steps but stayed close enough to hear their conversation.

Johnny knew the father of Crazy Horse and through him learned the secret location of the great war chief's grave. Not his grave exactly, not like a Christian grave. "His heart," Johnny said with downcast eyes. "His family buried his heart on Wounded Knee Creek."

McGillycuddy stood staring for an instant, then, "We must keep this a secret. But I want to go."

Johnny nodded. "I have horses saddled," he said.

McGillycuddy looked up to Fanny and she nodded. "Careful," was all she said.

Crazy Horse had been dead for only sixteen months but it seemed much longer. The first six months had been consumed by General Crook arguing with Red Cloud and Spotted Tail about where their reservations would be. Then a couple months in moving them to the Missouri River where they did not want to go because of its proximity to whites. There had been half a year of turmoil in getting their supplies to them, then a few months in moving them the two hundred miles back to where they had begun. McGillycuddy had been only the surgeon assigned to the fiasco but the confusion and expense associated with the search for a proper reservation insulted his Presbyterian sense of order. The inefficiency was staggering and the results utter failure.

McGillycuddy was rid of all that nagging responsibility now. He hoped to forget the year-and-a-half nightmare and move on to a career with the Army Medical Corps. He attributed the troubles that he and Fanny had been having to the pressure of the situation. The living conditions had been miserable, cold, and wet, with very little in the way of conveniences. It was no place for a woman and Fanny had been the only woman on the post. She had insisted on coming and he had not stopped her but now he knew that he should have put his foot down. Had he made her stay at Fort Robinson, or even travel to stay with her family in Michigan she would never have made the acquaintance of Lieutenant Olsen. *Baah.* The thought of the man made every muscle in McGillycuddy's long, wiry, body strain. *I should have thrashed the bore. I might still.*

The lieutenant was young, about McGillycuddy's age, and handsome. But he was brash with his long flowing Custer curls. *An insult to the general's memory no matter what you thought of him.* He was glib and, like many others, was attracted to Fanny. Unfortunately he knew Spanish, a language that Fanny had always wanted to learn and Olsen was, of course, more than willing to tutor her. It all seemed innocent until the lessons began to take place while the doctor was on duty at the post hospital. He didn't like that arrangement and let Fanny know. She laughed at his jealousy but it was more than simple jealousy.

By then they had been married for four years and McGillycuddy had begun to wonder about children. To that point, their conjugal relationship seemed to him to be normal. Fanny had begun to tire easily but overall seemed healthy. In such a situation, it was common to ask if the lack of children might not have to do with the husband's shortcomings. It was a question that McGillycuddy did not want to ask and he certainly did not want to feel it from the eyes of a brash and shiftless army lieutenant turned Spanish tutor. Upon returning early from the hospital one day, he detected such questions in the lieutenant's smirk. He lost his temper. He took the lieutenant by the arm and led him to the door and out onto the makeshift porch. He had been quite ready to pummel the upstart but the look on Fanny's face made him know that her intentions, at least, were innocent and that she did not understand the reason for his actions. Instead of the beating McGillycuddy still believed the lieutenant deserved, he settled for an icy stare that thinly veiled the threat. "You, sir," he said, "might one day find yourself with an arrow in your gut. I am the only man for two hundred miles with the ability to save such a patient. Consider that and never darken this door again."

The aftermath of that incident continued for most of their time at the temporary Red Cloud Agency. Fanny had been livid over what she saw as his implied insult of her. He would not budge on the issue. All he would say was that Olsen had been improper and even when he cooled down and realized that perhaps he had been too hasty, he did not relent. Lieutenant Olsen wrote a letter demanding an apology but McGillycuddy ignored it. He stuck to his position and insisted that Fanny have no more communication with the lieutenant. He got his way but their relationship suffered. While he could not understand the lack of children in the first four years of their marriage it was easy to understand why Fanny had not become pregnant in the months since the incident with Olsen. She had become decidedly cool to him and it was his fervent hope that the trip to Washington, D.C., might again warm their relationship and set them on the road to children and family.

That was the reason he had arranged a lovely dinner and purchased tickets to a production of *As You Like It*. *Othello* had been playing the week before their arrival and McGillycuddy was glad they had missed it. The theater was one of Fanny's fondest diversions and already she was searching the papers for schedules of the week to come. But *As You Like It* was getting marvelous reviews and would certainly be the high spot of their theater tour of the capital. McGillycuddy wanted everything to be perfect and, knowing his own brooding nature, feared the meeting with Hayt might distract him from his original mission in Washington. He was a man who became upset easily and after meeting with Hayt he might well have difficulty forgetting it and focusing all his attention on Fanny.

McGillycuddy returned from the meeting with the commissioner of Indian affairs too late to call at the office of the Army Board of Medical Examiners. The meeting at the Department of the Interior, which included Indian affairs, had not only ruined his day from a time standpoint; it had set his mind to racing about the events on the Dakota prairie. And once the Dakota prairie had entered his mind he was consumed by the problems, disorder, and injustice that ran rampant on those rolling grasslands. It was a ridiculous place to expect to find one's fortune and he was trying hard to break away from the land that had so captivated his imagination. He told himself that he wanted to break away for Fanny's sake. When he put it to her that way she denied that she was unhappy on the plains. She claimed to love the sweep of the land, the wildness, and even the Indian people who populated that lonely, desolate place. McGillycuddy believed that she loved Dakota because he too loved it. *Love it and hate it.* It was such a hard place. None of the finery that they craved and took advantage of in Washington. Yet there was something so alluring about all that space that it confused McGillycuddy. He was an ambitious man and felt he had the talents and skills to make a success of himself in the broader world. But that damned waving grass, the buffalo, the Sioux, and the turmoil ahead attracted him like a magnet attracts horseshoes.

That's the kind of thing his talk with Hayt got him thinking about and as he dressed for the theater he vowed not to bother Fanny with any of it. She knew, of course, that he'd spoken to the commissioner of Indian affairs and was dutifully impressed. But he said only that they had talked about the present conditions at the Red Cloud Agency, not that the commissioner had got him thinking of all that was wrong and ways to right those wrongs. She knew that his jumping into the solution stage of a problem was his curse and had she been in a reflective mood she would have known what was going through his mind. But she was too excited for such talk and that was just fine with McGillycuddy. It was the way he had hoped she would be—part of a solution for another problem. He vowed not to spoil their evening with ruminations about the Sioux. As they dressed, he tried to keep his talk light and comical but he felt the distracted hollowness of his banter and feared Fanny felt it too.

For fifteen minutes she sat in front of the mirror and combed her long auburn hair. When it shone silky and fell from the brush like something rich and liquid, she braided it into a long rope and coiled it tightly on top of her head. Then she began to apply her makeup and all the time McGillycuddy tried to engage her in light conversation and get the evening off to a good start. She tried to join in and their talk limped along, but they were not wholly successful. In the end, McGillycuddy fell to fussing with his starched shirt and brown waistcoat. He fumbled with the studs and cuff links and wished she would help him, but did not ask.

When she was satisfied with her appearance she stood up for his inspection. She was dressed in a lavender gown that played nicely with her light green eyes and showed her shoulders and neck to great advantage. Her neck was draped with a string of small pearls that McGillycuddy had given her for their wedding. A sash of a darker purple wrapped her waist tight and McGillycuddy smiled to himself when he thought of McClellan saddles cinched to strong healthy horses.

"And what is so amusing?" Fanny said with a smile of her own.

McGillycuddy felt caught. He could hardly say that she reminded him of a horse. No woman could understand that as a compliment. "You look lovely. Truly."

The green eyes sparkled. *Why do clothes and society please them so?* She tilted her head in acknowledgment of the compliment. "And you, sir," she said, "look dashing."

It was a term McGillycuddy would never associate with himself. To him, a better term to apply to Valentine McGillycuddy would be dashed. Galloot and gangly came to mind too but he had learned that the perception of a woman was often very different than that of a man and demanded to be simply accepted. "Thank You, Lovey. I feel a bit like we are off to a masquerade ball but I agree that our costumes are remarkable. Who could guess that three weeks ago we were saddle sore, wind-burned, and a hundred miles from the nearest permanent dwelling?" He fingered the lapel of his coat. "Fine clothes are fine camouflage."

"Nonsense, we're as elegant as any couple in this town." She rolled her fan out and smiled coyly over it. "You are particularly elegant."

"A thistle compared to your blossom." It sounded silly but he meant it and she took it that way. He stepped up to her and lightly kissed her on the forehead. She reached out and held him tight.

"I mean it," she said into his starched shirtfront. "You are an exceptional man. You belong in the highest circles of power and society."

She sees herself in those circles. Such hubris was an indulgence that McGillycuddy could not bear to embrace. He had always admired humility and knew that he must fight to sustain it. "I am a simple contract surgeon."

"But your superiors hold great store by you." She pushed back and looked up into his face. "And so do I."

McGillycuddy laughed. "Let us hope they hold enough store in me to allow me to take the army medical exam, and let us hope I am elegant enough to pass the damned thing so I can become a full-fledged commissioned army surgeon."

They were both smiling now, gathering up their fur coats and readying to leave for the theater. "They shouldn't even bother with an exam. You know more than any of them. They should just make you a major on general principles."

McGillycuddy was holding the door for his wife. "Well, if they see you, they just might. The military balls I've been to could stand a little sprucing up."

*   *   *

In the capital city it was fashionable to eat after the theater, and so that is the way McGillycuddy arranged it.
They ate at an Italian restaurant situated just where the
city touched the Potomac River. The spicy red sauces
and pasta of Italian cuisine were quite the rage in the
capital and the wife of General Crook, McGillycuddy's
commanding officer during the Sioux Wars, had recommended this restaurant, Cusma, by name. She said it
was likely that they would be dining with senators and
generals. Even President and Mrs. Hayes were known to
appear at Ristorante Cusma.

Fanny was thrilled, the exact reaction McGillycuddy
was hoping for. They sat at a corner table and talked
about the production of *As You Like It*. Fanny had
found it uplifting and acted beyond compare. McGillycuddy thought it was a bit frivolous but entertaining
and likely worth the price of admission. They laughed
at the thrifty nature for which he was known and Fanny
used that reference to urge him into a bottle of wine that
he would ordinarily never have consented to.

As they drank the wine they glanced at the sophisti-
cated people in the restaurant and guessed at what government office they held. The men's mouths were
draped with thick whiskers much like McGillycuddy's
and the women were dressed in gowns that billowed
below the waist but were cut low like Fanny's. Though
McGillycuddy would never admit it, he wondered what
the women looked like under the dresses. It was innocent enough but an urge he was not proud of. His justi-
fication was the fact that he was male and the
knowledge that there was much about Valentine T.
McGillycuddy that no one would ever know. He judged
what was below the dresses by the ladies' faces. There

was a bony one. Over there, a pockmarked and pimpled one. Few, if any of them, promised the voluptuous curves obscured by Fanny's bustle.

For Fanny's part, she felt slightly out of place, conspicuous, leered at by the gentlemen. But she held her head high and did not let on to McGillycuddy that the attention bothered her. Though he too felt more at home on the prairie, he would not have wanted her to let on that she was even remotely intimidated. Oysters were on the menu and, though Fanny had tried them once at her family home in Detroit and not cared for them, she had heard from the wife of Captain Dougherty that oysters fresh from Maryland were excellent indeed. McGillycuddy had never tried oysters and was not sure that he wanted to, but she pleaded with him in a playful way and he gave in to trying one.

They were actually quite good and Fanny smiled at McGillycuddy to see if he agreed. McGillycuddy shrugged. "Well?" she asked.

"They're excellent," he said. "Best mucus I've ever tasted."

"Valentine!"

"No," he said, "they really are good." *For mucus.*

"Well, they certainly aren't as good as buffalo steak," she said.

"Hmm," he said. She knew he was lamenting the fact that buffalo steak was getting exceedingly difficult to procure. McGillycuddy was prone to complaining that there had been tens of thousands of buffalo when he first went to the plains and now only the occasional wanderer could be seen. Those that still existed had a bedraggled look from being pursued most of their lives. Unlike horses, buffalo could not be tamed and did poorly in fences or as beasts of burden. Many times

McGillycuddy had referred to them as an emblem, a
metaphor for most of the prairie, which included the
Sioux. If the Sioux proved to be as incapable of civilization as buffalo were to domestication, McGillycuddy
knew the Great Plains were in for turbulent times.
McGillycudd forked an oyster and held it up for a
close look. She knew he was comparing it to the buffalo
he liked so well. "Indeed," he said.

But he did not become maudlin. He raised his glass of
Chianti and toasted her beauty. He was trying very hard
and she knew it. It felt good and by the time the main
course of pasta and tomato sauce came to the table she
had had two glasses of the wine and had twice leaned
over to whisper in his ear that she loved him. It embarrassed him but also made him very happy and he ate
and drank with gusto. He was tall and thin but wiry and
very strong. Though there were few men as tall as
McGillycuddy, those who were often outweighed him
by twenty pounds. When not consumed with worry and
thought, he could eat with the heaviest man in the bat-
talion. That was the way he was that night and Fanny
was glad to see that he had put the problems of the Red
Cloud Agency and the bureaucratic struggle to be accepted into the Army Medical Corps out of his mind.
He was a man who could deal with several challenges at
a time, but he preferred to focus on one and was troubled deeply when his concentration was interrupted.
That night he was concentrating on her and Fanny rev-
eled in his attention.

After the dessert and sweet wine arrived, McGillycuddy was ready to reach across the table and touch her
hand. It was a show of public affection that was rare for
McGillycuddy, and Fanny was excited by the feel of his
rough hand. She modestly slid her hand away and

looked to the ladies and gentlemen seated beside them at the next table. The men were clearly some sort of government officials and both Fanny and McGillycuddy had a great deal of respect for such people. But McGillycuddy leaned over the table and whispered, "Oh damn them." He reached for the hand again but this time his sleeve dragged in the ice cream and chocolate sauce. "Double damn," he said. He spoke out loud this time and the people at the next table looked as if he had uttered a grave vulgarity.

McGillycuddy grimaced, nodded an apology, and leaned to Fanny. "Are you ready to get out of here?" She looked at him with a quizzical expression. "I'd like to take you back to our room."

"Oh," she said. "Well. Yes." She smiled. "Yes."

"Yes. Well, good," he said and raised his hand for the check.

Once outside the restaurant, McGillycuddy flagged down a white carriage pulled by a team of grays. "Madison Hotel," he called up to the coachman, who was dressed in an otter-skin coat and beaver top hat. The harness was polished black with silver accoutrements and bells that rang like icicles falling from a roof. They burrowed into the buffalo robes that cushioned the seat and wrapped them tight around themselves. McGillycuddy tucked Fanny's head beneath his chin and she could feel his mustache against her temple. The carriage rocked and the sound of the horses' hooves on the cobblestones was like holding an ear to the inner workings of a grandfather clock.

When they arrived at the hotel, McGillycuddy stepped down and tossed the driver a dollar gold piece. He was feeling expansive and Fanny felt his focus upon her. He helped her from the carriage and snuggled her under his arm for the climb up the stairs to the lobby. Gaslights shone on the porch, and through the lobby windows they could see the waving shadows of the fire that burned in the huge fireplace on the far wall. McGillycuddy pushed the heavy door open as if it were made of feathers and Fanny hurried to keep up with his eager gait.

But when he asked for the key the clerk passed a note over the desk even before he turned for the key. "Seemed quite important," the clerk said. "Official government messenger."

McGillycuddy glanced at Fanny before he opened the envelope. He read it to himself as the clerk found the key and laid it on the counter. Already he was preoccupied and Fanny picked up the key herself. When the clerk stepped away McGillycuddy read the note aloud to Fanny.

Dr. Valentine McGillycuddy,

Please come to my office at the Bureau of Indian Affairs. Tomorrow morning nine o'clock sharp. The Secretary of the Interior would like to make your acquaintance.

Commissioner Hayt

"The secretary of the interior?" Fanny was flabbergasted. "What could Secretary Schurz want with you?"

McGillycuddy was looking at the note and shaking his head slowly. "I don't know," he said. His facial features had become deep-set with thought and Fanny knew that she had lost him for the night.

2

The waiting room outside Commissioner Hayt's office was too comfortable for McGillycuddy. He had not slept well the night before and even though he was interested to meet the secretary of the interior, the immobile wait was too long and the overstuffed chair sucked him down. The walls were walnut wainscot to three feet, with a cloth wall covering of browns and yellows framed in columns of the same walnut to the ceiling trim. Centered in the panels hung oil paintings of historical moments in the United States' dealings with Indians. Whoever painted the pictures had never seen an Indian. At least he had never seen a Sioux or Cheyenne. The poor creatures represented in the oils looked more like the swarthy Italian waiters at Cusma's than Indians. Their hair was wild instead of the tight, shiny braids that were the norm of McGillycuddy's experience. Preposterous headdresses made of the feathers of birds from the painter's imagination made the scenes comical. The subjects were caught in all sorts of ridiculous acts. The cliché of simple-minded savages viewing with awe the ships of Columbus. The proverbial table spread with trinkets and beads in front of innocents being hoodwinked by a couple of fellows in idiotic hats. There was even a missionary holding a cross over praying tribesmen.

McGillycuddy was only thirty years old but had already been in Indian country for six years, fought in wars against the Sioux, spent hundreds of days and nights with Indians, counted many as friends. They had come to his clinic with babies and ancients for the same reason anyone would come to a doctor. He'd never seen anything like what was depicted on the walls of the waiting room of the U.S. commissioner of Indian affairs.

He hadn't noticed the silly paintings the day before because he had not been made to wait the day before. As he was commanded in Hayt's note, he arrived at nine o'clock sharp and found the halls nearly deserted. It looked to McGillycuddy as though the government did not rise early. He, himself, had been up for almost five hours and so was already quite full of coffee when Hayt's secretary—a prim little man with a close-cropped mustache and wire-rimmed glasses—offered to bring him a cup. McGillycuddy took him up on the offer, hoping more coffee would make him alert. Twice more before ten o'clock the officious secretary checked in on McGillycuddy. On the last visit he leaned forward and, in a conspiratorial way, whispered, "The commissioner and the secretary of the interior are conferring with the president."

It was clear that the man felt more important and perhaps superior for being able to deliver that information but McGillycuddy could not let the little fellow gloat. "Was the president's appointment before nine o'clock?"

The man looked at McGillycuddy as if he had broken wind. "The president of the United States," he said.

"I see," McGillycuddy said gravely. "I assumed they'd be talking with the president of Austria."

The little man chose to ignore the last comment. "A question of propriety," he said.

"Umm. Propriety."

At a quarter after ten o'clock the secretary returned and, as if they had never spoken, showed McGillycuddy to a leather chair in the anteroom where he settled heavily. "Well," he said to the much smaller man. "I'm progressing."

His hands, rusty brown with skin peeling from recent sunburn, massaged the arms of the chair as he squinted at the new set of paintings that surrounded him. *The men are too rigid and there is no sign of even a breeze in anyone's hair.* But the leather of the chair was genuine. It was dangerously soft. McGillycuddy lifted his hands slightly and moved them in small circles to graze the leather with his calluses. He closed his eyes, and though his curiosity about what such a high government official as Carl Schurz could want of him had occupied his mind since the night before, he was not surprised to find himself imagining Fanny's skin—the velvety smoothness on the underside of her breasts. But the animal in that chair rose up and moved under his fingertips. Suddenly the chair was alive and all he felt was the fender of a McClellan saddle, rocking, rocking, and the surge as a good horse carried him to the top of a washout. One of a thousand washouts, a thousand draws and coolies crossed on their way from White Clay Creek on the Nebraska border to the Missouri River in the center of Dakota. The muddy Missouri. The cursed and hated Missouri. Five hundred soldiers had escorted the bands of Red Cloud and Spotted Tail from the Nebraska border where they wanted to settle, to the Missouri River where they did not. Thousands of people strung out in a ten-mile line of march. They crept over land for months on their way to the river port that made delivery of supplies easier. But the chiefs insisted that their people could not live in such close proximity to the new white settlements and by the end of the winter had prevailed on their powerful political friends to reverse the march. So, without ever establishing permanent dwellings and after suffering a dismal winter, the march was reversed.

McGillycuddy was influential in the route of travel and, both coming and going, was questioned about his choice to skirt the upper valley of Wounded Knee Creek. By this time the people were tired, hungry, and sick. The politics of Washington and their own chiefs had rained suffering down on them. They did not need more miles to walk. To his superiors McGillycuddy created acceptable reasons for the deviation. But only Johnny Provost knew the real reason. Only Johnny Provost had seen McGillycuddy fall to his knees and press both his hands to the disturbed earth where the heart of Crazy Horse was buried. "No one can know this place," he said. "The soldiers hate the freedom he represents and would dig up the heart and feed it to the dogs."

Johnny nodded. "And the chiefs are jealous and would do the same."

So the horrid, insane, and futile march had taken the long way past Wounded Knee Creek and by the time McGillycuddy had traveled from Fort Robinson to the Missouri and back to White Clay Creek he had worn finger holes in the fender of that McClellan saddle where he used it to mount and dismount. *What a debacle. Handled about like this nine-o'clock-sharp meeting.*

His eyes had only been closed a few minutes when the officious assistant reappeared. He announced himself with a falsely tactful and annoying cough. "A western man," he said with a smile. He acted as if he might suspect that McGillycuddy was hungover or daft.

McGillycuddy opened his eyes without apology and looked slowly up to his tormentor. "Just a man," he said. The little man nodded to let McGillycuddy know that he did not approve. Then nodded in a different way to say that Commissioner Hayt was ready to see him. The man's gesture was smug and for an instant McGillycuddy wondered what it would be like to stand up and pummel him there surrounded by oil paintings and walnut panels. He had awakened McGillycuddy from a reverie and that, along with the fact that he was Washingtonian and felt himself well placed in the Indian department, seemed to have made him self-satisfied. It would have been good fun to wake him from his drowsy existence with a lanky leap in his direction. *Enough for now.* McGillycuddy simply rose to full height and lingered over the little bureaucrat for an extra instant before moving toward the commissioner's door. *There will be a chance.*

Hayt met him at the door with an eager smile that McGillycuddy had not seen the day before. As soon as he stepped into the office, he guessed the reason for Hayt's deferential attitude. Secretary Schurz was seated in a chair near the fireplace. The great man rose from his chair and moved to shake McGillycuddy's hand. He was tall and though much older than either McGillycuddy or Hayt, moved with that spry sort of dignity that is often found in leaders. McGillycuddy knew that this man had been mentioned as a potential presidential candidate and he immediately understood why. *He has wisdom.* He took Schurz's hand, felt the solid grip, and knew that this was no patronizing public servant.

McGillycuddy had not thought he would be so impressed but it was obvious that this was the rare sort of man that he admired and tried to emulate. Schurz was like General Crook in that sense and his sobriety was undeniable. Schurz looked at him not with the piercing eyes of a man intent on domination, but with an intense desire to understand. What McGillycuddy had assumed would be merely another session of bureaucratic debriefing of a man who had been at the center of a grave and pressing problem, now seemed to be something different, something personal and sincere. "It is good to meet you, Doctor." He motioned toward a second chair near the fire. "Please."

Hayt found a third chair but was relegated to a subordinate role of nodding first at Schurz's questions then again at McGillycuddy's answers. "I would guess it is colder in your Dakota on this January day than we Washingtonians can imagine."

"It is cold here too. But different. There's moisture in the air here that makes it unpleasant for me. But no wind. Wind is the nemesis that we live with on the plains."

"Oh, the plains. I've never been there, you know. It must seem absurd to you that the man ultimately in charge of so much public land and all the Sioux and Cheyennes has never even seen your country."

"My realm is a very small portion of the department of the interior. Your job is immense," McGillycuddy said.

"Indeed. But right now a great deal of my time is taken up by answering the complaints and questions of citizens concerning the Sioux problem."

"Yes. The Sioux problem."

"You might as well know, Doctor, that your name has come up in meetings with Generals Crook and Sheridan.

Commissioner Hayt informed me of your presence in the capital and told me of your talk yesterday. You are young, but you are a man of experience with the Sioux." McGillycuddy was humbled and had trouble meeting Schurz's probing eyes. "I've invited you here to ask your advice."

"My advice?"

"Yes. There is a great deal of debate here in the East. One journal in particular, Dr. T. A. Bland's, *The Council Fire,* has taken exception to nearly everything with regard to what has happened to our policy toward the Sioux." Schurz paused and looked kindly at McGillycuddy. "In your opinion, Mac—may I call you Mac?— I've been told your friends call you Mac." This knowledge by a highly placed administrator surprised McGillycuddy.

"Of course," he sputtered.

Schurz grinned. "Well then, Mac, what should be done with Red Cloud and his agency?"

McGillycuddy balked. "I don't feel qualified," he said.

"Nonsense, Mac. Every man has an opinion and I've heard that you often hold strong ones. I would like to hear what you think." *Does he want the truth?* "I want your true assessment."

McGillycuddy took a moment for listening to his own senses. He sat quietly but felt no intrigue on Schurz's part—only a genuine interest and a curious mind. His question was not a trap. "Very well. After the tragedy at the Little Big Horn it was necessary that the Sioux be put under the control of the army. However, the army is not qualified to civilize the Sioux. If the goal is to bring the Sioux into the citizenry, and I assume that it is, then a firm but understanding hand must be employed."

"Agent Irwin has been trying." Schurz spoke without conviction and it encouraged McGillycuddy.

"May I speak freely?"

"Of course."

"Agent Irwin is weak. He came quickly under the control of Red Cloud. Had it not been for the army's influence, Red Cloud would have been running his own agency, controlling the immense food-stuffs, the immense wealth that is being supplied by treaty, and likely funneling great quantities of it to the Sioux who are still hostile. He would like nothing more than to get the United States government to supply the fighting men who are waging war on that same government. It is the sort of irony that he would find amusing."

"Red Cloud is fond of irony?"

"He is an obstructionist. He stands in the way of his people's advancement toward civilization."

"You know him personally?"

"Yes. We've spoken many times. Eaten in each other's homes. Our wives know each other," McGillycuddy paused to find the very best way to put this next part. "But he is flawed like all of us. His esteem is very important to him and it makes him difficult."

Schurz nodded thoughtfully. "He is a defeated war chief. Wouldn't you expect him to be difficult?"

"Of course. Keeping the pot stirred is understandable. But not acceptable. Many Sioux—I would hazard a guess that most Sioux—would like to put the past behind them and move, as they say, down the white man's road."

"You are a liberal in that sense."

"In one sense, yes. But I believe that for all men, work and enterprise is the only way to betterment and, in that sense, I believe there are people in this city who would find me conservative."

Schurz was nodding. "I have petitions from those

people on my desk right now. They seem to believe that the Indian should not be encouraged to farm like white men but be left to his old life. Never mind that the buffalo are gone and with them, the old life."

Hayt found an opening. "And I have petitions on my desk insisting that all the Sioux be exterminated so the Black Hills can be opened for settlement."

There was a moment of silence as they pondered the disparity of the extreme positions. "I've seen the Sioux in their natural state," McGillycuddy said. "I have to admit that if I had the power I would have them remain as I found them when I first arrived on the plains." His voice took on a distant quality that he fought to hide. "But progress is a beast without regret. The Sioux will never again be the way I found them. Like all of us, they must accept change or perish." *God forbid that they should perish.*

"Well, Mac, just how should Red Cloud's Sioux be driven down that white man's road of industry?"

McGillycuddy tried not to hesitate. "That is a matter of public policy," he said as a way of stalling while he gathered his thoughts.

"Of course, but what would you do?"

McGillycuddy had, of course, considered this question but he wondered if this was the time to speak his mind. He looked at Schurz and found him patiently waiting. *What the hell.* "I'd remove the army from the picture. Then institute strict orders in all things from the influence of nonofficial whites to the apportionment of land to individual families. I would treat the Sioux like white men, insist on education, hard work, and individual thinking."

"Individual thinking? Doesn't that run contrary to tribal life?"

"No sir, I don't believe it does. The Sioux I knew were individuals indeed. To paraphrase Whitman, 'they tipped their hats to no man.' "

"Not even Red Cloud? What would you do with Red Cloud?"

"I'd subvert his negative influence."

"You'd break down the native power structure?"

"The power structure that is in place on the reservations is a creature of the white man. No historic chief ever had the power to control food or behavior. The Sioux were always free to obey or not. The land was immense; if a chief ever tried to assert such power the smaller bands just moved away from him. No, a chief for war is one thing and Red Cloud was the epitome of that species. But the social and economic notion of a chief being in charge comes from us. It is foreign to the Sioux."

Schurz was nodding and looking into the fire. "If that's so, Mac, it sounds reasonable. How can we best help them avoid extinction? How can we get the Sioux to accept the control of the United States government over their affairs?"

McGillycuddy had warmed to the topic and did not have to think for long. "As citizens of the United States none of us should accept control of the government over our affairs. The government exists to assist us in our affairs. If we treat the Sioux as we treat any white man, show him the value of order and law, he will submit as all of us have submitted."

Schurz sat for a long minute before speaking again. He did not look at McGillycuddy. "Would you mind, Mac? I think Commissioner Hayt and I would like a moment alone."

McGillycuddy was surprised. "Of course." *Have I*

overspoken? He rose and let himself out of the office and into the anteroom. The oil paintings of Indians instantly assaulted him.

But he did not have to suffer the paintings for long. In less than five minutes Hayt came for him and with an even more solicitous smile ushered him back into the office. Schurz was standing now with his back to the fire. He looked regal in his trim gray waistcoat and starched shirt. He did not ask McGillycuddy to sit down. "I understand," he said, "that you are here in the capital to apply to the army medical board for admittance into the medical corps."

"Yes."

"It would be a bit of a promotion for you."

McGillycuddy was hesitant to discuss his personal life. "Yes," he said, "it would set me on track for a military career."

"More money I suspect. More prestige."

"Yes." *What is this man getting at?*

"You are young, so what I am about to say will make a lot of people mad. They are opposed to any catapulting ahead in salary and prestige, but Commissioner Hayt and I agree that you are something different than we are used to dealing with." He looked directly at McGillycuddy. "Changes are needed at the Red Cloud Agency. We have decided to change the name to the Pine Ridge Reservation and we want you to be the first Indian agent."

3

Schurz gave McGillycuddy two hours to make up his mind. There was something about presenting the nomination to the Senate immediately to ensure confirmation before the makeup of congress changed in late January. But McGillycuddy did not fully understand such inner workings of government and felt it best not to learn. Making such a monumental decision in two hours was preposterous but perhaps that too was one of the inner workings of government. He was instructed that an official government courier would call at his hotel.

McGillycuddy found himself standing on the street in front of the department of the interior in a sort of daze. The sky was a dull gray that he had not seen much of since his childhood days in Wisconsin. There was no such color in Dakota Territory—at least for a sky. It was more like the faces of dead men and those were not so rare. Suddenly he was thinking of mortality—what it could mean to die, what it could mean for a man's life to come to an end, children, Fanny, a career spent in the land of the Sioux.

When he roused from his thoughts two carriages had pulled up at the curb in front of him and the drivers were arguing over who would get the fare. Both drivers were standing and urging their teams into the other as they jostled to pull in front of McGillycuddy. The drivers called to him as they snapped the rumps of their horses with the heavy reins. "Sir!"

"It was me, sir. I was here first." The driver of the black team was a large man in an immense bearskin coat. His whiskers were the same muddy brown as his coat and he controlled the blacks easily with mittened hands the size of great melons. The other man was dowdy in comparison. He was obviously the victim of hard times and though he was pushing his team hard to move the better-appointed carriage away, it was clear that he would soon give up. He drove a team of white-socked bays and was wrapped in a bundle of tattered buffalo fur that McGillycuddy recognized as a worn greatcoat like those issued during the Yellowstone Campaign. Once he realized that the man was a veteran of the Sioux Wars he understood the significance of the white-footed bays—a famous cavalry general had insisted on white-footed bays for his best troopers. McGillycuddy approached the man, necessarily walking past the slick blacks and the man in the bearskin, and laid a hand on the rail where the veteran pressed a knee for balance. He nodded toward the horses that were still fighting to gain the curb. "General Terry?"

The man looked surprised. He was not a young man. His face was hard and showed traces of defeat but his chin came up as if he were ready for a confrontation. "I served with Reno," he said defiantly and snapped the bays hard enough that they moved ahead and the blacks were cut off.

The giant carriage driver called out angrily. "Ta hell with you then. Ride like a pauper, if you like." He spun the team with great flair and they stepped off smartly down the cobblestones.

McGillycuddy watched him go then turned back to the driver of the bays. "You're from here?"

"Maryland. Sir."

"The rebellion?"

"Indeed. Sir. That's where I got my start."

"And Reno."

"The finish of it, sir."

McGillycuddy looked up at the older man and imagined what it must have been like to be pinned down on a point of land and watch helplessly as the rest of the Seventh Cavalry died in a brutal swirl of frantic Sioux directed by his friend Crazy Horse. He wondered what it was like to be forever accused unjustly of cowardice.

"I want to go to the Madison Hotel."

"My pleasure, sir." The man sat down on the seat, obviously relieved that there would be no accusations about his courage or the courage of Reno.

McGillycuddy extended his hand and touched the man's hands that held the heavy leather reins. His gloves were worn with the fingers cut away. "I was there," McGillycuddy said. "A day later I was there." *I likely cared for some of your mates. Maybe even you. I watched them bury Custer. Or at least the mutilated pulp that passed for Custer.* McGillycuddy considered telling the man what he had seen but knew it was no use. This tattered soldier had seen it too. He had seen even more: that pulsing mass as it engulfed Custer. He'd seen Crazy Horse and Sitting Bull at their zenith. What would he say if he knew that McGillycuddy was considering becoming the defender and advocate of Red Cloud?

The man was looking down at him curiously. It was

a huge decision and he needed more time before he took the proposal to Fanny. McGillycuddy dug into his pocket and took out his purse. He unsnapped it and took out a dollar gold piece. "On second thought, take me along the river first. I'd be honored to be drawn by your white-footed bays."

The old soldier smiled and showed that he was missing teeth. "I'll drive you all day for this, sir."

"That won't be necessary. Just some air, some time to think."

"Let me help you, sir." And the driver started to get down off his seat.

"Nonsense," McGillycuddy said. He pulled the carriage door open and put a boot on the iron step. He took hold of the doorjambs and swung up and onto the upholstered seat. He motioned for the driver to proceed.

The cobblestones vibrated the carriage but the springs cushioned the effect. They passed by several government buildings and then turned right along a wooded gravel road. He watched the Potomac pass on his left side. The position of Indian agent would mean a huge raise in pay and prestige. His power and influence over the events in the soon-to-be-state of South Dakota would be greatly enhanced. In that way it was a tremendous opportunity. He would be in charge of a budget of tens of thousands of dollars. He would become known nationwide and he welcomed that. But there would be difficulties: no matter what his policies, there would be detractors by the score, there would be danger, and he would have to forget about his medical and military career. There would be little time for medicine and no commission in the army. In fact, his comfortable relationship with the officers on the frontier would likely suffer. While it appeared that Generals Crook and Sheridan had supported him as a choice for the job he would be no one's puppet and resolved that if he did become Indian agent he would he his own man.

It was slightly after noon and the day was as warm as it would be. He extended his arm and hand from the carriage window to feel the air. For a minute he thought of nothing. Then came the familiar emotion that had visited him occasionally for most of his life. It was an excitement borne of imagined possibilities for the future. He had learned to be wary of this swelling inside his body because it was not always trustworthy. It felt like a call to greatness and perhaps it was. But from experience McGillycuddy knew it could prove to be more akin to a simple desire for fame. He knew he was prone to pridefulness. It was always hard to tell when the feeling first hit him. If it turned out to be the common, debased version it was not worth having and in fact could be as dangerous and destructive as the classic sin of hubris. Sometimes the feeling that came over him was of nobler stuff, a calling to higher pursuits. Two hours was not enough time to divine the nature of the beast that had crawled inside of him. But he rode on along the Potomac River thinking of the confused and nearly impossible situation he was being asked to jump into.

He thought of Machiavelli—there was that much intrigue. The stakes were easily as high as that famous prince had ever played for. A people wrenched from the Stone Age into a powerful and violent world they had little chance of understanding. It was not as simple as the corruption of innocents. The Stone Age that the Sioux were emerging from was no idyllic pastoral. It was every bit as cruel and even more superstitious than that of the conquering civilization. The solution, if indeed there was a solution, would not be easy and would likely be unjust. *Only in the practical. Not without casualties.* He longed to call up to the driver to take him back to Hayt's office. He longed to stride in and tell the man that he was exactly the man for the job.

But what of Fanny? What of family and what of home? There would be controversy and danger. There would be few chances for plays or Italian food. He smiled at the thought of the meal they had shared the night before. He knew that Fanny would agree to this change of plans and see it as the fortuitous opportunity that, in the most obvious respect, it was. She would be thrilled with the new prestige and would embrace the hardships as she had embraced other hardships. But he had great power over her as she had great power over him. Was he being selfish? Was he taking a chance with true happiness? Would he be putting her into a position similar to the position she had found herself in at the temporary agency on the Missouri where she would have only company like Lieutenant Olsen? *The hog slop bastard.*

They had both been looking forward to the life of medical officer in the United States Army. With his duty record and a commission there would be no more remote posts with typhoid, malaria, drunkards, and savage warriors to contend with. He had done his time with that sort of thing. He would no doubt be put in charge of at least part of an army hospital. It would be a city job without risk. There would be politics of course but nothing like the politics of Indian agent. It would be a safe existence—a nurtured and nurturing life. He stared out the carriage window at the broad, gray river flowing past. The movement of the water took away the sense of movement along the street. The river steamed from the disparity of temperature between the water and the January air, and McGillycuddy was momentarily struck by this river's relative tameness. The new Pine Ridge Reservation was located on the White River—a chaotic watercourse that oscillated between near dryness and muddy tumult a half mile wide. It was a river that regularly rolled cottonwood trees as big as any of the hardwoods that had stood by any of these eastern rivers since George Washington crossed the Delaware to surprise the British. *The most spunk these tired old rivers have seen since Christ was a corporal.*

And that got him thinking about Washington: the courage to suffer for positive change, the terrible risk of action, the winter of deprivation at Valley Forge. A hundred years ago now, somewhere just down this road near Philadelphia. It crossed McGillycuddy's mind that he might be able to lean out of the window and ask the driver to take him to Valley Forge. But he had only two hours and no real idea of how far it was from this city named for Washington to the sight of his great trial. He had seen the effects of cold on soldiers and civilians alike but it was hard for even him to imagine the masses of men under Washington's command submitting to actually living out of doors without shoes, blankets, or, in some cases, shirts and pants. He had endured many miserable nights and seen many cases of frostbite but he had never been asked to sleep on snow without so much as a greatcoat. What would make men do such a thing? And not a few men, but tens of thousands.

An idea. The concept that life might be made better for generations to come by the sacrifice of the present generation. He watched the tired old river pass for a few minutes longer, then leaned out of the carriage and called up to the driver. "Turn us around mate. I'm ready to go to the hotel now."

He expected to find Fanny dining at the restaurant on the ground floor of the hotel. It was not exotic food like they had had the night before but adequate for his tastes and he hoped she would be there dressed in her blue woolen dress with the matching bow tied discreetly in her shiny hair. He stood at the doorway of the restaurant and felt the heat from the fireplaces both in the lobby and beside the waiter's station. When the waiter looked up McGillycuddy waved him off. There were only three people in the restaurant and Fanny was not among them.

As he walked to the desk he reached out to the fire and only then realized that he had let his hand get too cold, hanging it out the carriage window as his mind coursed from Machiavelli to Red Cloud. The desk clerk stood leaning on the counter and McGillycuddy wondered if Fanny had left him a message. He hoped that if she had gone out he would be able to find her. An hour of their two hours had already passed.

The man had a very thin mustache and a lugubrious expression. McGillycuddy could not like him. "Any message for me?"

The man looked as if he might cry but he also looked extremely disingenuous. He tried a pitiful smile as he turned to the pigeonholes behind him and began an extensive but mock search. It was plain to see that all the holes were quite empty. "I'm so sorry, Doctor," he said as he turned back. "Not a thing. I'm so sorry."

McGillycuddy took an instant to stare at the man. "It's quite all right," he said. He couldn't help himself. "I guess if there is no telegram that my mother is still alive, I'll have the key for suite 212." The clerk started to say something but couldn't think of what it might be. He turned and retrieved the key with an uncharacteristic fumble.

"In about fifty . . . ," McGillycuddy looked up at the huge clock on the wall above the clerk to make his calculation, "fifty-four minutes an official courier from the Department of the Interior will arrive. Send him to my room immediately."

"Absolutely, sir."

The man still wore his doleful expression and McGillycuddy thought of giving him another verbal jolt but knew it was only his Irish mean streak fighting to be exercised. It was one of the duties of civilization to do one's best to censure such demons and McGillycuddy moved away without another word.

Gibing the clerk wasn't worth it. It would be more humiliation to him than to the clerk. Besides, now he was filled with anticipation about finding Fanny in the window room of their suite. He thought of her sitting in the chair by the wavy glass overlooking the street and the park beyond with yellow winter light filtering in from the murky eastern sky. It had become her place the instant they arrived at the hotel. She had staked her claim like a housecat and that was the way McGillycuddy preferred to think of her: warm, cuddly, perhaps purring. But that is not the way he found her.

When he unlocked the door and stepped through, the closeness of the suite struck him as oddly familiar. It was nothing profound or even identifiable—just a tickling of déjà vu that passed quickly as he shut the door behind him and looked to the window cove where he hoped to find Fanny. A slice of the winter sun slanted across the green velvet chair the way he had imaged. But there was no Fanny. The bathroom door was open and he walked the six steps across the room to see if she might be combing her hair. The room was empty, cool and dark, and so he moved to the bedroom door and pushed it open slowly. Again the tense, familiar feeling came to him as the door swung open and this time it was accompanied with an ineffable twinge of dread. The dread accelerated when he saw Fanny lying perfectly still on their bed. She was dressed in a cream dress with her hair braided and wrapped on her head. For an instant he thought she was dead.

But he had seen too many corpses to be fooled for more than a desperate second. There was too much color in Fanny's skin, more resilience in the muscles of her face. She was sleeping like a baby and McGillycuddy would not have thought of waking her, had they not been under such pressure for time. He would sit on the bed and stroke her face into wakefulness but not before he took an instant to gaze at her.

Some would think her less than beautiful but to McGillycuddy there was no doubt. The auburn hair was thick, and a shade like no other. Her cheekbones were high and aristocratic. But as McGillycuddy looked closer he noticed the hint of puffiness that had recently come into her face. *Age?* Fanny was certainly not old. But age is a progression and he couldn't help wondering if their chances for children were slipping away. *Nonsense! A healthy young woman.* He touched her face lightly and traced a renegade lock of that special hair. He stroked the cheeks and lips. Then the eyelids, until he felt them flutter. He was touching the cheeks again when Fanny roused and her eyes came open.

"Oh," she smiled. "I was dreaming."

"A dream?"

"Of colors and Maypoles. A schoolyard back in Detroit."

McGillycuddy smiled to think of her as a small girl. "A happy past."

"A very happy past." She smiled and let her head loll on the bed.

"Well, I'm here to talk of the future. Are you fully awake?"

Suddenly Fanny was embarrassed and sat up even with McGillycuddy's hand on her shoulder. "I'm so sorry, Valentine. I don't know what's wrong with me. Some mornings I am so tired."

Tired?

She rose and stood for an instant, as if she were dizzy. *Tired.*

The odd feeling of déjà vu came over McGillycuddy. He felt the closeness of the room. *A sick room?* "Our future?" Fanny said.

"Yes," McGillycuddy said. "Our future."

"You've talked with the medical examiners?" This was his old Fanny. She was still groggy from sleep but smiling and making a gallant attempt to catch up. McGillycuddy found it charming. "No, no one so mundane."

"Oh, oh, of course. You were with the secretary of the interior." She smiled and reached out to touch his shoulder. Then she went serious. "Our future?"

Now he was standing in front of her and looked down with what he hoped was a neutral expression. His hands were on her hips. "I . . . we have been offered a job."

She looked up at him, obviously confused. "A hospital?"

"No. Regretfully, there is nothing medical about it."

Her eyes narrowed with what could have been suspicion or confusion. "It would be a substantial raise in pay. A house. Expense account for the home. There would be entertaining."

Now she was smiling. "Out with it."

"A great amount of responsibility."

"A political appointment?"

"Indeed."

Now her eyes were laughing. "What then? Where?"

McGillycuddy watched her closely. It was the answer to this question that worried him most. Though she had always professed to love the plains he could not believe her. It was he who had the great connection to the frontier and he felt certain that she was hoping for a posting in the East. *Here goes.* "Dakota."

The eyes neither brightened nor dulled. "Dakota."

"Indian agent. They want me to take Irwin's position."

They sat staring at each other. "It is an unimaginable opportunity," McGillycuddy said weakly.

My God. They are beginning to sparkle. Sparkle. Sparkle and smile.

"Valentine! That is wonderful. Just wonderful." She threw her arms around his neck. "Agent McGillycuddy. Agent and Mrs. McGillycuddy." She kissed him: first joyfully, then with a passion that surprised McGillycuddy. He pulled away to see into the eyes to be sure that she was not simply being a supportive wife. It was clearly genuine.

"I've always known you were made for greatness, Valentine."

"Now, now." He was thinking of that sin of hubris again. "Now, now."

She kissed him and he kissed her back. "Then you approve?"

"Approve? Good heavens, yes." She laughed. Then she looked very seriously into his eyes and he believed she would speak. But she did not. She kissed him hard and pressed her body against his. It was suggestive and would have been unseemly had McGillycuddy been able to refrain from a response. She licked at his mouth and McGillycuddy licked back. When she pushed he fell back onto the bed and spread his legs so she could settle on top easily. Passion surged as it had not surged for many months and they struggled at each other's clothes for the feel of skin tight along the length of their bodies.

When the knock came on the door McGillycuddy at first jumped and scrambled for his clothes. But when he realized that both dignity and timeliness were impossible he gave up. When the voice of Hayt's smug assistant came through the door he smiled. *My chance.* To the sound of Fanny's muffled laughter he strolled toward the door naked as Adam before the fall. He reached into the bathroom as he passed and took a towel from the rack.

Fanny could see him from the bed where she lay with the covers up to her eyes. "Valentine, no." But she was still laughing and continued to do so as he wrapped the towel around himself and swung open the door. There stood Commissioner Hayt's diminutive assistant with eyes as big as buffalo chips.

"I . . . I." The little man was mortified.

"You've been sent for my answer." McGillycuddy said. He held both hands out as if he were orating to the multitudes. "Tell the commissioner and Secretary Schurz that I accept. I await their orders."

Fanny could not resist.

She called out from the bedroom. "Tell them he stands ready to serve his country."

Part Two

Pine Ridge

SPRING 1879

4

It took more than two months for McGillycuddy to adequately familiarize himself with the policies and procedures of the Bureau of Indian Affairs. There had been a barrage of telegraphs back and forth to Fort Robinson where McGillycuddy engaged Johnny Provost, to again be his assistant and interpreter. He also arranged for a woman to help Fanny with the household chores. Word had been sent up to White Clay Creek, where the agency buildings were being constructed to have the house ready for the McGillycuddys by mid-March. With the exception of this time spent studying the Bureau of Indian Affairs, McGillycuddy and Fanny continued to live at the Madison Hotel. McGillycuddy was constantly aware that such living was very expensive. In reality his salary had taken a substantial jump and they could now afford such living but lavish expenditure had always bothered him. It was simply more money than McGillycuddy's conscience would let him enjoy spending and only Fanny's delight kept him from moving to less expensive rooms. For their entire stay in Washington he justified the extravagance by reminding himself that the day was approaching when luxury would come to an end. And now, on

the tenth of March 1879, as he stood on the snow-
strafed railroad platform at the edge of the struggling
frontier town of Sidney, Nebraska, he knew that day
had come.

With the help of the station manager McGillycuddy
got Fanny settled in the drafty station beside the strain-
ing woodstove and plunged back out into the wind to
secure their baggage. Most of their belongings had been
shipped ahead and that was, no doubt, how the solicitous station manager had found out that McGillycuddy
was the new agent at Pine Ridge. Though it was nearly
two hundred miles distant, nearly all supplies for the
new reservation were flowing through Sidney. The citizens of Sidney were quite aware that huge quantities of
supplies would continue to pass through their city as
long as the Sioux were dependent on the United States
for their subsistence. It was in the station manager's interest to have McGillycuddy's confidence. But the fool
was trying too hard—hustling on and off the train with
the bags as if the Indian stevedores who stood with their
backs hunched to the wind did not exist. When the pile
of luggage was finally assembled, McGillycuddy tipped
the Indians in full view of the manager as if they had
done all the lifting.

McGillycuddy wore a long woolen campaign coat
and a beaver fur hat that felt familiar and let him turn
to the hunkering station manager as if it were a balmy
summer day. "And what of our conveyance?" McGillycuddy's back was to the wind and the manager was facing it. The man was inadequately dressed and
McGillycuddy wondered if he would have enough sense
to move to the side so that his eyes, nose, and mouth
were protected. When he did, McGillycuddy took note
that this man might be all right after all.

"A Mr. O'Donald sent an ambulance to fetch you to the Red Cloud Agency."

"Pine Ridge Agency."

The manager smiled. "Of course. Pine Ridge." The man's eyes were beginning to water and McGillycuddy took a devilish pleasure in testing to see how long he would stand in the wind with the station door not five feet away.

O'Donald had been hired by the Bureau of Indian Affairs to help with the Oglalas resettlement on the new reservation. He was in charge of beginning construction of the agency buildings and easing the transition between the old agent, Irwin, and McGillycuddy. "Is Irwin still up there?"

"Hasn't come through here, sir," the manager said.

It seemed odd that the old agent would remain at Pine Ridge for two months after he had tendered his resignation. "The ambulance?"

Now the manager's eyes were watering fiercely. *For heaven's sake, man.* "The drivers are at the boarding house and the team is stabled next door."

"Have you sent word that we are here and ready?"

Now the man was shivering. "Today?" McGillycuddy did not bother to answer. He only stared with clear eyes and the knowledge that icicles were beginning to form on his mustache. The manager nodded. "I'll just pop in and have my assistant run down and rouse them."

Four days later McGillycuddy and Fanny arrived at Pine Ridge. They made stops every night but only for enough time to change the horses and give the drivers a few hours of sleep. Most of every day McGillycuddy sat looking from the window of the ambulance as Fanny

snuggled deep into the buffalo robes she had arranged
on the seat like a mother lion. There was little to see
from the ambulance window except shifting snow and
the dark lines of dormant trees snaking the draws and
drainages. Occasionally McGillycuddy noticed prairie
chickens teetering from the bare branches or a string of
antelope blending into a mottled south slope where the
sun and wind had removed enough snow to make the
hillside near perfect antelope camouflage. Only once did
one of the drivers tap on the roof to draw his attention
to buffalo. It was a small band of survivors who were
already running for all they were worth. *They used to
stand*. It made McGillycuddy sad and he thought of Red
Cloud's people who waited for him at the end of this
journey.

While he was in Washington he had met, as per
Hayt's wishes, with Dr. T. A. Bland, the founder of the
National Indian Defense Association. Bland was famous, or infamous according to one's politics, for the
extreme position that Indians should be left alone and
not required to adhere to "civilized" standards unless
that adherence came from their collective initiative.
McGillycuddy found this point of view naive for many
reasons, not the least of which was the assumption of
some sort of democracy in Indian culture from which a
collective initiative could be gleaned. It also struck
McGillycuddy that a failure to adhere to civilized standards left only the option of being uncivilized and he
wondered if Dr. T. A. Bland had ever been witness to
truly uncivilized behavior—say cutting the nose off a
woman for adultery or the enslavement and exploita-
tion of other Indians captured on raids. Bland was an
East Coast liberal and editor of a journal called *The
Council Fire*. Even a cursory reading had led McGilly-

cuddy to the conclusion that the man was an idealistic romantic, likely wealthy and pampered, who had no real grasp of conditions on the Great Plains. Before their meeting McGillycuddy had honestly tried to see the Indian situation from Bland's point of view and, by contrast, found himself focused on the most drastically opposing view. He thought of men who believed that Indians were simply members of defeated nations and must submit to their conqueror's cultural structure or perish. When he considered the chilling but popular phrase, "the only good Indian is a dead Indian," he began to see that Bland's quixotic position had value, if only to balance out the views of the most barbaric elements of the "civilized" culture. There was a great deal of room between the poles of possible Indian policy.

McGillycuddy, though he had strong feelings favoring a Yankee work ethic, also found great appeal in the nomadic way of life he had found when he first ventured out onto the plains. As the ambulance bounced along the last twenty miles from Fort Robinson to their final destination at the new Pine Ridge Agency he vowed to redouble his efforts to be reasonable. This new challenge was very important, for the nation, the Sioux, and his family. He looked across at the opposite seat where Fanny snuggled under buffalo robes with Louise, the mulatto girl they had picked up at Fort Robinson to be their domestic helper. *A servant. My, my Dr. McGillycuddy. What would your immigrant mother have to say?* Their skins were dramatically different shades, Louise's an olive brown and Fanny's white as ivory. He watched them sleeping and wondered if Fanny's skin was too white. He wondered if these two sleeping beauties were all the family he would ever have. The question forced him to look back out the window at the rolling snowscape. High above a black eagle circled with broad, long wings and then, finding direction, narrowed the wings and began a long flat stoop that would take him over the distant rim rock where grew the first of the coniferous trees that gave Pine Ridge its name. In fact, they were western red cedars, and McGillycuddy wondered if anyone knew or cared that the reservation was misnamed.

"First," Bland had said, "my group does not approve of the new name for Red Cloud's reservation. My reports indicate that the few trees hearty enough to live are not pine at all."

"Cedars," McGillycuddy said.

"Exactly. It is insulting to that noble old chief to remove his name, particularly at the cost of gross inaccuracy."

"The names of the chiefs have been removed from all the Sioux reservations."

"A plot to break down their societal structure."

"Our social structure. An artificial power structure."

"Artificial?"

"In the sense that it is a construct of military rule over the Sioux. In fact it is ironic that the social structure of the present reservation is a poor imitation of this nation's. It looks slightly like a democracy but the leader was appointed by a foreign power."

"Red Cloud is a hereditary chief."

Liberal dreamer. Do not lose your temper. "In my humble experience the notion of hereditary ruler is a European concept." *One our revolutionary fathers died to oppose.* "Of course, I could be wrong."

Bland had started to come out of his chair until he heard McGillycuddy qualify his statement. "Well," he said. "I should think that you might indeed be wrong and my hope is that my good friend Red Cloud does not suffer under any such misconceptions."

Time to give the devil his due. "He is an exceptional man. An excellent military man with a keen mind and great capacity for reason and dignity."

This made Bland smile. "Dignity is the key."

"You've met the man?"

"Absolutely. Once on his 1870 tour in New York and once here in Washington in '75. Both triumphant trips." McGillycuddy, like most Americans had been kept apprised of these trips via immense newspaper coverage. As he watched the light come up in Bland's eyes at the recollection of the great chief's visits to the enemy capital, he couldn't help wondering if Bland considered them triumphs for all the Oglalas or for only Red Cloud. "It was on the New York trip, when he addressed the city that his dignity was most apparent." *Perhaps mostly a triumph for Dr. T A. Bland.*

Bland began to quote from Red Cloud's now-famous address to the so-called Indian Peace Commission in the Cooper Institute in New York City. McGillycuddy was well versed in the speech and noted that Bland did not bother to include the fact that every word had been translated by a sympathetic interpreter, whispered into the ear of Rev. Howard Crosby, then reinterpreted by that well-known orator for eastern liberal causes. "I came to see our Great Father that peace might be continued. The Great Father that made us both wishes peace to be kept . . ." Bland was clearly delighted but McGillycuddy thought it sounded a little like a Christian sermon.

"When," McGillycuddy asked, "was that speech delivered?"

"June of 1870."

"Of course. Six years before the tragic death of Colonel Custer at the Little Big Horn."

Bland realized that he had been trapped. "I resent your implication, sir, and hope it is not an indication of your attitude toward your new job. To imply that Red Cloud was in any way associated with the Sioux who massacred Colonel Custer is inflammatory. Those Indians were provoked and openly hostile."

McGillycuddy smiled sadly at the recollection of that scene on Little Big Horn Creek. "Hostile," he said. "Yes, they certainly were."

They certainly were. But this was a new era. A time to begin a new path and to set things right. He looked across at his slumbering wife. A time to look to the future and to perform duties to the best of one's abilities. When he looked out the window again they were winding down a snowy road to a tiny set of buildings constructed along the banks of White Clay Creek. They had arrived at the Pine Ridge Reservation and he took a moment to close his eyes before he leaned and gently shook Fanny to wakefulness.

Louise came awake too and they watched the buildings grow from an idyllic miniature, nestled in a snow-covered cradle of the river bend to the rough-hewn and only partially completed conglomeration of mismatched dwellings. No one stirred from the buildings but beyond the immediate agency site, where the black, leafless trees were thickest, came a string of Indian children. The road wound down a hill now and McGillycuddy felt the ambulance lurch forward and he listened for the grunts of the horses as the wagon's weight came to rest on the cruppers. The coachmen spoke to the horses as they rounded a knoll and, from the window, the river was revealed from a different perspective. Suddenly, north of the buildings, tepees became visible in the trees. The closest one was decorated with a huge red buffalo that McGillycuddy recognized as the symbol of Chief Young Man Afraid of His Horses and both Fanny and Louise pointed to it with delight. But beyond the lodge of Young Man Afraid were the prickling tops of other tepees. Many tepees, McGillycuddy thought. And Indians, now by the score, continued to emerge from the brush along White Clay Creek.

Red Cloud's Oglalas were supposed to be spreading themselves out over the thousands of square miles of Pine Ridge Reservation but, *good God,* there were tepees all through the trees of the creek. This was not the way the reservation was intended to operate. Now, McGillycuddy could see that the Indians were not only camped north from the agency buildings but also south. Every level space seemed to be taken up with a tepee. Hundreds of tepees. What of utilization of the reservation? What of sanitation and health concerns? What of potential for unrest?

By the time the horses came to a stop there were perhaps a thousand Indians gathered in groups, clutching their blankets at the neck and staring on with interest. No white men emerged from the buildings and, as McGillycuddy stepped out, he saw that the two coachmen had not budged from their buffalo robes except enough to be sure that their sawed-off shotguns were clear and ready for action. He pounded twice on the side of the ambulance. "It's quite all right. Come down from there. Unload the baggage." *Important to be firm.*

"Fanny, come out." He leaned into the ambulance and whispered, "Neither of you act scared, now. Come ahead," he said in a confident voice.

But far beneath the vision of anyone, McGillycuddy himself was nervous and had to fake his composure until a familiar face emerged from the gathering throng.

"Sir." It was gentle Johnny Provost pushing his way kindly through the comatose crowd. "Perhaps it would be best to unload the baggage down by my tepee."

McGillycuddy could not help smiling. "Tepee?"

Johnny smiled back. They had been in complicated situations before and Johnny's timid smile told McGillycuddy that they were in another. "What the devil?"

"A mix-up, sir."

Now Fanny was standing beside McGillycuddy. She reached out and touched Johnny's hand and that made the half-breed pull his hand back and smile again. "What mix-up, Johnny?"

"It seems that Agent Irwin is still in your office."

"Ex-Agent Irwin," McGillycuddy said.

Johnny shrugged shyly. "He claims that you're not agent until you sign for the inventories."

There was a gust of excitement in the crowd and slowly the Indians began to part. "For the love of Christ," McGillycuddy grumbled. He turned from Johnny to face the small but gloating entourage of Irwin's. Foremost in the group emerging from the only building that looked to be completed was Red Cloud. Ah, yes. *The great man himself.*

He did not let Irwin and Red Cloud come to him but met them halfway with an extended hand toward Red Cloud. Now that he knew the problem his confidence had returned. "Red Cloud." The chief smiled and McGillycuddy smiled back. And, true to form, after a few pro forma words of greeting, the chief launched into an impromptu speech that was only partly understandable to McGillycuddy. He could fumble along in

Lakota but Red Cloud's orations were too much for his understanding. Fortunately, he felt Johnny Provost at his side and so watched the chief carefully as he waited for Johnny to translate into his ear.

"He says he heard that you were coming. That he was surprised the United States government would make such a young man his agent-father." McGillycuddy gave no sign that he understood what Red Cloud was saying or that he was getting the translation from Johnny. He simply continued to look at this man who had suddenly become the second most important person in his life. He was a grand representative of his race, large boned and still sinewy strong even in his middle fifties. He was known for his oration but was a warrior first and McGillycuddy could not help wonder how many men this wily fighter had killed. Many of his exploits in war were well known to Indians and whites alike. As McGillycuddy listened to the surpassingly high-pitched voice, and watched the sparkling eyes set wide above the exceedingly long nose, his mind rested on one of the many incidences of Red Cloud killing an Indian with his bare hands. He had once heard Red Cloud tell the story himself.

A successful war party had routed a band of Utes. The last Ute to flee was wounded and when he tried to cross a river he separated from his horse in the current. The warrior seemed lost in the flood and the Sioux war party pulled their horses up to watch him drown. But Red Cloud, streaked with Ute blood and flushed with the excitement of battle, forced his horse into the river and swam the horse hard to catch up to the Ute. He grasped the man by his hair and, at risk to his own life, held on until the man was dragged ashore. It was a fine story, fit for the legend of Galahad. But the Great Plains were never Camelot. Red Cloud, cheered on by the rest of his war party, summarily scalped the man and left him to bleed to death on the riverbank.

It was impossible for McGillycuddy to follow the on-going speech of Red Cloud. But he had been in this position before and knew that pretending to listen was enough. McGillycuddy knew with whom he was dealing. Since his glory days as the main leader of the only nation ever to fight the American army to a standstill, Red Cloud's main goal had been to confound his old enemies, white and red, and to employ his considerable political skills to remain the recognized chief of the Oglala Sioux.

McGillycuddy listened to his ramblings but would not let himself be fooled into feeling superior. He knew Red Cloud to be a man of great intelligence but self-centered by white standards and capable of antics that would make a six-year-old blush. He talked on about his hopes for the future and began his standard litany of complaints against the government and the Bureau of Indian Affairs, which was hardly appropriate for this meeting. McGillycuddy had heard all this about treaties broken and gifts not delivered before. It was certainly grounded in fact, though it left out any mention of promises broken by the Sioux. He wanted to interrupt the old chief but knew that he must wait until he had finished.

The gist was this: Red Cloud would not accept McGillycuddy as agent until his "good agent-father" was officially relieved of his duty. McGillycuddy turned to Irwin, already understanding the game that was being played. "And you want me to sign inventory sheets that make me responsible for every item on them without doing an inventory of my own."

Irwin smiled. "I'll not have your Republican friends tacking fraud charges on me when you claim that commodities and materials are missing."

"And you expect me to take a Democrat's word that all items on the lists are indeed here at this"—he waved his hand around to indicate the jumble of ill-conceived and mismanaged buildings and tepees—"this agency? I'll wager that you are leaving this position a richer man."

"You impugn my honesty?"

"You impugn mine." McGillycuddy, rising to the ridiculousness of the discussion, added, "And I have a better right to impugn. You, I understand are an ordained minister and experienced at defrauding the Indians on other reservations."

Irwin was dumbfounded. "You are impertinent beyond belief. You should never have been allowed on the Red Cloud Agency."

"Pine Ridge, sir. And you are the intruder here." He was about to take one more step toward Irwin when another white man fought his way to the front of the crowd. Without an introduction, McGillycuddy knew this was O'Donald, who had been sent out to facilitate the transfer and felt obliged to weigh in on this discussion. But McGillycuddy did not give him a chance. "You must be O'Donald," McGillycuddy said. "Find me a horse. I'll be riding to Fort Robinson forthwith." He turned to Johnny. "Find my old friend George Sword and have him put together a dozen men for an escort."

Then he turned to Irwin who was looking to Red Cloud for support. "It will take me most of the day to get to the fort. But I will be back by midday tomorrow." Red Cloud was ignoring Irwin's pleading eyes and McGillycuddy could see that Irwin was beginning to fold. This was good because McGillycuddy did not relish the idea of a cold, two-day ride to bring troops to install himself as agent. Now he was confident and raised a finger to Irwin's face. "Your last chance, sir. Surrender this agency to me immediately or plan to spend the next months in the military brig awaiting treason charges."

There was silence all the way around. McGillycuddy felt the eyes of Red Cloud, Irwin, Johnny Provost, Fanny, and O'Donald. But he did not let his eyes fall away from Irwin's. *I certainly hope this works.* Finally he saw Irwin crack. His head began a nearly imperceptible nodding and McGillycuddy pressed forward. "I'll have those inventory sheets and put Provost here to work on them." He was moving toward the solitary finished building. "We'll be moving in." He raised a finger to the ambulance drivers and indicated where they should take the luggage. He extended an elbow to Fanny and a nod to Louise. Then, ignoring everyone but his wife, he smiled. "Mrs. McGillycuddy. Let me escort you." Her look of surprise turned to a smile. "Mr. Irwin can perhaps impose on the hospitality of his good friend Mr. Red Cloud. I'm sure he will be quite comfortable in the chief's tepee." He winked surreptitiously to his wife. "Temporarily. He will be leaving Pine Ridge in the morning."

5

The night of their arrival they slept on the floor of the administration building. Irwin's possessions were packed and ready to be moved, which indicated that his show of defiance was more theatrical than actual, and McGillycuddy had the belongings moved to a storage tent. But Fanny would not move into the sleeping room until it had been cleaned thoroughly. Since there was no time that night, she made beds of buffalo robes and woolen blankets for her husband and herself in front of the woodstove. Louise slept on the buffalo robes along the south wall. The next morning, while McGillycuddy arranged his desk in the front room, Fanny and Louise went to work with hot water and soap.

The building was less than a month old. It was newly constructed by O'Donald, and McGillycuddy pronounced it well built. There was still a great deal of sawdust in the corners and the smell of the green wood, combined with the knowledge that it had been inhabited by Irwin, drove Fanny to a sweeping and scrubbing frenzy. It was only the administration building—their residence was being built a hundred yards to the south. It would serve, temporarily, as their home and it would be the reservation office for years to come. The building's appearance and cleanliness were a reflection on the new agent and his wife and Fanny was determined to establish herself as the mistress of the reservation.

McGillycuddy was known for his tireless work habits and she was determined to match her husband effort for effort. By nine o'clock, McGillycuddy had arranged his office so that administration could be conducted and Fanny had cleaned the sleeping room and moved their essential personal possessions into place. A half hour later Johnny Provost had been given a list of people that the agent wanted to interview and been sent to the outlying camps to arrange appointments. It was a list that McGillycuddy had been compiling for months and included the leaders of every faction or clan that he could think of, but especially four men. American Horse was the representative of the old warriors. Young Man Afraid of His Horses, the leader of the progressives. George Sword was a proletarian warrior that McGillycuddy had known for years and respected for his cool head, progressive attitude, and his commanding bearing. Last, but certainly not least, Red Cloud, the aging patriarch. He told Johnny Provost to call the people to a council on the following day. He intended to lay out his plan for the rehabilitation of the reservation and the Oglala people.

O'Donald came at ten o'clock to conduct McGillycuddy on a tour of the ongoing construction of the storage buildings, trader's stores, and residences, council building, and the agent's home. He was a large Irishman with a pleasant personality and a reputation for getting the job done. He'd been a troubleshooter for the Bureau of Indian Affairs and had seen the inner workings of many reservations but took particular pride in his work at Pine Ridge. He knocked briskly on the front door and came into the office with his hat in his hand and a grin on his face. By that time Fanny and Louise were scrubbing the floor of the office and were forced to look up from their knees as the big man came into the room. "Don't get up," he said. "I know you've got work to get done and I know how that is."

Louise blushed and continued to scrub but Fanny scrambled to her feet. She moved too fast and was grateful for O'Donald's strong hand to hold to while the flash of dizziness swirled once, twice, and was gone. She tucked in an errant lock of hair and smiled. "Mr. O'Donald," she said. "Nice to find a friendly face in this place."

"Oh, there are many friendly faces," O'Donald said. "They just need to know the new game." He winked at McGillycuddy who was coming from behind his desk and smiled.

McGillycuddy reordered his face to retain the friendly smile. "Well," he said, forcing himself back on task, "we will certainly do our best to explain the rules to them."

"I must say it is about time. That clever old Red Cloud had Irwin doing parlor tricks." O'Donald laughed a pleasant honest laugh. "Only Indian in the system to run his own reservation."

"Indeed," McGillycuddy said. "To the detriment of his own people." His expression folded briefly into his own thoughts and there was short pause in the conversation. McGillycuddy forced the smile to return and O'Donald responded in kind. "But I'm here to straighten that out."

"And straighten it out you shall. You got off to a proper start."

"I hope so." McGillycuddy was pulling on his bearskin coat.

"You played her just right, sir. Irwin is loading his kit onto the ambulance that brought you as we speak. He won't be bothering you again."

Fanny brought McGillycuddy his otter-skin cap. "Thank you, my dear." He turned to O'Donald. "Politics," he said with a wave of his hand. "I don't worry about Irwin or any of his Democratic bleeding-heart friends." He laughed. "I don't worry about anything. But there is a legacy to contend with."

"That's true, sir." O'Donald was opening the door on the cold but brilliantly sunny day. "But we got a leg up on defeating that primitive legacy. Wait till you see the civilized buildings we're puttin' up."

McGillycuddy leaned and kissed his wife. "I'm off," he said, "to my first day of work."

On such a clear, calm day the new agency grounds were a swarm of activity that made McGillycuddy grin. His smile grew broader when he saw five of Red Cloud's warriors loading the last of Irwin's belongings onto the ambulance. He refused to let his eyes linger on Irwin who stood sullenly beside the carriage. He gave the defeated ex-agent only a fleeting glance and felt sure it was the last he would have to suffer from Irwin, save perhaps an editorial in Bland's *The Council Fire*. McGillycuddy continued to smile as O'Donald conducted him among the workmen who were measuring, sawing, and nailing roughly cut boards to the frames of several buildings at the same time. Thirty men busied themselves with the construction and McGillycuddy saw that the layout of the agency was good. There were even a few Oglalas helping the carpenters. *Only as helpers. No Indian carpenters.* And it was a cold day for any man to be out sawing and nailing. It was good to see that there was at least a nascent sense of industry on the reservation. If there was only one thing that could be done to assist these people into the new world that was being thrust upon them, a sense of industry was it.

The arrangement of buildings made immediate sense to McGillycuddy. The administration building, where they had spent the night, was at the eastern end of a circular road that encompassed a central commons. The road emptied out onto the main wagon trail from Fort Robinson, sixty miles southwest, to the Rosebud Agency, ninety miles east. Along the circular drive that was the main street of Pine Ridge were a few small older buildings and already an additional half dozen buildings under construction. Because there had been several years of confusion regarding the exact location of the agency within the greater Sioux reservation, the civilian contractors—the traders, freighters, livery men—had only recently felt secure enough to begin construction of their establishments. O'Donald was well along with the government buildings and the civilians were pushing hard to have their stores and residences finished before the spring trading season.

As with nearly every concession on the reservation, the positions of agency traders were political appointments. And as with most concessions there had been a weak attempt to cloak the selection of the required two traders as a guarantee of competitive free enterprise. McGillycuddy knew that, in reality, George Blanchard was well connected with the Republicans and T. G. Cowgill was associated with the Democrats. He had never met either man but knew that the sooner he did so, the better. As if in an attempt to bring the concept of choice out from the beginning, the traders had chosen building sites adjacent to each other and seemed locked

in a race to raise their establishments. There was only
an inch of snow on the ground and the temperature was
warming enough that the foot traffic and the wheels of
freight wagons were turning the road into a quagmire.
McGillycuddy and O'Donald stood on the common
ground across the road from the growing traders' stores
and McGillycuddy laughed. "Looks as if they even retained the same architect."

In fact the buildings were very similar and the future
proprietors stood before the laboring crews and shouted
orders like mirror images of each other. "Which is
which?" McGillycuddy asked of O'Donald.

"Cowgill on the west. Blanchard on the east."

"And which should be approached first?"

O'Donald laughed. "If we had a telegraph I'd advise
contacting the Department of the Interior for a ruling.
Blanchard is a good chap. Family man. Guess I'd start with
Cowgill to ensure that your day will be ever improving."

McGillycuddy nodded and started across the road.
When O'Donald made to go with him McGillycuddy
held up a hand. "Let me establish myself." O'Donald
nodded and struck out to supervise the ongoing construction of a small stout building that could only be the
guardhouse. McGillycuddy stepped deliberately off the
untrammeled snow and into the muddy wagon ruts.

Cowgill was a blocky little man with a full beard and
long hair that hung thatchlike from under his wool knit
hat. He was busy with a large and awkward diagram of
what the store was supposed to look like when finished.
He had the plans rolled out on the top of a barrel and
was talking with a New England accent while pointing
to a particular corner of the building with a chisel. A tall
thin workman with white skin and very blond hair
squinted in an attempt to understand his meaning.

"Gables," Cowgill was saying.

"Gaable?"

"Gables." Cowgill tapped the plans with the chisel. "Gables."

"Ya, ya, Gaable."

"Ya, ya," Cowgill said and the man seemed pleased.

McGillycuddy took this opportunity to engage Cowgill. "Norwegian?"

"I don't know," Cowgill said. "He's dumb enough to be Norwegian." The little man squinted up at McGillycuddy. "And you?"

"McGillycuddy. I'm your agent."

Cowgill laid his chisel down and thrust out his hand. "Well, now. I heard you were young but I had no idea you were just a boy."

McGillycuddy arrested his own hand at the understanding of this slight. But then he went ahead and took Cowgill's hand. But he did not let his expression go soft. "Young perhaps, Mr. Cowgill, but not without experience." He gripped the hand tight and felt Cowgill squeeze back hard. "And certainly no boy." Neither man changed expression as the muscles of their hands and forearms contracted with enough strength to crack walnuts. They stood that way until tiny beads of sweat appeared in the furrows between Cowgill's eyes.

When McGillycuddy relaxed his grip the smaller man did not press the point and let go too. "I'm sure it will be a pleasure," McGillycuddy said, "to work with you for the benefit of the Oglala Sioux."

Cowgill nodded. "A pleasure," he said with a laugh. He rubbed his right hand with his left. "Indeed." And both men laughed.

Then McGillycuddy looked to the partly finished store. "When will you be open for business?"

"Soon. April. I've got a mule train due in with supplies on the fifteenth."

"Excellent. Plenty of plows and harnesses?"

"More than these brutes will ever use."

"Oh, come now, Mr. Cowgill," McGillycuddy said with a smile. "Given a little time these valleys will be more like the sublime fields of Iowa than the reservation of the wild Sioux."

This made Cowgill grunt and nod with what seemed honest good nature. "Ah," he said, "the optimism of youth." McGillycuddy had started to walk away but when he looked back Cowgill grinned and held up his hands. "Youthful optimism I said. Nothing boyish about it."

Blanchard's store was slightly further along than Cowgill's. So far along, in fact, that the owner had set up an office in one of the rooms. It was a large room and had no roof but the back section was covered over with a tarp and McGillycuddy could see, through a sheet that had been pulled away to admit light, that the trader had installed his family and that the area was clean and tidy. There was a hint of hominess and McGillycuddy marveled as he always did when a home was established where there had been none, where the nurturing industry of a woman had transformed space from the geographic to the spiritual.

Blanchard was honing a saw blade but as soon as he saw McGillycuddy he stopped his work and thrust out his hand. "You must be Irwin's replacement," he said.

"I am."

Blanchard was a good-looking man of medium build with long brown hair combed back in a ponytail and no hat. He was only slightly older than McGillycuddy and stood straight with his shoulders back and one eye slightly cocked in thought. He seemed to be appraising McGillycuddy, trying to tell if this man was as stern as he appeared or if he could appreciate a little humor. "Can't say I hate to see old Irwin go."

He's a good fellow. Careful but down to earth. "I'm sure you're not alone."

The sharpening file was still in Blanchard's left hand. "Would you care for coffee?" He didn't let McGilly-cuddy answer. "Margaret." He called into the parti-tioned back of the room and the woman appeared instantly. She was a pleasing, fine-boned woman with a lovely smile. "Do you have coffee?"

"Nearly finished," she said with a curtsy to McGilly-cuddy.

"This is the new agent. Mr. McGillycuddy. My wife, Margaret."

McGillycuddy removed his otter-skin cap and felt the warm winter sun on the top of his head. "A pleasure," he said.

"The pleasure is mine," Margaret said. "I'll send Julia out directly."

Still holding the file in his left hand Blanchard pushed a stool toward McGillycuddy and dragged another up for himself. "We were talking about those that would, and those that would not, be happy at Irwin's leaving." It was not like McGillycuddy to talk unguardedly with a stranger but Blanchard's confidence and good humor were infectious.

"By my reckoning," Blanchard was saying as McGillycuddy slid one cheek onto the stool and laid his hat on the workbench, "there would be only a few who aren't plumb tickled to see him go."

McGillycuddy watched Blanchard's face, thinking. Taking his time. Considering.

Why not?

"Would Red Cloud be one of them?"

"Eureka." Blanchard laid the file down on the table. "Red Cloud and a few of his devotees in the cities."

McGillycuddy nodded but did not leap to declare himself with regard to Red Cloud. "The question, Mr. Blanchard, is this: are there those who are glad to see me come?"

"Certainly, some. And by what I understand of you there will be many more who will be eventually glad."

McGillycuddy looked directly into the intelligent dark eyes of this trader. *Might as well see what he's made of.* "And what do you understand of me?"

The dark eyes did not look away. "That you are a man who chose this land. Not a man who is here on a political whim to make his fortune and leave with the gold." McGillycuddy felt pressure to answer but Blanchard was not finished. "You're known and respected out here. Military, Indians, settlers. You been out here with the rest of us. You know what makes this place tick and it ain't the way some folks figure it. The romance is just that, romance. These are real people out here and just like any other people, cheating won't do. Putting them up on a pedestal won't do. What's needed are solid principles and hard work." Blanchard had become excited. Though he had pulled the stool up to the workbench as if he would sit down, he was still standing. He had even picked up the file again and was using it to punctuate his speech. "Just people. Indians, sure, but just people all the same. Ain't devils and ain't angels."

Now McGillycuddy was smiling and Blanchard was suddenly embarrassed. "No, no," McGillycuddy said. "Go on. Hold forth." *A marvelous man.*

Blanchard was crimson. "I'm afraid I've held forth a bit too much. I hardly know you."

McGillycuddy heard a stirring behind the hanging sheet. "We know each other a bit better now."

"At least you know me better now." He looked beyond McGillycuddy. "Ah, the coffee."

McGillycuddy was energized and smiling. "And you will get to know me much better very soon." He turned with a smile to accept his coffee and met the blue eyes and long lashes of a fourteen-year-old girl. She was holding a tray with two cups and smiled with perfect white teeth, save a charming chip from the corner of one of the incisors. Her head was tilted with the promise of stunning womanhood and she seemed to take great enjoyment in overhearing the discussion.

"Aha," Blanchard said. "The apple of my eye. My darling daughter, Julia."

6

On the morning of McGillycuddy's first general council with his Oglala clients the agency grounds began to fill just after sunrise. It was a chilly April day but promised to warm in the afternoon to further push the cottonwood and box elder buds toward leafing out into full spring. He and Fanny had made the move from temporary quarters in the administration building to two rooms of their new residence. The rest of the house was still being worked on but Fanny was already beginning to clean right behind the workmen. The front porch was finished and McGillycuddy had fallen into the habit of taking the morning air from that slight vantage point. Some mornings he smoked a cigar but on this morning he was sufficiently anxious to forget that he carried two fine Virginia panatelas in his vest pocket.

He was too busy watching the participants of the council arriving and going over what he wanted to communicate to them to think of smoking. Too preoccupied even to think of breakfast. But Fanny was tenacious on the necessity for a good breakfast and had already sent Louise to the porch twice to call him in. This time she came herself. "Oh, my," she said when she saw how the parade grounds were filling up. "For the council?"

McGillycuddy was leaning on the unpainted railing and did not turn from his appraisal of the gathering crowd. There were perhaps four hundred men, women, and children already coming together in colorful blanketed groups. A few men on horseback sat slumped in crude saddles as comfortably as if they were in rocking chairs. It all reminded McGillycuddy of a few years before when these same Oglalas were hostile. They were not as impressive with so many afoot, with leather and feathers turned to cotton and ribbons. But they were perhaps more dangerous now than ever. No animal, certainly not man, can maintain tranquility when crowded together. It was the main thing that he wanted to talk about at the council. "These are mostly the common people. Just come in for the festivities. There will be a lot more and we'll slaughter a half dozen beeves. The headmen will make their grand entries in a few hours." He turned from the railing and looked at Fanny. She continued to gaze at the Oglalas, moving now to where the sun was beginning to warm the ground.

He knew that she had not slept the night before. She had cuddled into him with her cotton nightgown against his bare chest. He began to unfasten the blue ribbon tie beneath her braided hair but felt immediately that it was not good. Instead he stroked her soft hair and held her close. For a while he thought that his bony chest might have lost its appeal for her and soon he only lay silent, staring at the black ceiling and caught in his thoughts of the coming day. Some time later she had slipped from the bed and did not return. Now, even in the morning light that had always made her complexion vibrant with health, she looked tired. There was puffiness in the face and, indeed, a general swollen appearance to her bare arms and hands. *Too much work.*

Cleaning, worry about this place and position. "Do we know any of these people?" Fanny asked. She turned to him and the smile was still as fresh as it had been five years before on the banks of Lake Michigan where they had fallen in love.

"Of course we do. Perhaps not these people right here." He indicated the scene in front of their house. "But there will be people we knew from two years ago at Fort Robinson, all the wives you got to know on the Missouri last summer. Mrs. Young Man Afraid, Mrs. Red Dog. The Blue Robes. Black Shawl. *The wife of Crazy Horse.*"

"And men you fought against."

"And men I fought against." McGillycuddy laughed. "Though I was never much of a soldier."

"Surgeon."

"There will be a contingent of men and women I treated." *I'm afraid my fighting with these people has only just begun.*

Now Fanny was looking hard into his eyes. "Why, Valentine. You're anxious." He shook his head and tried to smile the accusation away. But she took his trim goatee firmly in her hand. "No. I can see it. You're nervous about today."

McGillycuddy knew he was caught. Fanny always had a way of calling him on his feelings and he had come to know that it was usually easier to admit them to her—though he would never admit them to any other living soul. "I'm not worried about just today. I'm worried about all of it." She continued to look deep into his eyes and nodded her head. "A great deal rides on my ability to get these people to understand that the United States government has expectations." Fanny continued to nod her head but now a tiny smile of pride was working the corners of her eyes and mouth. "I'm in a unique position," McGillycuddy said. "I have genuine prior knowledge of their lifestyle. I know how fast it is disappearing. I, perhaps only I, know that accepting a radically new lifestyle is their only salvation."

Now Fanny's smile was full blown. "If anyone can do it, you can."

Strange how words can double or halve the weight on a man's shoulders.

Louise knocked discreetly on the doorjamb as she stepped out onto the porch. "Madam? Doctor? Stove is hot, coffee boiling." She glanced up from where she had been staring at the floor and McGillycuddy was pleased to see her smile.

"Well then," McGillycuddy said. He was relieved for the excuse to end the discussion. "I am resolved to succeed. But first I must have a good breakfast."

"Right you are. A good start is essential." Fanny became all business. "Fresh bacon and eggs from the trader."

They moved into their house. "Which trader?"

"Blanchard. He is a kind man."

"He is," McGillycuddy said as he took a last look at the congregating Indians. There were nearly a thousand now. "But we must use Cowgill too. Don't want any charges of favoritism."

The council was held in one of the dilapidated buildings left over from years before when the White River had been a hub for fur trading. It was a huge log structure built of ancient cottonwoods. The chinking was long gone and the roof had failed a decade before so the council became instantly unique because it was held indoors while still being open to the great blue prairie sky.

It seemed quite fitting to McGillycuddy and he commented to Johnny Provost that the venue seemed to him a good omen—half white, half Indian.

Large as the building was, there was still only room for the chiefs and headmen of the different bands. Exactly how it was determined who was a headman was a tricky matter. Johnny told McGillycuddy that the word from the bands was that there was a lot of jealousy and that many who wanted, and felt they deserved, to attend the meeting had been superceded by older or more politically adept tribal members. Some had even boycotted the council in protest. But the protests were not against McGillycuddy or the U. S. government. They were among the Indians themselves—perhaps even personal—and McGillycuddy tried not to concern himself with the inner workings of the Oglala social structure. It was important and he would have to come to understand that structure. But that day, on the first opportunity to lay out his plans for the reservation, it was not a priority. He walked through the crowd of common people knowing that there were likely many disgruntled among them. But today was for the big picture and as he and Johnny Provost threaded their way through the crowd and as he shook hands with many who reached out to him, his mind was going over exactly what he needed to say to create the proper first impression.

Once inside the scene became quiet. All the chiefs and headmen were already there—a half hour before the appointed time—the lesser men stood around the perimeter of the room and the old established chiefs were seated on benches in a circle with places left for McGillycuddy and Johnny.

McGillycuddy was slightly disappointed because he had wanted to be the first to arrive so that he could set a precedent of punctuality. He had been to other councils that had begun days late because one or another important chief had not deemed punctuality important. *I should be glad they were all here on time but it is serendipity that they arrived early. It could as easily have been late.*

Old Man Afraid of His Horses, named for the fact that his enemies were even afraid of his horses, sat in a prominent seat with his son Young Man Afraid. McGillycuddy nodded to them as friends. The old man was clearly a head chief and had been a fine warrior. He was old now but could potentially still lead men in battle. The son also was a chief and well respected. McGillycuddy had gotten to know him during the winter on the Missouri and found him intelligent and progressive. Little Wound and the short, powerful Little Big Man were there. Against the back wall stood Man Who Carries the Sword—George Sword—common man but a man of uncommon courage and fighting skill. Red Cloud, of course, held center stage with a seat right beside the chair supplied for McGillycuddy. He smiled and motioned toward the chair.

McGillycuddy smiled back. It had to be admitted that Red Cloud was quite magnificent. He was at a magic age for men who wear it well and Red Cloud wore it very well. His face was the prototype of the white man's image of the red man. The cheeks were very high and the nose long and broad. His hair was still raven black and though he was not a big man, he was clearly powerful. It was not hard to imagine him performing the physical feats of bravery, skill, and stamina for which he was famous. Every time McGillycuddy met him he reminded himself that this was the man who shot the wounded chief of another band of the Sioux in the head and led the successful resistance to the whites in the Powder River Country. It was important to keep in mind that Red Cloud was the killer of untold men. He was also an icon for white America—the best-known and best-loved member of his race and far more famous than all the other people in that room would ever be.

McGillycuddy and Red Cloud nodded to each other and Red Cloud smiled. Beside Red Cloud sat Nick Chappell, his brother-in-law, and as white as McGillycuddy himself. The little Frenchman exercised too much influence over Red Cloud and had no right to be at the meeting except that he was Red Cloud's official interpreter. *Need to be sure Johnny listens to make certain old Nick is giving it to Red Cloud straight.*

Red Cloud motioned toward the chair and McGillycuddy considered taking a seat on the bench like everyone else. It was a natural impulse to resist what could be construed as a command from the presiding chief. But there was no sense getting off on the wrong foot. He took the chair and laid his briefcase and rolled maps down on the floor beside him. "Good." Red Cloud said. He did not speak English but it was a trait of Red Cloud's to use English words when he could and McGillycuddy had wondered for years if the old chiefs facility with the language was not a matter of convenience.

Red Cloud drew the sacred pipe from its leather case and solemnly pushed the bowl and the stem together. Little Wound supplied the tobacco and McGillycuddy recognized immediately when the match was held to the bowl that it was heavily mixed with kinnikinnick. The pipe was passed to him as the honored guest. *And me with two fine Virginia panatelas in my pocket.* He took the pipe and drew in the sweet mixture of tobacco and wild herb. Then he passed the pipe back to Red Cloud who pulled on the stem and passed it on to Old Man Afraid. It took twenty minutes for the pipe to make the round of everyone in the room and during the frequent reloadings McGillycuddy stretched his legs and fought the impulse to roll his eyes in frustration.

Finally the preliminaries were complete and Red Cloud launched into a speech. Johnny was a good interpreter and whispered into McGillycuddy's ear as fast as Red Cloud spoke. They were both prepared to hear the standard thirty-minute, homespun cataloging of complaints for which Red Cloud had become famous. McGillycuddy had heard Red Cloud speak before and read many more speeches in the newspapers. Like many others, he always wondered if the eloquence came from Red Cloud or from the sympathetic translators and newspapermen. He trusted Johnny and listened intently. *The devil his due. The man can turn a phrase.*

"Hau tayan yahi yelo," Red Cloud said. He was glad to welcome their new father to the agency. He spoke warmly with no detectable sense of irony in calling McGillycuddy his father. It was as if there had been no incident with Irwin, and McGillycuddy was greatly encouraged. The second surprise in Red Cloud's speech was its brevity. He was talking along in his rambling way about the new agency and all present expected him to go on for perhaps the best part of an hour. But suddenly, in what seemed to be the middle of a thought he abruptly stopped and turned to McGillycuddy. "Até wanna taktokanu kte kin unkokiyaka pi," he said.

Johnny whispered into McGillycuddy's ear. "Now, Father, tell us of your plans."

It caught McGillycuddy by surprise but he stood immediately to ensure that he would not seem confused. "I am happy to be here," he began weakly. As Johnny interpreted and the Indians leaned forward to hear first him, then Nick Chappell's version, McGillycuddy focused on his message.

He was responsible for eight thousand Oglalas, many still quite hostile to the U. S. government. Now he looked at the representatives of those people. They had agreed to give up the rights to many hundreds of thousands of acres in return for food, clothing, justice, and a decent chance at the white man's life. McGillycuddy took a deep breath. *Honest: plain, and simple. Honest: plain, and simple.* He touched his chest with the fingers of both hands. "Many of you know me. I have been a guest in your lodges and you have been guests in my home. I know your land and indeed feel that in some ways it is my land. We know many things together." Here he paused to let the translators speak. When the nodding and congenial grunts had died away he went on. "But I know things that you do not know. I know the white man's ways and because I know these ways I can see the future. It will not be easy."

McGillycuddy watched the chiefs, particularly Red Cloud—the old war leader—and Young Man Afraid of His Horses—the young progressive. Their expressions were identical, sad but otherwise unreadable. "We are in a bad place here. It is a dangerous place. The troops at Fort Robinson are strong and not friendly to you."

As the translation was doled out there was a stir of agreement. "We must leave this place and come to a safe place. But the only road that will get us to this safe place is the white man's road."

McGillycuddy let that soak in. He studied the eyes around the room and saw that nearly all agreed with him though he knew that none would admit to such agreement. "I know that road and I will guide you."

"Ogle to unki ob unyakowa pi kta helhwo." "You will chase us down that road with your bluecoated troopers," Johnny interpreted. The speaker was an Indian that McGillycuddy did not know. A common man standing against the back wall.

"Not if you will work with me. I propose to build an all-Indian police force of fifty well-mounted and armed Oglala men. These men will enforce the laws of the agency. And once this force is established, there will be no more bluecoats on this reservation."

As the understanding of McGillycuddy's proposal spread through the room there were smiles and even a few hoots of delight. McGillycuddy smiled back. He knew it was a bold step and that he would have to argue persuasively with the military but he believed that an all-Indian police force was the best way to secure the stability needed to move forward. He had expected that the idea would be popular with most Oglalas and he had also anticipated that Red Cloud would not agree. He saw the old chief conferring with Nick Chappell and readied himself for what he knew was coming.

"Red Cloud says there is no need for you to build a police force and certainly no use in such a little force. He will supply a thousand warriors to keep the peace." Chappell stood up to deliver this remark and remained standing as if to take some credit for the counterproposal.

McGillycuddy looked past Chappell to the real power. He stared right at Red Cloud in a way that he knew full well was not polite in Oglala society. His reply had been practiced and he was ready. *Time to put that first foot on the white man's road.* "That is impossible," he said. "An Indian can no more serve two masters than a white man. He cannot serve his chief and the agent at the same time. The responsibility for law and order on this reservation lies with the United States government and the agent is the representative of the government. At this agency the police will not be beholden to any quasi ruler. Indeed they may be called upon to arrest, or even kill that person, his friends, or family. We are working toward a civilized community here, where individuals will consult their own interests before they obey orders from such quasi rulers."

He looked away from Red Cloud with no suggestion that he should respond. There was no need to hear Red Cloud's response. He was confident that his proposals were honest, fair, and aimed at the welfare of all Oglalas now and in the future. The Great Sioux Reservation was not yet a democracy and there would be no debate. A stunned silence settled over the room but McGillycuddy felt that some were biting their tongues watching Red Cloud sitting chastised.

Now McGillycuddy reached for his roll of maps and nodded for Johnny to help him tack one to the wall behind them. It was a map that McGillycuddy had drawn and prepared himself. One like the hundreds he had made of these people's land when he worked for the Department of Geological Survey. The Oglalas were familiar with maps but still looked at them as a curious novelty. Their maps were in their heads and often more accurate than any McGillycuddy had drawn. But these chiefs understood the value of maps and leaned forward to hear what McGillycuddy had to say. "This is the Oglala section of the Great Sioux Reservation, Pine Ridge." He outlined the vast section of the map with a pointer. "Ten thousand square miles. Well over a square mile for every man, woman, and child." *Imagine what*

*the Irish might have done with more than a square mile
for every soul. Where is the equity?*

"It is a great deal of land. Enough to make you all
wealthy in the white world. But here." He pointed to
the clusters of tiny dots he had drawn along a short section of White Clay Creek—one of scores of creeks on
the map. "Here," he repeated, "are the lodges of your
people. Squeezed into a few miles of river bottom closest to the agency." He tapped the other creeks on the
map. "These are fertile rivers and the land between is
prime grazing land. It is the sort of land that many,
many Americans are now risking their lives and for-
tunes to homestead." He looked away from the map
and out at the Indians. He let the pointer relax against
his thigh. "We will supply you with plows, seed, oxen,
and still feed and clothe you. But you must move away
from these centers of idleness and work the land like
white men."

After the translation was understood, Little Big Man
spoke up. "Le tanhan unkiyapi kinhan oyate oma kin
talo k'apamni unkitawa kin ijupi kte."

"If we move away from the place of the beef rations
the others will get our share," Johnny said.

"No one will get your share. I am in charge of the
beef ration now and no one will get more beef simply by
hanging around the agency. In fact, I have devised a
plan to give *extra* beef to those farthest away. They deserve more for the effort it will take them to come in off
their land."

There were noticeable nods of approval and McGillycuddy was very pleased. He swung right into the nuts
and bolts of moving the people away from the agency
and out onto the land. "One hundred steel plows and
one hundred yokes of oxen will arrive at this agency

within the month. In plenty of time to begin spring plowing. I would advise that each band begin to stake out its areas." He turned to the map and began pointing to large blue Xs that indicated land he had looked over and felt was promising for agriculture. He expected some questions, but when he turned back to the Indians he understood why the buzz in the room had died away and that there were no questions coming.

Red Cloud had risen to his feet and was obviously preparing to speak. *Here we go.* Red Cloud wore his black hair braided tightly with silver bells wound along the length of each braid. He wore no feathers but his moccasins were decorated with more bells and quill-work of light blue and green. Under his red blanket he wore a yellow white-man's shirt and a black leather vest. He was stern and commanded the attention of everyone in the room. He smiled resolutely and held his hands out to all present. He made the perfunctory opening comments that Sioux protocol required, and Chappell interpreted them tersely to McGillycuddy who did not bother to check the translation with Johnny Provost. He waited for the meat of what Red Cloud had to say. And when it came he was dumbfounded.

Red Cloud addressed his remarks to McGillycuddy and seemed to sneer at him as he spoke. When Nick Chappell began, McGillycuddy let his eyes drift from the interpreter to the chief who stood with arms crossed and head held artificially upright.

"Father," Chappell smiled directly to McGillycuddy. "The Great Spirit did not make us to work. He made us to hunt and fish. He gave us the great prairies and hills and covered them with buffalo, deer, and antelope. He filled the rivers with fish. The white man can work if he wants to, but the Great Spirit did not make us to work.

The white man owes us a living for the lands he has taken from us."

McGillycuddy did not take his eyes off of Red Cloud. He was fighting to hold his temper and mechanically he spoke so only Johnny could hear. "Is that what the Chief really said?"

He saw Johnny's head nod from the corner of his eyes. "Very, very close, sir."

The hell.

Part Three

The Yeoman Sioux

SUMMER, FALL 1879

7

A few days after the first confrontation with Red Cloud, McGillycuddy left the agency and traveled to the eastern side of the reservation. Supplies for the agency were stockpiled there along the Missouri River where the Oglalas and Brulé Sioux had spent the previous year. It was more than a hundred fifty miles via horseback and though Fanny had made several rides of that length in the past, she stayed at the agency. She knew that Valentine had wanted her to go along. He had even said that he wanted her with him, that a wife's place was with her husband. But Fanny had demurred with all the sweetness she could generate. Ostensibly her reason for staying home was that there was still a great deal to be done to finish moving into their new residence. With spring coming there was also a garden to plan and prepare. She told Valentine that there was simply too much for her to do. But, in fact, she did not feel up to the trip. She had gained some weight over the winter and believed the extra pounds were causing a lethargy that gripped her on and off most days. She was tired but she still had enough energy by the third day of McGillycuddy's absence to finish painting the upstairs bedrooms and was now seeing to it that her two young Indian helpers plowed the garden.

There had been a great deal of moving of furniture
and all day long the house seemed terribly hot. Several
times that day she stepped outside to stand on the porch
and cool herself and rest. She had just come out of the
house for the fourth time to enjoy the lovely spring day
when she heard the boys at the back of the house. They
were chattering away in Lakota and she had no idea
what they were talking about but they appeared to be
happy in their work. She stepped around the building
and took a moment to watch the boys struggling with
the yoke of oxen and the plow. They were boys of four-
teen and fifteen with long black braids tucked up under
head scarves the way they had seen the white men who
came to teach the Oglalas to farm. The plow bucked
and jolted and with each bounce it sent the sinewy
young men this way and that. They did not have the
technique mastered and Fanny giggled at their antics.
But she also knew that these boys had not been trained
for such work. They could no doubt ride a horse at full
speed without a saddle. They could shoot bows and
even rifles with deadly accuracy. They had killed many
animals—perhaps men. Now they were determined to
be farmers and she wished that Valentine could be there
to see them.

Of course it was true that they were the sons of a
notable progressive and that they were only doing
what all children do: follow in the footsteps of their
parents. There were many other Oglala boys who
would not be plowing the earth this spring. Many
were lounging around their camps, whittling on
bows, listening to their elders talk of past glories,
dreaming of breaking out and heading north to join
their cousins who were still at war with the United
States. They waited for the monthly beef issue, hoping

that a few of the cattle would escape so they could be killed from horseback like the buffalo they were meant to replace.

Fanny walked out to the garden and had just leaned to pick up a clod to test it for moisture when she heard her name being called. She stood up and turned too fast and had to stand perfectly still for an instant to retain her balance. But the two men who were just now coming around the house did not notice her little setback. It was Brownie O'Donald and George Blanchard. They smiled as they approached but Fanny could tell that something had happened.

"Afternoon, Mrs. McGillycuddy," O'Donald carried a paper in his hand and pulled off his hat as he came. He had done a wonderful job of helping McGillycuddy set up the administration of the reservation and was talking of staying on as the agent's assistant. McGillycuddy was hoping he would accept the job and Fanny assumed that that was what he had come to call about. "Is the agent home from the Missouri yet?"

"Why, no. He's due at any time."

Fanny smiled first to Brownie then to George Blanchard.

"Afternoon," Blanchard said.

"Good afternoon, George." Then to both men, "Nothing terribly important I hope."

The men looked at each other. "Well," George said, "I'm not sure how important it might be. I think maybe Brownie here has squelched it."

"What? Squelched what?" Now the men looked at each other again, not knowing if they should tell Fanny what they were talking about. It was, after all, government business and they weren't sure yet if Fanny enjoyed the professional confidence of her husband.

But neither man was shy and Blanchard blurted out

that it was a letter. "From Red Cloud," he said. "Red Cloud and a few others."

Now Fanny looked sternly at the two and O'Donald, as honest as McGillycuddy, held up the letter and said, "It's a letter from Red Cloud and several other chiefs asking that your husband be relieved of his duties and that Irwin be reinstated."

Fanny's eyes narrowed. "And just who is this letter addressed to?"

"Well," said O'Donald. He looked at the letter as if he couldn't quite remember whom Red Cloud had written to. "It's addressed to Rutherford Hayes."

"President Hayes?"

O'Donald nodded.

"And you squelched it?"

"I did."

The three of them stood in a circle along the edge of the newly plowed garden with the letter to President Rutherford B. Hayes held out between them. No one could think of just what to say but finally Fanny asked the obvious question. "Was he put up to this?"

Blanchard had been wondering the same thing. "Irwin is still in the area. Just over the Nebraska line. I'm betting he's at the bottom of this."

"By God," O'Donald said, "if he is, he's in violation of the law. A private citizen influencing the Sioux against a United States Indian agent is serious business."

"Then there you go, Mr. O'Donald. I think you should ride over the river to the Nebraska side and dispel this whole thing. I can assure you that Valentine has enough on his mind and would be thankful for the assistance."

"I think I'll just do that. 'Spect he's holed up at Louis Shangrau's ranch."

"That's the word I get at the store," Blanchard said.

"Then I'll be off, Mrs. McGillycuddy," O'Donald said, tipping his hat. "When the agent gets back tell him not to worry about this. I'm going to scare the hell out of Irwin. I'll leave Red Cloud to Agent McGillycuddy. Red Cloud and that man of God that moved in with him."

"Man of God?" Fanny asked. But O'Donald was moving away, obviously pleased to have the mission of threatening Irwin, the enemy of his boss. When he was out of earshot she turned to George Blanchard. "Man of God?"

"Red Cloud invited him to move into the house the government is building for him. Not even finished. Must be camping on the floor."

"What sort of man of God."

"Oh. Father Meinrad McCarthy. Catholic as the Pope."

Fanny's hand came up to her mouth. "Catholic? Oh dear."

My bony Protestant ass. McGillycuddy faced the priest with a steely stare. "Your presence on this reservation, ecclesiastic or otherwise, will not be allowed."

He had run into the black-robed priest as soon as he stepped from the stable after turning his horse over to Ott Means, the livery man. "Feed her well Ott. She's a good animal, brought me from the Missouri in four days."

"She'll get all that's good for her, sir."

"And what's been going on in my absence?" McGillycuddy stretched his saddle-sore frame and looked out the stable door at his growing and bustling enclave.

"Nothing much that I know of," Ott said. Just then the priest walked past the doorway.

"What in the . . ." McGillycuddy sputtered.

"Nothing but that old mackerel snapper, come to convert the savages."

As if the savages aren't dangerous enough!

McGillycuddy stormed from the stable and it was then that he accosted Father Meinrad McCarthy with his sentiment about the father not being welcome in any capacity.

"But I have an invitation from Red Cloud and a letter from Abbot Martin," the dumbfounded priest replied.

"Ah, but you must have an invitation from me and a letter from God." The old priest looked at him with a combination of fear and repulsion. "In point of fact, Father, the reservations have been divided up among the different creeds, as I'm sure you know, Pine Ridge is the hunting ground of the Episcopal."

Just then Johnny Provost, having heard of McGillycuddy's return came trotting up. He was a bit winded and his gentle face showed a rare trace of excitement.

"I see you've met the father," he said, but no one was listening to him.

"But the chief wants Catholics," the old priest was saying in a kind voice. "He has called for us to come."

"That well may be but I am calling for you to go. And go now. Come along, let's collect your kit and get you off this reservation."

"I'm staying with the chief."

"Which chief? We have a hundred or so."

"Red Cloud." The priest's chin was raised high as if he expected McGillycuddy to relent when he heard who was hosting him.

"Red Cloud?" McGillycuddy pretended to be deep in thought then brightened with recognition. "Oh, the deposed chief. Come along, let's see if the old boy is awake."

Johnny's eyes were large and he stood as still as a rabbit in the presence of a great horned owl. "Come along, Johnny. We'll take care of this mix-up right away."

They walked in silence to the edge of the agency grounds and then across a tiny clear tributary of White Clay Creek to the site of what was becoming Red Cloud's compound. It had been promised to Red Cloud years before as an enticement to settle on White Clay Creek and the chief was quite proud of the fact that he would be "living like a white man."

It had been a month since McGillycuddy had seen the house and, though it was not yet finished, he was still quite impressed. *Damned thing's bigger than mine.* "Step right up here, Father." He called to a pair of Red Cloud's men. "Help the father out here, boys. Where's your gear, Father?"

The priest was incredulous but not angry. He was clearly frightened that the situation might escalate and wanted to avoid a scene. He hurried to the front door and when he pulled it open, there stood Red Cloud.

Johnny had already stepped away and the two men McGillycuddy had called to help the father pulled up short. It was only then that it dawned on McGillycuddy how dangerous this situation could be. *The killer of men. Careful, careful now Valentine.* He stepped up onto the porch beside the priest. *But don't let on, don't weaken.*

The two men looked into each other's eyes. When McGillycuddy began to speak, Johnny translated without being asked. "Father McCarthy cannot stay, Red Cloud." The staring continued and every man present knew that Red Cloud was capable of instant and extreme violence. Knife or bare hands, he could overpower McGillycuddy in any way but one. "I'm determined to see that he goes," McGillycuddy said. "It is the law."

Red Cloud took a moment to measure this young, petulant, white man. He considered his options and decided to talk. "The Great Father and also the commissioner told me that whenever and wherever I selected my place for a home, that there I should have schoolhouses and churches with men in them in black gowns." Here he paused and turned to Johnny and Johnny translated slowly and precisely. But McGillycuddy had already understood the gist of what Red Cloud was saying. *Why, with such genuine traditions would you want Papists?* "There is one of those men here now." Red Cloud pointed to McCarthy. "I want him to stay."

McGillycuddy did not have to wait for this to be translated. "You and I both know that is against the policy of the United States government. Pine Ridge has been reserved for the Episcopal Church."

"We want Black Robes to teach our children." *Your children will curse you.* "And I want you to write a letter and write it strong to the Great Father and the commissioner telling them these things."

McGillycuddy waited for Johnny to finish translating to be sure he had the meaning exactly right. What Red Cloud was saying seemed outrageous but McGillycuddy nodded. "I will send such a letter. But in the meantime Father McCarthy will be residing off the reservation."

By then McCarthy, an amiable and now very nervous older man was beside himself to avoid conflict. "Yes, yes." He waved the two braves to enter the house. "This way, this way."

They disappeared into Red Cloud's house and McGillycuddy and Red Cloud stood facing each other on the porch like two cats, until McCarthy reappeared.

With a curt nod, McGillycuddy took his leave and led the priest, followed by the two exotic porters toward the livery where Johnny was already arranging for a carriage. On the walk to the livery, McGillycuddy spoke cordially to the priest and by the time the old man was loaded up and heading for Nebraska they were joking and had regressed to speaking in the Irish brogues of their parents.

Later that evening, after he had reunited with Fanny and had his dinner of side pork and potatoes, she told him of the letter that O'Donald had "suppressed." She knew it would send him into a rage so she waited until he had a glass of whiskey in his hand and was comfortably seated in front of the potbellied stove. He had his boots off and showed his exhaustion from the long ride and the afternoon conflict with Red Cloud and McCarthy. It was her plan that these factors would conspire to mollify his reaction. Her plan worked to an extent. He stood up from the chair and cursed long and loud. He paced the floor as he sipped on the whiskey. He poured himself another whiskey. He sent Louise out to find Johnny with instructions to find O'Donald and ask him to come at once to the house. The plan worked only in the sense that McGillycuddy did not race out and confront Red Cloud, but that seemed a success to Fanny.

It was dark by the time O'Donald arrived and McGillycuddy met him at the door. Louise wanted to sit in the kitchen and work on a quilt that she and Fanny had been making but Fanny sent her to bed with a raised eyebrow and a nod. Then Fanny finished up the kitchen chores, busying herself and keeping up the pretense that, to her, the letter addressed to the president of

the United States and derogatory to her husband was
the smallest of concerns. The men were still standing
and O'Donald was explaining that he just arrived back
from the Nebraska ranch where Irwin was staying when
Fanny breezed into the front room, greeted O'Donald as
if nothing of importance were happening, and kissed
her husband good night.

She took her leave and mounted the narrow, freshly
painted stairs to the main sleeping room. As she passed
Louise's room she pulled the door tight but when she
went into her room she left her own door open so she
could hear what the men were saying. She undressed
quickly but quietly and was just ready to turn the lamp
down and step into her nightgown when her reflection
in the full-length mirror caught her attention. She stood
in white, wavy light and noticed how the shadows of
her full breasts diffused across her rib cage. Her pubic
area was in darker shadow and she could understand
how a female body captivated men. She ran her hands
over the breasts and down her sides to the round hips.
They were larger now than they had been only a few
months before. Valentine still found them inspiring but
the touch of her hands, indeed the touch of any hands
did not affect her the way it once had. She heard Valentine telling O'Donald what had transpired between Red
Cloud, Father McCarthy, and himself. "When did the
priest arrive?" he was asking. The mention of the priest
sent Fanny scurrying to her nightgown and the lamp.
She stepped into the nightgown and choked the wick
down in one motion. By the time O'Donald answered
she was under the covers.

"You hadn't been gone a day," O'Donald said and it
was clear from his unusually tenuous voice that the idea
of throwing a priest off the reservation made him un-

comfortable. Probably a Catholic, Fanny thought. She hoped Valentine would understand this and be gentle.

"Yes, well that's the way they often are, isn't it?"

"Well, I suppose they are, sir," O'Donald said and seemed as if he was considering saying something more about the old priest. But he changed his mind. "But let me tell you about Irwin."

"Yes, indeed. But would you have a whiskey? I'm having another."

"I would, sir. Yes, a whiskey would be appropriate."

"Appropriate? Are we celebrating?"

"In a manner of speaking, sir. Could be said."

In the silence that followed Fanny could almost hear the copper liquid burbling into the glasses. "Cheers," Valentine said. Then another short silence and Fanny heard the tiny, involuntary purring of the men.

"Well, then," Valentine said. "Tell me why we should be celebrating a letter that asks for my removal, demonizes the administrators that hired us, and no doubt canonizes the Democrats."

The uneasiness had disappeared from O'Donald's voice. Now there was the hint of humor. "It's not nearly that articulate, sir. Have a look." Fanny heard the rustle of paper as O'Donald retrieved the letter from his coat.

It took a moment for Valentine to read and digest the letter. "It certainly isn't Emerson," he finally said.

"Not Red Cloud either." Now O'Donald was certainly smiling. It was his usual state and Fanny heard it in his speech.

"Indeed not Red Cloud."

"I thought I detected the style of Mr. Irwin so I rode down to the outlaw ranch where he's taken up residence with cattle thieves and liquor runners. I confronted him."

"He's not good in a confrontation."

"No sir. He gets scared, like all people of weak conviction, then tries to cover his fear with indignation."

"He confessed to writing the letter."

"Blurted it right out."

"And you explained the law to him."

"Informed him that if his arse was not on the eastbound train tomorrow it would be cooling off in the brig at Fort Robinson."

"And he agreed to go?"

"Packin' before I was done talkin', sir."

Fanny heard Valentine's snort of amusement. Then, "there's no need to call me sir after hours. Call me Mac." More burbling of whiskey and a crystalline clink.

"In my absence things got a little Machiavellian. Democrats and priests running wild on my reservation."

"They did. But they're put to rights now."

"Well . . ." There was the remote rustle of paper again. "I tend to agree in general. But see here, Brownie." Fanny had never heard Valentine call O'Donald by his first name and she grinned in the dark of her bedroom. "This is quite a group of signatories."

"Twenty-one."

"Quite a list. I recognize most of these chiefs and many don't surprise me. Many are hostile, either just surrendered from the north or those with clear sympathies for going back to the wild." Then Fanny heard her husband mumble more to himself than to O'Donald and she would not have been able to decipher the words had she not heard him mumble them often before. "Can't really fault those sentiments."

"I'm sure the signatures were coerced."

"No doubt. Irwin's idea and Red Cloud delivered the goods." Another round of whiskey into the glasses.

"Oddly, though they are truly dangerous, I don't worry about the hostiles on this list. I know they are volatile and we must be prepared to deal with them. It is the others, the progressives on the list that trouble me. Young Man Afraid troubles me the most. And kind, good-hearted old Clearance Looking Dog. I met him years ago in Washington. I thought he understood that the old ways were gone."

"Both of those fellows are fine men and you can count on them. They and many others were deceived. I'm betting they didn't even know what Red Cloud and Irwin were asking them to sign. Their loyalties are strange you know. Not like ours. No real structure to compare to ours."

Fanny knew what O'Donald said was true. She had heard Valentine say much the same many times and was not at all surprised to hear him agree. "It's us, Brownie. They never had a hierarchy like ours. Every man was free to do as he pleased. There was no order as we know it."

"Not sure I'd call that an inferior culture." Fanny could hear the smile in Brownie's voice.

McGillycuddy said, "All I know is that is how we beat them on the battlefield. It was only our notion of discipline, division of labor, and authority. They were the better horsemen. They knew the country. The country knew them." McGillycuddy sipped his drink and paused for thought. "No, political leadership was mostly our idea."

"And we ended up with men like Red Cloud."

"An extraordinary man but with no notion of leadership beyond the battlefield and no philosophy of society, compromise, or vision of the future." Both men had had enough to drink but Fanny heard the sound of whiskey one more time.

After the pause, O'Donald exhaled with regret. "We both know it's a bit of a powder keg," he said. His voice was very serious now. "I don't know the Oglalas the way you do. Maybe no literate white man does. But I been on lots of reservations for the department and I know Indians. They want their old lifestyle with the guarantees and compassion of civilization. Won't happen. There's bad times ahead if they don't listen to you."

"Civilization is not like hunting or war."

"Not nearly as exhilarating."

Now Valentine chuckled. "Downright boring, sometimes."

And there was merriment in O'Donald's voice too. "Going to all be all right, sir."

"Mac."

"Going to be all right, Mac. You should just put this letter out of your mind. Don't even worry about it. It was all trumped up and doesn't mean a thing."

"I believe you're right, Brownie. I won't worry about the letter. But I'm a little worried about you." Fanny could tell that there was a joke coming even though the words were serious. "I understand you've been aiding and abetting the enemy."

"Beg your pardon?"

"That may be a trifle strong. Contributing to the opposition?"

"Oh. I think I know."

"Of course you do. McCarthy spilled the beans. Turned out to be quite gregarious once he was reconciled to the fact that he was headed for Nebraska." The thoughtful chuckle. "We must be paying you too much if you have an extra twenty dollars to contribute to the old boy's missionary work."

O'Donald had caught on to the joke but he still

wasn't sure if he was in trouble or not. "Missionary work off this reservation only. I'll send him a note to earmark it as such."

As soon as Valentine began to laugh O'Donald joined him and Fanny drifted off to sleep with the pleasant sound of men laughing in her living room.

But an hour later, when Valentine finally came to bed, his mirth had disappeared. She felt him undressing a little shakily in the darkness then the dullness of air that accompanies the presence of a person standing close. She was afraid that the liquor had made him amorous but when he slid into bed he only laid his head on her shoulder as a child might do. She was at once relieved and heartsick, but glad to hold him tight against her until his breathing became steady and deep.

8

O'Donald's prediction turned out to be correct. McGillycuddy restrained himself from confronting Red Cloud about the letter to President Hayes asking for his removal and the issue simply evaporated. But by the middle of the summer another issue had risen to prominence and was taking up a great deal of McGillycuddy's day and likely most of Red Cloud's too. It was the issue of the Indian police force and McGillycuddy did his best to appear as if Red Cloud's opposition was of no concern to him.

At least once a week McGillycuddy rose before sunlight and rousted Ott Means from the livery. Once Ott was up and working at readying a saddle horse or buggy—depending on the day's destination—McGillycuddy walked back down what was now a graded street superior to many towns in Dakota Territory and entered Blanchard's store for coffee. George and his wife were always up early and the coffeepot seemed bottomless. He would chat with this pleasant family while his horse was being saddled and fed and more than once found himself envying the domestic scene of husband, wife, and children. They seemed extremely happy in their work of providing a home for their family. The younger ones often wandered into the store, still charmingly sleepy, looking for breakfast or simply affection. Often it was the oldest child, Julia, who catered to their needs and sometimes McGillycuddy would enter into conversations with her and her parents that were so pleasant that he hated to leave.

But often his destination was many miles from the reservation headquarters. His mission was to visit villages that, at his urging had sprung up along the most farmable river bottoms. These were villages headed by mostly young progressive chiefs like Young Man Afraid; the heir apparent to Red Cloud's imagined throne. Only one older chief had shown signs of breaking away from Red Cloud's tyranny. Clearance Looking Dog was a chief from the older generation and even though he had passively opposed Red Cloud he was still respected and loved by all. That Clearance Looking Dog was a good man was perhaps the only thing that McGillycuddy and Red Cloud agreed upon.

When McGillycuddy visited his village he took extra time to spend with the old chief who worked his fields like the rest of the two hundred men in his band. When he spoke, Clearance Looking Dog's eyes glistened with excitement. "It will be all right," the old man had learned to say in English. "Better days are ahead." *The power of the dreamer.* And dreaming was part of McGillycuddy's message.

He had encouraged this conversion from warrior/hunter to yeoman farmer knowing that the latter was perhaps the crueler life and so he felt obligated to show his continued support. Not simply by supplying equipment, but by his physical presence. So each week he toured on horseback a section of the nascent agriculture that was blossoming all around the reservation. He encouraged the planting of the new wonder crop called alfalfa. He oversaw the planting and harvesting of the hay. He beamed at the surprise and pride in the faces of the Indians as pumpkins, corn, and beans began to ripen. As the summer progressed he took Fanny along when he took a buggy and the Oglala farmers always showered her with the best of their produce. At the lodge of Young Man Afraid Fanny was whisked away by the women hungry for the knowledge of cooking with pots and vegetables. McGillycuddy would be gone for hours observing the men at work and when he returned he found Fanny kneeling on a hide with giggling girls and women all around. The weather was perfect that summer for farming and McGillycuddy gloated inwardly at the Cassandras who had predicted that Dakota was not fit for farming. It was a great triumph for his policies and the chiefs of the bands who had moved out from the agency were coming steadily into McGillycuddy's political camp.

He would have liked to see more, encourage more, assist more, but too often he had to hurry back to his office to deal with the establishment of the Indian police force. It seemed that while he was out developing an economic base for the Oglalas, Red Cloud was organizing opposition to a police force of his own people that would guard the new economy from threats both internal and external. It was all completely understandable to McGillycuddy. Who would want an independent police force when you were used to having your own private army? Red Cloud had been made a monarch by the government's insistence that he was the chief of all the Oglalas and monarchs, no matter how they derived their right to rule, were loathe to surrender power. The battle to establish the Indian police force had raged all spring and summer. Man Who Carries the Sword, rechristened George Sword, had finally convinced fifty warriors that Red Cloud would not be allowed to kill them if they took the well-paying job of Indian policemen. He had come up with good men who seemed very willing to enforce the laws of the United States and the yet-to-be-established tribal courts.

Sword appeared to be taking his duties seriously and, if physical prowess equated to effectiveness on the job, there was no doubt that he would be an efficient police captain. He had been a celebrated warrior only a few years before when the Oglalas were still in the north with Crazy Horse and Sitting Bull. He fought alongside Red Cloud in the Wagon Box Fight and, even though he was a commoner, traveled to Washington with Red Cloud and a cadre of chiefs in 1870 after they had defeated the United States in Red Cloud's War. But unlike many of the other notable warriors, Sword had retained his independence from Red Cloud and stood firm against the ever-present threat of some who wanted to break out and rejoin the hostiles. He had been to the eastern cities of the whites and understood the military hopelessness of breaking out. Now he was determined to see that his people become a nation of laws like the whites and was ready to fight in this new way to see it happen.

Captain Sword was large for an Indian, nearly six feet tall, and surprisingly heavy through the shoulders. His cheekbones were extremely high and his eyes narrow and Asian in appearance. He had always worn his hair in very long braids in the traditional way but after an interview with McGillycuddy had agreed to cut it short, more in keeping with the tradition of a white policeman. For this he was chided, and some even went so far as to make fun of him for less than a manly appearance.

His old commander Red Cloud dismissed him as inef-
fectual as a warrior and even though the chief was older
and softer than he had been when he killed several men
in one day with his bare hands, few would have taken
long odds on Sword.

But McGillycuddy had known Sword since just after
the Custer fight and saw in him exactly the sort of common man to lead the Oglalas into a new life. McGillycuddy was quite aware that the stakes in this Indian
police force game he was playing with Red Cloud were
very high. McGillycuddy was putting his money on
Sword—on Sword and the power of the philosophy of
law that stood behind Sword.

To make sure that his captain and policemen had every
advantage, McGillycuddy not only supplied them with
good horses but traveled to Washington to convince Secretary Schurz that first, the Indian police force was a
good idea, and second, that they needed to be armed with
rifles. The idea of an Indian police force was accepted
readily but the idea of firearms in the hands of Indians
who were constantly being tempted to break out and join
their still very hostile brothers was not taken seriously.

"Dr. McGillycuddy, the best police forces of this
nation—cities like Philadelphia, Chicago, and New
York—are armed with clubs and do excellent jobs of enforcing the law."

"With due respect, Mr. Secretary, when you visit the
Pine Ridge Reservation in the fall you will see that we
do not live in an enclosed environment. Our crimes do
not occur in dark alleyways or smoky poolrooms. It is
a land of distance, great vistas, and sweeps of terrain
that render the noble billy club as useless as a cigar."

"But to arm the Indians who are only partly sub-
dued . . . It would not be allowed by the military."

"The military understands my position."

"Indeed, that is why they would never stand for it."

"They might." McGillycuddy was being crafty and Schurz knew it.

"Well, Mac." Secretary Schurz was smiling at his entertaining, if petulant, junior agent. "As you know, the military has not agreed with any suggestion of this department since before the Custer tragedy. If you can get the blessing of the Department of War to arm the enemy I would be forced to defer to its inspired judgement."

Now McGillycuddy smiled. He had anticipated Schurz's reaction and had visited General Sheridan before coming to the Department of the Interior. Sheridan and McGillycuddy had known each other since General Crook had asked that Sheridan assign McGillycuddy to his command before the Yellowstone Campaign. He knew that the Departments of War and the Interior had been fighting over Indian policy for years and presented his request for rifles in such a way that Sheridan saw a denial on his part as agreement with Schurz. "I have a letter right here," McGillycuddy said, "authorizing the transferal of sixty-four Spencer rifles from the armory at Fort Robinson to the Pine Ridge Agency."

Schurz reached across the desk and took the letter. He slid his glasses down on his nose so that he could focus on McGillycuddy and still read the letter. He took his time and as the seconds ticked along a smile crept onto his face. Finally he pushed the letter back across the desk to McGillycuddy. "It is good to see that I was right."

"Sir?"

"Right about you, McGillycuddy. I knew you were sly enough for the job. Now I'm hoping you are not too sly. You make sure your Indian flatfeet are careful with those rifles. There is huge potential for embarrassment and tragedy."

He brought the rifles back to the reservation and gathered Captain Sword and his fifty men around to take them from the cases. The policemen removed them from the boxes as if they were delivering children into the world. These were weapons that they had never imagined possessing. Here was power and they touched the blued barrels and shiny walnut stocks as lovers touch each other's skin. Pride swelled from the guardhouse where this ceremony was taking place and within minutes the word was spreading across the reservation.

To the rifles, Red Cloud made a formal protest and came to McGillycuddy's office in person to lodge the complaint on the same day that ten boxes of uniforms were delivered. Red Cloud was accompanied, as he often was, by white men who had married into the tribe. These men were disparagingly referred to as squaw men and were well known to have undue influence over the chief. That day it was the ubiquitous Nick Chappell and Todd Randall, both suspected of illegally selling whiskey to Indians and clearly living off the beef issue intended for the support of Indian people only. McGillycuddy had no time for either man but had to put up with them because Red Cloud was entitled to an interpreter. It was unfortunate that he chose these two men. Particularly unfortunate that Chappell had pressed his advantage of being married to Red Cloud's sister and insisted on the preposterous salary of $1,200 per year from the United States government, $700 more than was appropriated for any translator and half of McGillycuddy's salary for running the entire reservation. As a result of this extortion and the fact that his marriage entitled him to free food from that same government, Nick was perhaps the richest man on the reservation and that stuck in McGillycuddy's craw.

Johnny Provost had heard that the delegation was coming and warned the agent. Johnny, McGillycuddy, and O'Donald met Red Cloud and the two white men, who dressed like Indians, on the porch where the boxes of uniforms were stacked. Captain Sword, who had heard that the uniforms had arrived and was very anxious to see them, came from the other direction and Chappell and Randall sneered at him as they met. Sword did not sneer and neither did Red Cloud. *Still respectful. Wary campaigners caught on opposite sides of the lines.*

"The chief has something he needs to say," Randall began.

"Let me guess," McGillycuddy replied. He looked at Red Cloud. "You don't like the idea of my police force having rifles."

Johnny began to translate but Chappell interrupted. "You're damned right he doesn't. Those traitors shouldn't have rifles."

McGillycuddy spun and put his finger in Nick's face. Both Sword and O'Donald moved instinctually closer. They knew Chappell's reputation for violence with a knife. "I'm speaking to Red Cloud," the agent sputtered. "I'll thank you to be silent except to translate." McGillycuddy was aware of Chappell's reputation too, but had flashed red at the greasy little man's impudence.

Johnny remained cool and went right on with the translation. Red Cloud seemed already to understand and spoke calmly to Randall. "Says those guns rightfully belong to him."

"Nonsense," McGillycuddy said. "Which one of you put that idea into his head?"

"He's got his own mind," Randall said.

"He certainly does and I'd be glad to listen to him. But not to you." McGillycuddy turned to Red Cloud. "The police force is commissioned under Captain Sword." The agent indicated Sword with his right hand. "It is being trained with the assistance of Mr. O'Donald." He indicated O'Donald with his left. "They are legally armed with Spencer rifles donated by the United States Army and will act as surrogates for the army in enforcing the laws of this nation and reservation. It is an effort to keep the regular army off this reservation and is a courtesy to you and your people."

Red Cloud was nodding to Johnny's gentle translation but clearly was not pleased. "Furthermore, the police force will be dressed in uniforms." Knowing of the red man's love of uniforms McGillycuddy was both deviling Red Cloud and rewarding Sword whom he now motioned to open a box of the uniforms.

Red Cloud spoke and Nick Chappell began to translate in surly fashion. "He says you don't have the right to start up your own army. He's got lots of warriors."

"He has no warriors. He signed a treaty of peace."

Sword was more interested in the uniforms than the argument he had heard for months now. He tore at the boxes as Red Cloud listened to Chappell then spoke indignantly in Lakota. "Says he is not afraid of your little police force," Chappell translated. "He could crush it any time he wanted."

This got Sword's attention and he looked up seriously holding a crisp new gray woolen uniform in one hand. Todd Randall began to laugh heartily. "For Christ's sake," he said. "I know that uniform. I wore one for three years fightin' for the Confederacy." Then in Lakota to Sword, "You and your boys are going to make wonderful targets for the cavalry. They're used to shootin' those uniforms." His laughter infected Red Cloud and Chappell and Sword looked down at the uniform as if it were poisonous.

"They are not Confederate uniforms," McGillycuddy said. He knew them to be uniforms created for the Columbian Guard at the Centennial Exposition in Philadelphia in 1876 but when he saw Sword's face he realized that the police would never wear them. They looked too much like the uniforms of the United States' great, defeated enemy.

It took six weeks before the uniforms could be replaced with ones more like the cavalry uniforms that Sword and his men respected. It had come to light that Brownie O'Donald was not only an excellent clerk but had been a sergeant in the army before going to work for the Bureau of Indian Affairs. He took an active interest in the proud but ragtag force of Indian policemen and volunteered his expertise to drill Sword's men. As he put it, "Brave and tough, you bet. But they need a bit of discipline and discipline is my specialty." When he could, McGillycuddy walked out to the edge of the settlement to watch them train. There was always a crowd of spectators: young women pretending to happen by the eligible braves honing their skills, boys engaging in a bit of hero worship, proud mothers, and always a few intractable older warriors who supported Red Cloud in his attempts to intimidate prospective candidates. These men refused to farm and if they saw McGillycuddy watching them, they elevated their heads and looked beyond him.

But on the occasions when McGillycuddy was able to stand unnoticed at the edge of the trees that surrounded the drill field he could see that the old warriors looked

on with longing. The Spencer rifles and excellent army
horses were objects to be coveted and the precision ex-
ercises that O'Donald ran the force through incessantly
seemed to arouse the fighting blood in these warriors.
One such day in September when McGillycuddy had
slipped along the creek to his usual observation post he
was amazed to see that Red Cloud himself stood with
the recalcitrant warriors as Sword's men drilled in the
hot sun. Immediately McGillycuddy smelled a rat.
O'Donald had told him that the men were working very
hard and McGillycuddy had arranged to roast a steer as
a sort of celebration. At the edge of the field the steer
turned on a spit while a half dozen boys tended the fire.
No doubt the news had spread and that was the reason
for the extra spectators. But, since the feed was a re-
ward for hard work and a celebration for the great
progress the force had achieved, the presence of Red
Cloud seemed odd indeed.

   McGillycuddy did not think that Red Cloud had noticed him in the shadows of the trees but at the sound of
running pony hooves the cunning chief turned and
looked square at the agent. As the sound intensified and
the police force looked around from their marching in
the hot sun Red Cloud smiled. When the first of his two
hundred mounted warriors broke from the river's trees
and onto the drill field the chief laughed. Most of the
horses were poor, but a few were illegal war ponies with
fine heads and chiseled muscles running from their
painted withers and rumps to their hard black hooves.
When he thought back on it, McGillycuddy believed he
responded properly to Red Cloud's sophomoric trick.
He ran to the center of the drill field with his hands
raised, not to try to stop the onrush of Red Cloud's
men, but to restrain the police force. O'Donald had

read the situation exactly the same and stood with Sword at the head of his troops with his arms outstretched in a gesture that quelled the rush of blood in each man. The Spencers were loaded but only one man unslung the weapon from his shoulder and Sword himself rushed to grasp the muzzle in his iron grip. Red Cloud's men were armed only with lances and bows but rode down on them with whoops of glee. The policemen did not break formation. They stood their ground, ready to accept the order to shoulder their weapons and fire if necessary. And Sword stood before them as brave as Stonewall Jackson and stared poison at the first warriors to ride past. They circled the pitifully small band of policemen then strung out for the roasting steer. The fire-tending boys broke and ran as lariats snaked out and jerked the beef from the spit.

At this point McGillycuddy looked back at Red Cloud who was enjoying the show immensely. Along with the other older men Red Cloud pointed and laughed. Two of his men held the steer between their horses and in an uncanny feat of horsemanship turned back in the direction from which they had come. Before the band of marauders was off the drill field McGillycuddy had stalked up to Red Cloud and was sputtering in his face. "You—" he said.

Already O'Donald and Sword had their hands on McGillycuddy's shoulders restraining him from getting too close. "You and your silly games!"

Red Cloud was perfectly calm. He glanced at O'Donald and Sword, daring them to assault him or release McGillycuddy. Finally, when he saw that no one would accept his challenge. He looked to McGillycuddy and spoke five words in a flat, frightening English, "It is no game, McGillycuddy."

9

In the aftermath of the Custer tragedy, Sitting Bull had fled to Canada and from that safe haven continued the Sioux hostilities toward the United States. His men raided south of the border and envoys sent to entice reservation Indians to come back to the warpath slipped on and off Pine Ridge constantly. McGillycuddy and his fledgling police force tried to intercept the illegal traffic of messages between Sitting Bull and the Pine Ridge chiefs but intelligence of such communication was very hard to come by. The old chiefs and young warriors who embraced the notion of joining Sitting Bull in one last battle for the old way, threatened the progressives who saw their only salvation in becoming farmers—equivalent to the white homesteaders who longed to get at Indian lands if the Sioux failed at McGillycuddy's experiment. Within the white community there were rumors of the "tame Sioux" breaking out to join their "wild" brothers and the specter conjured up by the union of the two great masses of Indians terrified the land-seeking immigrants amassed in tiny frontier communities.

As agent, McGillycuddy was forever accused of allowing cross-fertilization of his charges with the hostiles of the north. The claim was that the Oglalas of Pine Ridge were supplying the Hunkpapas of Sitting Bull with warriors and the materials of war gleaned from the commodities issued to them by the very government they intended to ravage. This scenario had indeed played a part in the Custer massacre and was fresh and raw in the minds of taxpayers. McGillycuddy and every white man except perhaps the liberal, eastern reformers of T. A. Bland's ilk saw an uprising of hostile and "friendly" Sioux as a very real and horrible possibility. McGillycuddy had always felt that the best hedge against such a catastrophe was to break Red Cloud's grip on the Oglalas by encouraging younger, less bellicose leaders, some with more right to the title of supreme chief, to step to the fore. That is why he was particularly excited when on the fifteenth of September of 1877 Young Man Afraid of His Horses sent a secret message that he would like to meet.

The message came through Johnny Provost who was related to the young vibrant chief through marriage and was delivered after McGillycuddy had retired to his home for the day. "He says he has information for you," Johnny said.

"Information?" McGillycuddy had just finished his favorite dinner of pork, potatoes, and apple pie and was pouring himself a whiskey. "What sort of information?" He looked hard at his assistant of four years and knew by Johnny's averted eyes that even if he knew what Young Man Afraid had to tell him, he wasn't going to say. "He wants to meet?"

"Could you come to his village as if it is just a visit to see the farming?"

"That's what he wants?"

Johnny nodded and McGillycuddy understood that

Young Man Afraid did not want the rest of the reservation to know that he was supplying information to the agent. "I plan to go out at the end of the week to inspect the new irrigation channels."

"Tomorrow," Johnny said. "Early."

It was not like him to make such a commanding statement. "Tomorrow morning then. You'll send a message to Young Man Afraid that we are coming?"

Johnny nodded again and slipped out the door, leaving McGillycuddy intrigued and slightly uneasy about the secrecy of it all. He walked to the bookshelf that Fanny had built to store his most prized volumes. He took a cigar from a wooden box on the top shelf and gazed absently at the leather-bound collection of Shakespeare. His eyes fell on the Henry plays, then *Hamlet, Macbeth, King Lear.*

"Valentine?" He turned with a start to see Fanny standing at the kitchen door. She still wore her apron and her face was an open expression of puzzlement. "I thought Johnny was here. I have a piece of pie for him."

"Well, he was here. He must have been feeling his Indian side this evening. He was a bit shy and stealthy." McGillycuddy smiled, shrugged his shoulders, and chewed off the end of the cigar.

Fanny smiled back at him. "You're a bit stealthy yourself. What was it?"

McGillycuddy shrugged again. "A breakthrough? An outbreak? I'm not quite sure." He delicately spit the cigar end into his hand and walked to the door.

Fanny stepped into the room. "All right, Dr. McGillycuddy. Out with it. What is happening?"

McGillycuddy opened the door to toss the cigar end into the yard but the cool autumn air so enticed him that he waved gallantly to Fanny to join him on the porch. She smiled at his foolishness but removed her apron, tossed it back into the kitchen, and walked toward the open door. He held the door for her and they moved out into the crisp evening where they stood for a moment, dumbstruck by the quiet and closeness of the prairie stars. "My, my," was all Fanny could say.

The unlit cigar was still in McGillycuddy's hand when he pointed to the southeast. "Orion," he said. "The old dog is back for the fall hunt." Then nearly to himself, "Pity there no longer is a fall hunt." He remained staring up at the enormous sky.

Fanny had seen sadness descend on her husband before. It could come at the tiniest suggestion of the times before the Sioux Wars. It was about his love of this adopted land. The fact that he had known it before the Sioux Wars, before the troubles, when it was all the hunt, fast horses, and uncrowded space. She knew the road that McGillycuddy was peering into at that moment and she did not want him to start down it. She called him back. "What was it that Johnny wanted?"

It took an instant for McGillycuddy to shake the memories of war, the hunt, and freedom from his mind. "Johnny, Johnny." He turned to Fanny and pushed the cigar into his mouth. "A secret meeting at the camp of the heir apparent to Red Cloud's throne." He was fumbling in his pockets for a match. "Not really sure what it's all about."

"A meeting with Young Man Afraid?"

"Precisely." He located a match and now took the cigar from his mouth.

"He's a good man."

"He's the Oglalas' best hope. Intelligent, reasonable." McGillycuddy struck the match on the porch rail and held it to the cigar. "A man who can see the future."

They both watched the cigar begin to glow as McGillycuddy rolled it in the flame. When it was evenly heated McGillycuddy held the unlit end to his mouth and drew. The cigar caught in earnest and Fanny breathed in the smoke that had always reminded her of gentlemen and pleased her very much. But the giddy feeling that the presence of men had given her once was no longer there. Now the cigar smoke was little more than smoke and it sometimes heightened the vague nausea that plagued her daily. "And what is this clandestine meeting about?"

"I don't know. Something important. I imagine a treachery of some sort."

"Valentine, don't make light. You don't know who else may be there. It's not unheard of for officials like yourself to he lured to such meetings for mischievous purposes."

"Young Man Afraid will keep our meeting to himself. He and I see the future of the Sioux in a similar way." McGillycuddy puffed on the cigar and looked back up at the stars. They were so close and the horizons so low that the little house seemed to be floating in the night sky. He did not really see the future much like Young Man Afraid saw the future. Or at least he did not relish that future. If he were to be honest he would have to admit to admiring Red Cloud's vision more. It was the only case he could name where he felt deception was the best strategy. "No, Young Man Afraid will see that I'm safe."

His voice had trailed off with that last statement and Fanny knew that he was back on the Tongue River. The Cannon Ball. The Knife. She knew he was reliving the buffalo hunts he had experienced, knew he was wondering how things on the plains had come to such a pass.

She had heard him talk of it many times. But not for more than a year. He only talked of his great passions when his maudlin, Irish heart was moved by the life around him. Otherwise he kept his dearest thoughts to himself.

Johnny was waiting for McGillycuddy at the livery. It was six o'clock and the early morning promised to bleed into an exceptional autumn day. But the days had begun to shorten and so it was only partly light. There was no good road to Young Man Afraid's village so Johnny had ordered saddle horses and Ott Means was busy preparing them. McGillycuddy and Johnny leaned on the hitching rail while they waited and McGillycuddy fidgeted. He had never liked letting another man saddle his horse; it smacked of something un-republican. As he thought of that he smiled. Republican in the constitutional sense, not necessarily the political sense. But at any rate he longed to stride back into the stable, sling a saddle onto a horse, and get on with it. But Means, big, amiable, and politically connected was an appointed contractor. It would not do to appear contemptuous.

They waited and finally McGillycuddy asked if Johnny had had his coffee. He was hoping that Johnny would say that he had not and it suddenly struck McGillycuddy that he wanted an excuse to go to Blanchard's store. In the cool morning air he imagined the warmth of the room. Perhaps just the woodstove.

But Johnny had already had his coffee and upon receiving that news he imagined Johnny's bachelor cabin but could not imagine enough heat from his stove to warm even yesterday's coffee. He was staring at the ground as he was thinking this and must have felt

Johnny's stare because, when he looked up, the soft, dark eyes were just moving away. "Here you go, fellas." It was Ott with the horses prancing behind him. "Brung you the bay that you like, Doctor. He's a dandy."

McGillycuddy couldn't help smiling. Both horses were fine animals and the bay particularly fine. It reminded him of a horse he had ridden after the Rosebud Creek fight where he had been in charge of fifty-six wounded men. His first battle, his first field surgeries. He felt the bay's chest and neck, guided the stirrup to his uplifted boot, and swung up into the saddle. His lanky body had always formed itself well to horses and he felt happy and at home in the saddle.

Johnny was a different story. He might be half Sioux but riding brought out his French side. He sat his saddle willing enough but he always looked uncomfortable, as if the seat were wet or very hot. They had ridden many hundreds of miles together. But Johnny's slightly pudgy body always appeared perched on the horse rather than settled into it, like McGillycuddy's. But despite this awkwardness, Johnny was game. They headed out at a fast walk down the main street of the still-sleeping community but as soon as they got to the other side of White Clay Creek McGillycuddy urged the bay into a lope. Johnny, flapping his elbows like Sancho Panza, stuck right with him.

But they did not ride through the idyllic Spanish countryside. They rode the rough country between the breaks of White Clay and Wounded Knee Creeks where only grass, sage, and a few stunted cedars grew. It was a wonderful day with almost no wind and McGillycuddy relished the thought of the twelve miles to Young Man Afraid's village. They kept up a cadence of loping a mile, then walking a quarter until the tip of the tepee poles came into sight. The village was still a mile off and McGillycuddy took that last mile to let the horses blow so that, except for the dark sweat stains, they might pass for a pair of riders simply out to inspect the progress of the farming operation. It was then that McGillycuddy most appreciated the bay. Once the pace slackened the animal let out a single tremendous puff, shook himself from head to toe—which made McGillycuddy smile—then raised his muscular head and stepped smartly down the trail and into the Indian village.

Young Man Afraid of His Horses had men posted on high ground awaiting their arrival. When McGillycuddy saw one riding toward the village he looked to Johnny but Johnny had already seen him. He gave a small shrug and nodded toward a large field along the creek bottom where dozens of men and women walked the green rows of beans. They were pulling and chopping weeds and were dressed in the cotton work clothes given to them under the terms of the treaty. Several left off their work and raised hands to greet the agent. Farther along the creek fifty men, their shirts off and backs bent to the shovels they held, worked to dig an irrigation ditch that would be finished in time to catch next spring's floodwaters. *Planning for the future. Wonderful!* The laborers looked up and paused. The foreman called out and they stopped their work to lean on the shovels and shout hellos.

McGillycuddy altered their path to ride through the men and survey the project. One man smiled broadly and shouted out in Lakota. "Sung'wakan o'wang sica nitawa kin he mayaku kin Owoké wasté mitawa kin luha oyakihi." The entire crew broke out in laughter, a few convulsing so hard that they collapsed and rolled on the ground. "What?" McGillycuddy asked. He looked at Johnny and found him smiling too.

"He says he would trade his beautiful shovel for your ugly horse."

McGillycuddy laughed. "Tell him that his shovel is too slow."

The men had just managed to get their laughter under control when Johnny shouted out McGillycuddy's response. This set them off again and now a dozen were too affected to stand. They sat down in the ditch and pointed at the man who had tried for the bargain and now stroked his shovel with affection.

But when they turned toward the village, Young Man Afraid and the kind old chief, Clearance Looking Dog, were riding slowly to meet them. McGillycuddy, who had been laughing along with the laborers, regained his composure and touched the bay with his heels. The horse broke into an easy lope and that brought another merry shout from one of the men. There was more laughter at McGillycuddy's rear and he would have loved to hear the translation but saw by the two chiefs' expressions that the time for levity was through. He took a quick glance over his shoulder to see that Johnny was coming—elbows flapping and a smile still on his face. They loped to within a few feet of the chiefs and pulled their horses up, facing the painted ponies of Young Man Afraid and Clearance Looking Dog.

The ponies were nowhere near the quality that McGillycuddy remembered from the days before the reservation. They were typical Indian paints but smaller than the hunting and war ponies that these men were famous for riding so well. These ponies were listless, like men in a prison camp, but McGillycuddy knew their potential. *It would be a mistake to think that, in such able hands, these ponies would be anything but lethal.*

"Hau Young Man Afraid. Hau Clearance Looking Dog."

"Hau Agent McGillycuddy."

McGillycuddy liked the two chiefs very much as men and was depending on Young Man Afraid to pick up Red Cloud's mantle when it was finally passed. He had always been at ease with these men but after their greeting an awkward pause settled on the four riders. Finally Young Man Afraid took the initiative. "Nunpila wounglakin kte.

"They want to talk where no one else can hear," Johnny said.

McGillycuddy looked around. "Well . . ." He gestured to the top of a grassy rise above the creek.

Young Man Afraid grunted his approval and Clearance Looking Dog smiled. "It will all be all right," the old man said in English.

Both the pair of Indian ponies and the horses from the livery were trained to ground tie so they were turned loose to graze the hilltop while the four men seated themselves in a circle and Clearance Looking Dog pulled his pipe from a feathered leather case. *Ah, the sacred pipe. The devil's device for elongating meetings and building suspense.*

Clearance Looking Dog was a religious man and took the sacrament of the pipe seriously. He loaded it with tobacco and kinnikinnick and spoke Lakota words that McGillycuddy recognized as borrowed from Catholic liturgy. He watched the old man and was reminded of his mother. She had accepted the Protestant faith of her Northern Irish husband but in old age had reverted to hybrid religion much as Clearance Looking Dog seemed

to have done. In later life his mother had begun searching for meaning that McGillycuddy did not believe existed. As he watched Clearance Looking Dog cradling
his pipe in huge rough hands as if it were the Christ
Child, he wondered if flights of spiritual fancy in the
aged were not one of the common touch spots of all cultures. That thought made him more patient and able to
look on the old chief with a tenderness reserved for
someone of his mother's stature.

Finally the pipe made its rounds and it fell to Young
Man Afraid to explain why he had called the meeting.
"Lakota Oyanke el taku ecetusni."

"He says there is trouble on the reservation," Johnny
said flatly.

"Tatanka Yanke etanhan wahosi wan hi hunh
tawacin kin owanjila hanpi okihi pi sni."

"There have been messengers from Sitting Bull. Some
are restless."

McGillycuddy leaned forward. Usually he worked to
retain his aloofness but these men were friends and he
knew that this was an act of faith on their part. He
wanted them to know that he was taking what they had
to say seriously.

Now Clearance Looking Dog spoke in the tone of the
gentle grandfather that he was. "Koskalaka kin nahan-
hci we kin pta ojula pi." His left hand gestured toward
McGillycuddy and then to his own chest.

"The younger men still have fire in their blood. They
do not see that we are all brothers."

McGillycuddy was only tantalized by what these men
were saying. It was taking too long for them to get to
their point and it was all he could do to keep from asking them directly. *Wait. This beating around the bush is
their way.* He expected that Clearance Looking Dog

would go on because for the younger man to yield to the older was the Sioux way too. But when Young Man Afraid began to explain in slow, precise words McGillycuddy realized that what they had to say was too important to be entrusted to the older, less charismatic man. Young Man Afraid looked McGillycuddy in the eyes, another break from the old culture, and it was clear that this was a man of noble bearing. McGillycuddy studied him as he spoke, judging that he could and would fill the shoes of Red Cloud.

"Koskalaka kin Lakota Oyanke kin etanhan iyayapi Tatanka yanke wicakize okiyapi kte," he said.

"We want to inform you that young men are leaving the reservation to join Sitting Bull to fight the Americans."

McGillycuddy sat up. "Who and when?"

The chiefs looked at each other as if to affirm that they were both committed to what would be considered by some to be treason. It was Young Man Afraid who took the plunge. "A band under Spotted Wolf is preparing to leave today."

Spotted Wolf. Young, lesser chief. "How many men?"

"Ten, perhaps twenty."

"Their camp is on Wounded Knee Creek?"

"Cankpe opi Wakpala el tipi eglep: hwo," Johnny asked.

"Hau," said Clearance Looking Dog.

McGillycuddy knew he should remain seated and smoke the pipe again but he could not. "Thank you," he said. "You have done the proper thing. You will be rewarded for guiding your people down the best path. Tell them I must go, Johnny. Say what needs to be said to excuse me. Tell them I am sorry. I must get to Sword immediately."

He caught the bay horse and was up in the saddle in

the same movement. It took all his self-restraint to keep
the horse at a walk until he was down from the meeting
knoll and behind enough trees to hide the surge of the
horsepower that splattered fresh earth in a muddy cascade behind the bay.

McGillycuddy would have liked to have galloped the
entire way back to the agency but he knew the horse
could not take it. He was not one to overwork a horse.
He had done it under battle conditions but carried guilt
for it even though it might have saved his life. He kept
to a regimen of lope–walk, but lengthened the loping
and shortened the walking. When the bay got his second wind, the condition the Sioux whipped them into
before a battle, he smiled. *A grand horse with a bottom
as deep as the ocean.*

Both the bay and McGillycuddy were stained with
sweat when they came down the main road of the
agency. He loped within sight of Red Cloud's house,
past the livery, past the administration building, and on
to the guardhouse. Sword must have heard the hoof
beats because he and two of his men were coming from
the small log building before they heard McGillycuddy
calling them. When he swung down, one of the policemen took the reins as efficiently as any staff officer of
any army. McGillycuddy pointed to Sword and then to
the guardhouse. "We should talk inside."

Sword was one step behind and shut the door to give
them privacy. *Calm now. Communicate the importance
and exactly what must be done.* McGillycuddy deliberately slowed himself and sat down at the desk. "Sit," he
said to Sword.

The powerful police captain sat down across from
McGillycuddy and the agent was filled with misgivings.

I know this man but I don't know what is in his mind. All the way from Young Man Afraid's camp McGillycuddy had gone over what must be done. He had accepted that it would all depend on the man now sitting across the desk from him. With the good bay moving under him, McGillycuddy knew Sword was capable and trustworthy but now he wasn't sure if this first test of the police force might not be too much. He took an extra moment to consider. *To hell. The Lord hates a coward.*

"Spotted Wolf is breaking out. He is on Wounded Knee Creek and ready to go north to Sitting Bull. You must not let that happen." Sword sat as cool as a panther and just as unreadable to McGillycuddy. The only sign that he understood McGillycuddy was an almost imperceptible nod. "He is no doubt armed with weapons hidden on this reservation. But your weapons are far superior. Take fifteen officers, capture the weapons, and bring Spotted Wolf back."

Sword answered slowly. "If he fights?"

"Bring him back. No one and no arms from this reservation can reach the hostiles. Bring him back dead or alive."

They stared at each other over the table. "Do you understand, Sword?"

"Yes."

"You'll know Spotted Wolf when you see him?"

Captain Sword was getting up. "Yes," he said. "We have fought side by side many times."

10

Little time had passed since the death of Crazy Horse. The reservations were still filled with sullen, anxious Lakotas. Surrounding the reservation were miners and settlers, many of whom had flocked illegally to the Black Hills in search of gold. Sitting Bull, the killer of Custer, waited on the Canadian border to rush southward and raise the reservation Indians in revolt. McGillycuddy stood on his porch each day and felt directly in the path of rolling peril. A wooden shed filled with oily rags. There were a thousand possible sparks in this wild landscape and McGillycuddy, who knew the gravity of the situation and was entrusted to predict where those sparks might be and to douse them quickly, wondered if he had not fanned one instead. It was ten days after Sword and his squad of agency policemen had ridden out to bring back Spotted Wolf, and McGillycuddy had not heard a word from his captain of police.

If Sword had not overtaken Spotted Wolf by then, he would never overtake him. By then the secret was out. The entire reservation knew that Spotted Wolf had broken for the north and that Sword had been sent after him. It was whispered around the agency that Spotted

Wolf's men had laid a trap for Sword and that the agency police were lying dead in their sleeping blankets. The other rumor was that Sword had caught Spotted Wolf but had been convinced to join him and now thirty well-armed men were riding to join Sitting Bull. This scenario haunted McGillycuddy. If it were true, he was finished as agent at Pine Ridge. If even the rumor of it got out to the frontier towns or to the liberals in the East, his career might be just as dead. The thought of what Bland would do in the pages of *The Council Fire* with even a hint of new military rifles and freshly trained men being supplied to Sitting Bull as a result of his orders made McGillycuddy close his eyes and grimace. But only in the privacy of his own front porch. In the presence of anyone except Fanny, he never let on that he was the least bit concerned about Sword. Only Fanny knew that he was not sleeping well, that he haunted the porch, looking out day and night in the direction from which Sword should come.

"It's late," she said from behind him.

His concentration on the dark distance was such that she had come onto the porch without him hearing. He had been imagining the meeting of Spotted Wolf's men with the men of Sword in some remote river drainage along the border with Wyoming. He knew all those drainages and wished that he could be there. But he was not in a remote river drainage dealing directly with the problem that threatened him. He was on his own porch, trusting in a man he hardly knew. "Late. Yes." He turned to his wife and was surprised to see, even lighted by only the thin lantern light through the window, that her face and neck were swollen and unhealthy. It had been coming on gradually but like the absence of Captain Sword, McGillycuddy only faced it during the prairie night. "I'm coming to bed just now." *Though for what reason I do not know.* He felt immediately sorry for his thoughts. He had reasoned that Fanny's loss of libido was a result of her malady and certainly beyond her control. He had considered taking her to the agency doctor but he knew that the man knew less about such illness than he did. It was frustrating and humiliating, but he and Fanny were in this alone.

"Right now," he said and reached out to stroke the hair that always reminded him of a horse's nose.

"You're worried about Sword."

"Mmmm." He continued to stroke the hair and began to wonder if it could be Fanny's chemistry. "He'll come back."

"Alive?" Fanny asked.

"Yes, alive."

"I hope so. He is a fearsome man but kind, I think."

McGillycuddy smiled in the dark. "It's a bit of a balancing act out here. That mix of the fearsome and the kind."

"Reminds me a bit of you." Fanny had moved in closer to the petting like a cat or bird dog let into the house.

"The fearsome or the kind?"

"The balancing act."

"Quite. I'm a nomadic hunter in my heart but employed as a salesman of agrarian pursuits." Now she was snuggled into him and it struck McGillycuddy that women were capable of a love that Aristotle could never understand—that ordinary men could scarcely grasp. "Reduced to the rank of mere salesman."

She giggled like a child. "You will never pass for a salesman. You are filled with passion that salesmen do not know."

"But, sadly, I'm capable of reasoning myself into that passion."

"Nonsense. It is a question of personal control. You have a great deal. Salesmen have little."

Ah, yes. Control. "Come now, George Blanchard is a reasonable and controlled man but capable of selling orange pits to the Indians."

"Neither of you would cheat them."

"No. But we might convince ourselves that there is a chance of orange groves on the prairie." They rocked there with Fanny nestled against him and his arms lanky but strong around her. "I wonder," Valentine said after a moment's reflection, "if I've convinced myself of the possibility of vegetables."

He felt her smile. "Vegetables are a certainty."

"In Blanchard's store."

"Not very good, I'm afraid. Little Julia brings me the best of them."

"Aha. Trading on your influence."

"She's a darling girl. Completely without guile and quite taken by you." A gentle laugh quaked between them. "Do you know what she asked me yesterday?"

"No idea."

"She asked if I thought you would marry her if I died."

McGillycuddy had been drifting toward thoughts of Sword somewhere between Pine Ridge and Sitting Bull's Canada but Fanny's comment froze his thoughts and halted his breathing. A cascade of images tumbled one on the other: Fanny—sick, Julia's angelic face, Fanny—dead, Julia as the woman she would soon become. *Good God.*

Fanny had felt him seize and turned in his arms. She ran her hands inside his jacket and tickled his prominent ribs but got no response. "My goodness, Valentine. It was nothing but the ramblings of a child." She stretched up on tiptoes and kissed him on the mouth.

He returned the kiss. *Too hard?* "It's just . . . It's the thought of you dead. I can't stand to even hear you say it."

A telegraph line was finally strung between Fort Robinson and Pine Ridge and McGillycuddy was in the office the next morning, waiting for the operator he had hired only the week before. The man's name was Arendt and he was not exactly what McGillycuddy had hoped for. He was a mousy, slovenly man with tendencies toward laziness and joining the worst of the squaw men in dangerous drinking binges fueled by illegal liquor. But he had been in the Army Signal Corps and could operate the machinery. And besides, there were not a lot to choose from.

When Arendt stumbled into the office at 8:20 he was surprised to find the agent sitting in his chair with his feet up on the desk. "Running a little behind aren't we?"

"Overslept, sir." He was tucking his shirttail into his pants and pushing his hand down far too deep for McGillycuddy's comfort. "The bunk ain't much and them damned Injuns was up squealing all night. Some heathen rite I'm bettin'."

"Yes, I heard them. It's a little late in the year for Sun Dances. I'm betting they were simply drunk. Who knows?"

"Who knows, is right." Arendt was shaking his head. He looked at the floor as if considering what heathen rite the Oglalas could possibly be celebrating. "Who knows?" he looked up at McGillycuddy. "I'm bettin' you want to send a telegram."

"Astute of you." McGillycuddy took his feet from the desk and swung them with the swiveling of the chair.

"What's that?"

McGillycuddy still sat in the chair with his hands on his knees. He wondered how this man could make a living dealing with the English language. "You are quite correct, Mr. Arendt. I am here in the telegraph office to send a telegram."

"You going to send the troopers after them Injun cops?" Arendt was smiling as if nothing would please him more than clicking out the telegram that would set the frontier ablaze. McGillycuddy was standing now and Arendt was moving into the chair with such delight that he didn't bother to look up at McGillycuddy's face. The face was gray and stormy. "I knew they'd break for Sitting Bull soon as they got the chance. You give an Injun a gun and a horse and—" Arendt began to rise out of the chair following his own shirt collar which was in the grip of McGillycuddy's long, strong fingers. He did not fully realize what was happening to him until he looked up into McGillycuddy's eyes.

"You are out of order." McGillycuddy hissed. "It is not your place to comment on official policy of this reservation and the United States government." He shook the little man only once. "This telegram is not about Captain Sword or his mission."

McGillycuddy eased Arendt down into the chair and turned him toward the telegraph key. "Dr. Randal Sweeney, Fort Robinson, Nebraska." Arendt's finger began tapping the line clear before he took his eyes off McGillycuddy. "Dr. Sweeney STOP." McGillycuddy hoped the man who took his position at Fort Robinson had not performed a complete housecleaning. "If you can spare the copy of Flavin's *Diseases of Mankind* please send to agency STOP." He let Arendt finish tapping out the sentence, then added, "It is on the shelf above the bed pans STOP. Sign it Dr. V. T. McGillycuddy."

As Arendt was signing off they heard the first distant wails of the women. It was a sound that McGillycuddy remembered well. It stirred the memories of the Little Big Horn, the battle at Slim Buttes, and the death of Crazy Horse. It was chilling, like the night sound of a hunting cougar, but there was something in it that attracted McGillycuddy. The two men were transfixed by the animal sound that they knew came from humans. They could hear the noise rise and spread through the camps along White Clay Creek. "Listen to them Christers," Arendt said. "They're startin' up again." But McGillycuddy had no time to consider Arendt. Something important had happened on his reservation. Someone had died.

He moved to the door and out onto the porch in time to see the head of the procession emerge from the trees. The riders were still a half mile away and, as they came, women materialized from the brush and followed. The death song pulsed in the cool morning air and McGillycuddy reached out to steady himself on the railing. The column advanced, serpentine and dusty. The reds, blues, and yellows of blankets, the wind-twisted feathers, and painted horses mixed with raven braids and earthy faces. McGillycuddy's head spun. *Wild as Africa. Wild as dreams.*

It was not yet clear to McGillycuddy what was happening. Riders in front. Women and now men falling in behind. *A dozen horses. No. More.* Twenty-five riders came slowly with Captain Sword in the lead. Sword. My God, Sword. The captain rode solemnly with his head erect and hands on the muscular neck of his horse.

His men came behind as sturdy as their leader. And in the center of the squad, pulled by a roan pony, a travois bent with a heavy bundle that forced the lodge poles into the ground and raised the red dirt in tiny curls of what might have been mistaken for the beginnings of twin prairie fires. McGillycuddy focused on the curls of dust and imagined that the travois poles had been raising such dust for hundreds of miles.

A hundred people followed the Indian police as they made their way to the agency headquarters and, as McGillycuddy came off the porch of the telegram office, children ran to him and danced around in a combination of joy and fear brought on by the electricity of their parents' emotion. He walked steadily to the headquarters and paused in front of the hitching rail to wait for Sword to cover the last hundred yards of a long journey. As he waited, McGillycuddy again traced in his mind just how that journey might have gone. Cheyenne, Bell Fourche. Grand. Moreau. Cannon Ball, Knife. Perhaps they had made it to the Yellowstone and Missouri. The horses were thin. *Perhaps beyond. Perhaps to the fringe of Sitting Bull's domain.*

When Sword reined his horse to a stop his eyes met McGillycuddy's and the trail-weary head gave a single nod. The rest of the force pulled up behind but no one dismounted. They would report and then take their mounts to the livery. The mourners crowded in and from their midst came a wave of excitement. It was Red Cloud, wrapped in a yellow blanket and followed by his entourage of hard-line, older chiefs. The spectators parted for the chief and McGillycuddy was revealed as he stood beside the burdened travois and the painted pony. The adversaries looked at each other for only an instant before McGillycuddy bent forward and cut the rawhide lacing with his pocketknife. When he pulled the canvas away from Spotted Wolf's bloody face the wails erupted anew. The noise was deafening but neither Red Cloud nor McGillycuddy seemed to notice. They stared directly into each other's eyes until Red Cloud could stand it no more. He covered his face with the yellow blanket and turned away.

Part Four

Eastern Politics

1880–1882

II

By the time winter settled on Pine Ridge the resentment of the United States and its agent, McGillycuddy, had gone underground. It is the way of the prairie, and therefore the way of the Lakotas, to use the winter to rest and mull over the events of summer. It is a time for staying close to the lodge and slowly consuming the bounty of the warm months. In years past the bounty took the form of buffalo, a few berries, and other meats, but mostly buffalo. Since the defeats in the north and the great killing of the buffalo by the whites there had been winters of suffering. Of late there was only the washy, stringy cattle supplied by the whites in accordance with the treaty of 1868.

That first year of McGillycuddy's tenure as agent, the complaints about the quality and quantity of the beef went on unabated. But only the hard-core obstructionists complained that the distribution system was capricious. It was not a winter like the good years before the white men but there were root vegetables and corn from the new farming and there was enough for all to eat.

McGillycuddy continued to visit the outlying villages to talk with the chiefs and subchiefs. He listened to their ideas about what should be done to improve conditions on the reservation and shared meals with them in the time-honored ritual of fellowship. When the weather was good enough to drive a buggy he took Fanny with him and she renewed her friendships with the pretty young wives of Young Man Afraid and Clearance Looking Dog's wise old wife, Fox. The women understood each other in a way that fascinated McGillycuddy. Though he and Fanny were learning more Lakota and the Indians were learning more English, their communication was more than simple increased facility with language. He watched Fanny and Fox considering the best use of the new iron pots and pans that had been supplied by the government. With snippets of words, gestures, and a large portion of intuition Fox asked Fanny about greasing the frying pan in a way that would make the food taste best. With a movement of her hand and a smile, she questioned the problem of cleanup. And with a laugh Fanny told her that she understood and that it was not that difficult.

Fanny worked on recipes appropriate for their simple kitchens and she lavished affection on their babies. The women showed her how the babies were strapped onto their boards and trained to be quiet and patient. When McGillycuddy sat talking or smoking with the men he became transfixed by the women fussing over the naked and helpless infants. He longed to go to them and hold them, but that was not something that was done by the men. It was the women's job to care for the very young—the men took over the care of the young boys when they were old enough to learn the ways of war and hunting.

By late winter, McGillycuddy realized that this division of labor in the rearing of children presented an immense hurdle on the path to the success of his plan to civilize the Oglalas. While the women's lives were still filled with traditional chores, the extermination of buffalo and the prohibition against warring with other tribes had left the men without a role. They had lost their function as providers, protectors, and as teachers of the boys. Idle warriors, in McGillycuddy's estimation, were a powder keg in the path of a prairie fire.

It was true that some of the bands had made great strides in converting to agriculture and that eventually the agrarian lifestyle and traditions could restore the men's value in society but that day was years off. The realization of this potential for disaster kept McGillycuddy awake on many long winter nights. By the beginning of February he had resolved to do three things: first, to accelerate more toward farming by every means including incentives and mild punishment, and second, to cushion that conversion by supplying at least symbolic opportunities to practice traditional ways. He determined to allow some religious observances including the sun dance and pipe ceremonies. He further resolved to fight for Oglala rights to engage in a fall hunt as long as remnant herds of buffalo remained. Finally, he decided to let the slaughter of cattle in the monthly beef issue be carried out by the Oglalas themselves. Until then the cattle had been killed and slaughtered by his staff, in the white man's way. He knew turning the procedure over to the Oglalas meant that the cattle would be released, ridden down, and killed by young men with spears and arrows. It was not a sight the eastern liberals who cried for Indian rights would relish but the scenes would warm the cockles of their beneficiaries' hearts.

He devised this scheme over a period of many weeks as he sat in his office after working hours and studied the medical book that Dr. Sweeney had sent to him from the hospital at Fort Robinson. He intended this first "faux hunt" to take place at the March beef issue and resolved to use the planning of the event as an olive branch to extend to Red Cloud. There would be nearly one hundred fifty animals killed that day and he hoped Red Cloud's imagination might be ignited by the possibilities for building the morale of his people as they waited for spring and planting time to arrive.

He studied Flavin's *Diseases of Mankind* in his office after hours because he did not want Fanny to see him reading it. As far as she knew he was finishing up extra government work but, in fact, he was poring over Flavin's reflections on the possible causes of such a combination of symptoms as weight gain, lack of libido, listlessness, and infertility. The great doctor speculated on the relationship between these symptoms and such seemingly trivial annoyances as sore feet and a craving for liquids. He read carefully to find a link between the first three symptoms and infertility. He felt frustrated that he, as a surgeon, did not understand more about the relationships between symptoms and diseases. And as he read and reread he came to realize that Flavin did not know much more.

At times he wondered if his imagination was not trying to manufacture an excuse that might soothe his male pride. Wasn't it normal that a woman in her thirties would put on some weight? Hadn't Fanny been working hard enough in this new life to justify fatigue? Wasn't a decrease in passion common in marriages? Weren't there many fine unions that produced no offspring? All winter his mind bounced back and forth between those thoughts and thoughts of turning the beef issue over to Red Cloud—between his very private life and his increasingly public life. Back and forth, back and forth in the long cold nights of the Great Plains.

McGillycuddy did not confide his private thoughts to anyone, but on the subject of the beef issue he brought O'Donald in to ask his opinion.

"It'll make a rowdy circus out of it," O'Donald said. "Course," he added with a smile, "I'm not opposed to a rowdy circus."

"But what do you think of the public reaction?"

"Depends on the public you're talking about. The locals will enjoy it greatly. Beyond that, it is hard to say."

"I agree with you about the locals but I'm concerned about the easterners. I read about this new organization, the Society for the Prevention of Cruelty to Animals, they call themselves. They lobbied the governor of Kansas to prohibit bullfighting in Dodge City."

"But those are Texas cowboys, Mac, white as you and me."

McGillycuddy nodded and pulled his goatee. "What you say might well be true, but I wouldn't be surprised that I will get blamed for any cruelty that occurs on this reservation."

"Some people will always twist things to fit the demons in their own heads—no matter how misinformed or naive."

"And ignoring these other men's demons is part of my job?"

O'Donald smiled. "They're not your demons."

McGillycuddy tilted his head and nodded in agreement. "Speaking of my demons brings us to the question of Red Cloud."

"Red Cloud?"

"I thought I might include the old boy in the planning

of this event, let him know that I still have some respect for him."

"Do you?"

Of course I do. He was an excellent warrior and is still a power to be reckoned with. "Not a great deal. He's a bit obsolete." *I hope.*

Now O'Donald nodded and McGillycuddy could see that he did not fully agree with what he had just said. "Be nice to include the old rogue though."

McGillycuddy had been sitting in his office chair and now slapped both hands lightly on the desktop. "No time like the present." He stood up and called to the outer office. "Johnny?"

Like a ghost, he was at the door in a blink. "Sir?"

"What's the intelligence report? Is Red Cloud at home?"

"Should be, sir. Very cold and I haven't heard that he's been out and about."

"Let's make a house call." McGillycuddy turned to O'Donald. "Would you care to come along?"

"Love to."

The three men bundled up in their fur coats and scarves, then stepped out into a bitter north wind. No one bothered to speak on the five-minute walk to Red Cloud's house. They passed no one on the road. In Lakota fashion, no one stirred on days like this unless absolutely necessary. A small drift of snow curled around the corner of Red Cloud's house and onto the porch. As McGillycuddy stepped to the door he saw Red Cloud's wife, Pretty Owl, peeking from the ground-level window not four feet away. It took several minutes for the door to be opened and McGillycuddy could not help wondering if weapons or war plans were being hidden. The three men stood waiting and looking over the newly finished, one-and-a-half story house that Red Cloud had insisted on having. There was an attached kitchen and McGillycuddy took some pride in noticing a curl of smoke from the cookstove chimney. The couple had only recently moved in and he knew that Fanny had stopped by to visit with Pretty Owl. She had reported that the house was adequate and that the only piece of furniture was a kitchen cookstove that Cowgill had given to the chief. Fanny reported giving Mrs. Red Cloud a lesson in cooking and operating the flue system of the stove.

There was movement behind the door and the idea that Red Cloud was loading a gun crossed McGillycuddy's mind. It was a silly thought but his last encounter with the chief had been contentious. On the day the Red Clouds moved into the house McGillycuddy made a contemptuous comment about the fact that the rest of Red Cloud's band was wintering in tepees. He was not proud of the comment but had not been able to resist the meanness that he knew would anger Red Cloud.

"I am a chief," Red Cloud had said with blazing eyes that fed McGillycuddy's predatory instincts. "I deserve a house like yours."

McGillycuddy had made a shameful humphing noise. *The petty resort of a petty man. For the love of God, Valentine.*

Finally the door opened a crack and Pretty Owl peered out with one eye. "Come in," she said in English. But she did not open the door. McGillycuddy looked around to Johnny.

"Winuhcala tiopa kin yugan yo." A look of surprise, then embarrassment came to that single eye and she backed away pulling the door wide with her retreat.

McGillycuddy, O'Donald, and Johnny Provost stepped into Red Cloud's house and Johnny closed the door behind them. The two windows in the main room let in enough light to illuminate three American flags tacked to the wood slab walls. There was also a wide-brimmed hat; a short, stout Osage orange bow; and a picture of the Virgin Mary. There was no furniture except a heavy wooden crate, no doubt another gift from Cowgill.

On the floor was an enormous buffalo hide and on the edge of the hide was Red Cloud, with his legs crossed tightly and a genial smile on his lips. "Hau tanyan wati el yahi," he said.

"Welcome to my house," Johnny said.

Proud as punch. They looked around for chairs but finding none, seated themselves on the buffalo robe across from Red Cloud who motioned for Pretty Owl to bring the pipe. Through Johnny, perfunctory greetings were exchanged while they waited for the pipe. When the elaborate buckskin case was passed to Red Cloud he extracted the pipe with great ceremony, fixed the pipe-stone bowl to the carved chokecherry stem, and took a large pinch of tobacco from a leather pouch.

McGillycuddy knew it was tobacco from the smell and did not fail to consider that the chief had upgraded his smoke from wild kinnikinnick. *Another gift from Cowgill?*

No one spoke until the pipe had made its round. Then Red Cloud spoke in Lakota, "Wati el wahi kin le lila maya yuonihan Eyas takuwe yahi helhwo?"

"He says," Johnny translated, "that he is honored to have both of you in his house and wonders what is the reason for the visit."

"Tell him that I have intended to visit him in his new

house for several weeks now but waited until I had good things to talk about."

Red Cloud listened to the translation, looked at McGillycuddy, and smiled. "Mr. O'Donald and I were wondering how you felt the beef issues were going."

Red Cloud frowned and launched into a familiar monologue.

"He says there is not enough," Johnny said, "and the meat is stringy and tough. He does not like the Texas cows or the way they are butchered."

O'Donald smiled, knowing that McGillycuddy had been dealt an ace but the agent's face was without expression. "Ask him if he thinks it would be better if the young men killed the cattle and the women did the butchering."

Before Johnny was finished talking a genuine smile came across Red Cloud's face. "Hau," he said. "Yes."

O'Donald was watching closely and was surprised when McGillycuddy turned to him. "I don't know anything about such slaughter and butchering," he said to O'Donald. "Who do we have on the staff that could oversee such a thing?" McGillycuddy watched Red Cloud from the corner of his eye and noticed again that the chief understood more English than he let on. He gave his full attention to O'Donald. "Who could we put in charge?" *Come now Brownie, play ball with me.*

"Why, who knows more about such things than our host?" *Excellent!* They both turned to Red Cloud who was looking at Johnny, pretending to wait for the translation. As Johnny caught him up, Red Cloud pretended to consider what had been said then began slowly to nod. But he did not answer.

He wants me to ask him officially. Okay. "Would you do that for us, Chief?"

There was more needless translation and grave looks of concern. Then came a considering silence until Red Cloud began again to nod. "Yes," he said, then mumbled another solemn sentence too low for McGillycuddy to hear.

But Johnny nodded. "He says he will oversee the beef slaughter and butchering for his people and for you, sir."

For me? "Tell him thank you, Johnny."

Now Red Cloud smiled unabashedly. He reached across the buffalo robe and shook O'Donald's hand and then shook McGillycuddy's. He picked up the pipe again and loaded it with Cowgill's Virginia tobacco.

As they walked back to the administration building O'Donald could not contain his exuberance. "My goodness, Mac. You played the old devil like a fiddle."

Even Johnny seemed to understand that McGillycuddy had managed finally to get Red Cloud to work with him. He was still nodding as if agreeing with a conversation in his own mind. "I'm not so sure," McGillycuddy said, though he felt himself being falsely modest.

They walked a few more yards in a wind that began to shed tiny snowflakes. "He seemed quite happy in his new house."

"He did indeed," O'Donald said. "Not unlike my own dear father back in Baltimore." He laughed out loud. "Save the buffalo rug and the lack of furniture." McGillycuddy grunted, engrossed in his own thoughts but listening.

They trudged on up the gentle grade to the administration building. The wind was stronger and the snowflakes had grown to the size of dimes. At the bottom of the steps, where they would separate and go their own ways, they paused and looked to the west where the snow was thicker and came in mare's tails over the ridge. "Make a request to the department, Brownie."

McGillycuddy was watching the snow roll down on them.

"Sir?"

"Ask them for authorization to buy some furniture. A few dishes. Things like that."

12

Families began arriving at the cattle corrals the night before the issue was to take place. For two weeks word had passed that the cattle would be killed and butchered in the traditional way and that Red Cloud would preside. The subzero nights and the steady wind did not deter the Oglalas. Young men had been taking crash courses from their fathers and uncles on the few poor horses that were left to them. The same mounts that pulled the family wagons were unharnessed and fitted out with war bridles, feathers, and painted with traditional talismans of the hunt. Their huge feet could be heard pounding the frozen ground at first light as the boys practiced shooting arrows and thrusting spears from horseback—some for the first time in their lives.

Most of the agency whites made their way to the corrals too. No one wanted to miss this symbolic hunt and a few even brought their young children to witness what they thought might be the last such spectacle on the face of the earth. By nine o'clock five thousand people surrounded the corrals and the huge snowy field onto which the cattle were to be released. These were Texas longhorns, lean and lithe from a thousand miles on the trail. They were not buffalo, but everyone expected them to run. A few Texans sat on good horses near the gates. They had been left behind by their cattle crews to see that the steers were properly delivered, and to collect the money from the agent. They shivered and swore in the Dakota wind. They cursed the Oglalas and their cruel land.

McGillycuddy, Fanny, and Louise arrived at the appointed time and pulled their buggy into line with the wagons of Clearance Looking Dog's band. The old chief stood watching his young men and boys thundering to and fro on the workhorses. His face was locked in a sad smile and his eyes were misty with burgeoning tears. No one bothered him because it was his way. The women gathered around Fanny and Louise as they sat bundled in the buggy. They chattered to them in half-understood Lakota and broken English, and Fanny did her best to respond while Louise only smiled shyly. Fanny's extremities were cold and she would not move from her bundle of woolen blankets and carriage quilts. Even when the Blanchards pulled up beside them she ventured only a brief hand of greeting from her warm nest.

When the Texas trail boss saw McGillycuddy he nudged his horse into a slow lope that caught the attention of every man on the killing grounds. It was the kind of locomotion that ignited the memories of the warriors, the dreams of the youth, and the envy of McGillycuddy. He was standing with George Blanchard and both men watched carefully as the horse changed leads coming around the wagon of Clearance Looking Dog. They strained their eyes to see what kind of signal the cowboy gave to the horse as it set its hind legs and slid to a dead stop in front of them. If there was any movement of rein or shift of body weight it was so subtle that neither man noticed. An involuntary smile swelled from that place deep in both men where love for horses dwells. When McGillycuddy looked to his left old Clearance Looking Dog stood beside him, watching. More tears teetering on his lower lids. The cowboy was dressed in his best winter finery. A black Stetson, wool coat, silk scarf, and woolly buffalo chaps. He looked down at Clearance Looking Dog with a vague contempt but did not object when the old man reached out to touch the horse's nose.

"I'm charged with seeing that no cattle die without gold in this purse." He held out a canvas mail pouch.

"Might not be a good idea to let the whole reservation know you'll be carrying gold." McGillycuddy had turned to the buggy and motioned for Fanny to hand him a similar bag. With difficulty she slid it to her husband and, with his help, hefted it out of the buggy. When her job was done she retreated again to her blankets.

"How come you think you're safe with this and I'm not?" The cowboy helped McGillycuddy hang the bag on his saddle horn and traded the empty sack back. He opened one side of the bag and began counting.

"I'm the agent," McGillycuddy said. He would have pointed out Captain Sword and his six officers watching from a respectful distance but the man was not listening.

It took several minutes for the man to count the gold coins. While his head was down Julia Blanchard moved up between her father and McGillycuddy. She was five inches taller than she had been the year before and McGillycuddy could not help noticing yellow curls dangling from her head scarf and the healthy pink of her frost-nipped cheeks. When the cowboy looked up he was smiling smugly from the feel of nearly a thousand dollars on his saddle. When he met Julia's eyes the smile went toothy. He touched the brim of his hat, then pulled a bill of sale from his coat pocket. "Far as I know we'll have another couple hundred head by next month. Guess the boss will telegraph you."

As he leaned to hand the receipt to McGillycuddy, Clearance Looking Dog stretched his fingers out and touched the buffalo hide chaps. "Tatanka," the old man said.

The cowboy pulled his leg away. "Yea, you old gut eater. But it's my tatanka." The horse backed away as if leaving was its idea. McGillycuddy made a point of watching the reins but did not see them move. In an instant the cowboy was loping across in front of the corrals to meet his partners who were coming in a similar lope. The cowboys and their horses merged into a single flowing ribbon and, with five thousand pairs of jealous eyes upon them, flew through the powdered snow of the killing field, mounted the distant ridge, and were gone.

The sadness and resentment was deep but brief. There was too much excitement in the air to dwell on the past and, within minutes, the boys were galloping their plow horses back and forth in the tradition of wearing war ponies down before a battle so they can fight on superior second wind. Even the day was warming and felt warmer yet because the air was still. Red Cloud's warriors were at the head of the cattle gates, taking the place of the Texans who had guarded the cattle from overzealous Oglalas for the last week. Now the men who had fought in the Wagon Box Fight, the Fetterman Massacre, the Little Big Horn sat their horses like cowhands. They had been instructed to do so by Red Cloud and waited stoically for their leader to arrive.

The younger chiefs were clearly piqued to see Red Cloud's men placed in positions of power on this day that would surely be remembered fondly by the common Indians. Now Red Cloud was pulling a typical trick by forcing everyone to wait. *Arrogant, calculated, and divisive.* As McGillycuddy looked from face to face he wondered if he had made a mistake in handing such a political plum to Red Cloud. He had hoped to bring Red Cloud into the fold of the progressives but, standing between wagons of the people, as the boys churned up the snow with their practice, McGillycuddy considered starting without Red Cloud. It would be an assertion of his own rightful authority. The more McGillycuddy waited and thought about what Red Cloud was doing the madder he got. Even the boys were beginning to ride toward the old warriors Red Cloud had stationed at the gates in mock charges that the men ignored. People watched the charges and cheered the boys on in their frustration at having to wait. The cheering emboldened the boys who rode the old horses harder and closer to the gatekeepers. Finally a particularly aggressive boy snaked a riding crop out and counted coup on a warrior twice his age. McGillycuddy stepped forward in anticipation of retaliation but the crowd roared with delight and the warrior smiled at the boy who was streaking back to the people.

Finally a murmur swept through the gathered Oglalas. Red Cloud was coming and all eyes turned to the ridge at the south of the killing field. Accompanied by six other war veterans Red Cloud loped a good horse onto the field. The honor guard was dressed in traditional winter gear but, despite the temperature, Red Cloud was stripped to the waist and as soon as all had seen him, urged the horse into a gallop. It was a horse that McGillycuddy had never seen before, far superior to the ones the cavalry had allowed the Sioux to retain. "So where's he been hiding that mount?" O'Donald whispered.

McGillycuddy shook his head and watched the chief circle the field. *Still a fine figure of man. My yes. Amazing.* No one spoke but the pride in this man from some quarters of the crowd was palpable. *A force for good or evil.*

Red Cloud must have been watching from the trees when the boy had counted coup on his elder because he rode hard for the boy and waved him to ride beside him. The six other riders fell away and Red Cloud slowed his horse so the boy could keep up. Riding abreast they loped toward the gate where a warrior was already opening the first pen. When the steer broke for the open field Red Cloud waved the boy ahead and slipped to the side to haze the steer as the boy fumbled with his bow. It took great nerve to hold the steer with his horse as the inexperienced hunter tried to steady his bow for the difficult moving shot. But Red Cloud was brave beyond belief and let the first wild arrow pass within inches without a flinch. With a hand motion he urged the boy to shoot again and this time the arrow found a vital spot and the steer tumbled headlong. The people roared with delight as one of the steer's enormous horns caught the frozen dirt and jerked the animal hard onto its back.

The steer's neck was surely broken by the wrenching but the animal kicked the air, rolled, and tried to regain its feet. The boy had ridden past and finally gathered up his plowhorse and turned it for another pass. The third arrow stuck in the steer's midsection and the steer bellowed and went down on its side. Without slowing his pace the boy baled off the horse and slashed at the neck while dodging the flailing long horns of the dying steer. Bright red blood spurted into the air and instantly the snow was soaked in a three-foot circle. Women from the boy's family squealed and raced forward on foot. They carried butcher knives, baskets, and hand axes. The animal was still twitching as they descended. Red Cloud sat the magnificent horse and remained at a distance until the women were at work.

As the steer was rolled out of its hide, Red Cloud urged the horse back into motion. He circled to the crowd and chose a second mounted boy but another boy could not be restrained and rode out too. When the second steer was released the crowd cheered and the sound of the women's eagle-bone whistles pierced the winter air. The boys rode their bellowing steer down but not before it had covered a quarter mile. This animal nearly made it to the trees of the ridge and after the first barrage dragged itself for a hundred yards before the second round of biting arrows broke it down. Another fifteen women ran to the site and Red Cloud rode another circle. But this time several boys galloped out to meet him and the warrior at the gate let three steers free. One steer ran toward the site of the first butchering and leaped the busy women who swung knives and axes at it as it ran. Two of the steers were brought to earth but the third looked as if it would make it to the trees and this prompted two grown men to whoop and line out for the escapee.

Now the remaining hundred steers began to panic and when the gatekeeper tried to let another steer free the rest of the animals rushed the opening and fifty broke onto the field. McGillycuddy saw what was happening and stepped forward as if he might try to stop them. But already twenty men were riding to make the first kill that they had made in the seven years since their captivity. Suddenly, cattle were being killed in a dozen ways. Blood stained the snow of most of the field and as the warriors and boys rushed forward followed by their women the remainder of the steers broke loose. When McGillycuddy turned back toward the white spectators he saw an array of human reaction: O'Donald and George Blanchard looked on with steely interest, Cowgill jotted words into his notebook, Julia clung wide-eyed to her father's arm, and Fanny peered horrified from the carriage seat.

McGillycuddy took one more look at the killing field. The Oglalas raced back and forth, smiling and calling to each other. Quarters of beef were being dragged to waiting wagons and many wounded animals still bawled as the final blows were delivered with axes. Everywhere the butchering proceeded. Trails of blood led off into the trees and mounted men pounded after them. The women laughed and the men played with each other on horseback. Children played with the bloody meat and sucked at the internal organs. *Absolute orgy of joy.*

It was bedlam to the whites. The last thing McGillycuddy saw before he turned back to his own people and raised his hands to command them back to the agency was Red Cloud, still bare chested, his horse lathered and prancing from butcher site to butcher site. The chief's chest was splattered with blood and his face was flush with pride.

13

McGillycuddy and O'Donald spent most of the spring trying to figure out what should be done about Red Cloud. The agent's first reflex was to call him into the office and chastise him.

"Chastise him for what?" O'Donald asked earnestly. "Only doing what you asked him to do." He smiled and shook his head. "Not exactly what you had in mind, I'll grant you."

At first McGillycuddy resented O'Donald's candid remarks. But finally, at least in the privacy of the office, he came to see the humor that O'Donald saw from the beginning.

"Still, the old goat flaunted the barbarity we're here to extinguish."

"Politics," O'Donald said. "Made himself quite popular with his people."

And a fool of me in the process? "Do you think it set back the movement toward farming?"

"The planting seems to be going on quite well. No, he was just flexing his muscles."

"Muscle flexing is a dangerous proposition on this reservation."

O'Donald's silence hinted that he believed all muscle

flexing was dangerous. "You're in a contest for the minds of his people."

"For the future of his people."

"I see that," O'Donald said, "but I'm not sure Red Cloud is capable of seeing things our way."

McGillycuddy nodded. "And we're incapable of seeing things his way."

"Something like that, Mac."

"And what of that horse he showed up on? Does he have guns stashed away in the same valley where he hides his war pony? Some of our spies say yes."

"Some say no. He may encourage an uprising but I don't think he would lead it."

McGillycuddy nodded. "I agree. He's too politically crafty for that." He was looking out the office window at the coming spring and thinking that he had been agent now for a year and a half. That was longer than most. But he had been lucky that Hayes had defeated Tilden in '77. The coming election could easily bring a Democrat to the presidency and make it very hard for him to keep his job. "Would the Democrats be unprincipled enough to exploit him?"

"You're damned right they would."

"I agree. Have to be careful." McGillycuddy turned from the window smiling. "The better question might be: would he be unprincipled enough to use the Democrats?"

Brownie O'Donald smiled. "No question."

McGillycuddy had rightfully sensed that Red Cloud was angling again for his removal. He suspected his efforts would surface in the form of political pressure after the fall election and that despite all the talk of civil service reform and opposition to the spoils system a Democratic administration would mean his demise as agent.

Garfield would likely be the Republican candidate and
if he won, McGillycuddy's job would be safe. It was at
this time in most Indian agent's careers that they began
to hedge their bets for a decent retirement by skimming
a little off the top of reservation budgets, demanding
kickbacks for beef and freighting contracts, and leasing
Indian land to white ranchers. These abuses were com-
monplace and nearly expected. McGillycuddy did none
of these things. It was not that he liked money any less
than agents on other reservations. It was just that he,
unlike most agents, had known his charges before they
were forced onto the reservations. He had seen the
Sioux when they were affluent and proud. He knew
what they had been and what they had gone through.
He had some idea of what they faced in the future and
knew that that future would be considerably more grim
if they were not led honestly to a civilized life. For
McGillycuddy, Red Cloud represented a major obstacle
to a bright and honorable future for the Oglalas. Red
Cloud of course believed that his people's future de-
pended on their ability to hold onto their traditions.
The idea of independent farmers threatened those traditions and, incidentally, Red Cloud's position of power.
For Red Cloud, McGillycuddy and what he represented
was the problem.

It was a thorny problem indeed and McGillycuddy
determined to hold his temper—never easy for him—
and to wait until Secretary of the Interior Schurz arrived in the fall. The trip had been scheduled for
September and it seemed clear that the timing was mo-
tivated by national politics. Both parties were trying to
show that they were attentive and sensitive to what
had come to be known in the national press as the
Sioux Problem—the Indians' reluctance to give up

more of their land, their bellicose threats, and the government's struggle to deal with it all. Because of Red Cloud's standing among eastern liberals, McGillycuddy had become a target for their wrath. Schurz had let him know that the Department of the Interior and the Bureau of Indian Affairs considered him an exemplary agent but that the Democrats were using him as a whipping boy. He also asked that McGillycuddy not give them any more fuel by inciting Red Cloud unless absolutely necessary.

So McGillycuddy did not call Red Cloud into the office and ask where he got the war pony. He did not chastise him for causing the beef issue to become a spectacle. He did, though, resume control of the beef issue, reinstating traditional white notions of slaughter and butchering. For all that summer he left Red Cloud alone. The disconcerting part of this strategy was that except for repeating his demand for Catholic teachers in the reservation schools, Red Cloud left him alone also. Things were a little too calm and by September McGillycuddy was sure that the old chief was up to something. On the day of Schurz's arrival it became clear that McGillycuddy's suspicions were correct.

As soon as McGillycuddy and Schurz were alone, Schurz handed the agent a copy of Bland's journal, *The Council Fire*. "Hot off the press," he said.

McGillycuddy had seen several issues of the journal in which he played a prominent role as villain and read this latest assault with comic, defensive disdain. The author was not identified but it was someone who wrote as if he had been at the horrendous February beef issue. What had been intended to give the Oglalas a sense of pride in their traditions was depicted in the pages of *The Council Fire* as the demonic wish of the incompetent agent. It painted the Indians as starving and driven to acts of cruelty and depravity. The whole ugly scene was laid on McGillycuddy's back as the result of gross mismanagement. He recalled Cowgill at the scene of the slaughter, scribbling in a notebook. Could he have written this absurdity? Was he that politically divisive?

McGillycuddy handed the journal back to Schurz. "And this from a group claiming to want the Sioux's traditions honored."

"Indeed," Schurz said. "They are not well informed and wrapped up in a idealism that is no doubt connected to their own shortcomings and guilt, but they are influential. We are already receiving mail from the American Humane Society and other do-gooders of similar ilk."

McGillycuddy was fighting to hold his temper in check but could not be diplomatic. "So what does this colossal misrepresentation mean to me?"

Schurz shrugged. "Nothing. We deal with outrages like this every day. We will have to give it the appearance of consideration but it is nonsense and all intelligent men know it is nonsense. My suggestion is that we go ahead with our meetings with the chiefs and inspect the farming projects and that you forget it." Schurz smiled and laid a fatherly hand on McGillycuddy's shoulder. "It's politics. They'd love to get you riled up just before this election. Don't let them. Just forget it."

But McGillycuddy did not forget that his attempt to honor Red Cloud had been turned back on him. He did not mention the article or confront Cowgill or Red Cloud but he did not forget. Now he knew the game and he would play it.

*   *   *

Schurz remained at the agency for a week, and twice Fanny organized dinner parties in his honor. There were local politics to play in arranging the guest lists. The first party represented the hierarchy as McGillycuddy wished it to be. It included the Blanchards, Young Man Afraid, and his favorite wife, Yellow Moccasin. Brownie O'Donald was to be in attendance and, of course, Schurz. The second party, representing the old order and again included O'Donald for his gaiety and good humor, but also the trader Cowgill, Red Cloud, and his wife, Pretty Owl. McGillycuddy would have liked to invite Father McCarthy, who had been camped off the reservation in Nebraska since his expulsion, because of his education and fine manners. But two days before the first dinner party, Schurz insisted on handling this problem in McGillycuddy's office. It was the first time the priest had set foot on the reservation for months, though Schurz had received continual letters of protest from his superiors.

Schurz handled the priest crisply, explaining simply that the Pine Ridge Reservation had been given to the Episcopal Church. "It is their hunting ground for converts and there is nothing we can do about it."

"But Red Cloud has asked for us specifically. He is a Catholic."

"Converted by one of your predecessors before the question of missionary work on the reservations was settled by the Bureau of Indian Affairs."

Although McGillycuddy had little respect for McCarthy's calling as a Catholic priest, he liked him as a man and regretted that Schurz was forced to reject McCarthy's request without appeal. McGillycuddy knew that Red Cloud would bring the expulsion up at his first opportunity and he hoped it would not spoil Fanny's party. As he led Father McCarthy to the door of his office, McGillycuddy again considered inviting McCarthy. He was, after all, a decent and intelligent man—just the sort for a lively dinner party. But his presence might make the party a little too lively. When they shook hands at the door McGillycuddy touched the priest's shoulder with his left. "Sorry it worked out this way."

Fanny ingeniously let word escape that the two traders would be invited to different parties. She let them know that she would be shopping at Blanchard's for the party he was invited to and at Cowgill's for the second party. She let them know long enough ahead of time so that a fierce competition developed over who could supply the freshest produce, the most tender meats, and the most exotic canned goods. McGillycuddy would not allow anything extravagant to be served. "Not appropriate," he said, "for a public servant to eat too high on the hog."

"But we can't appear common and coarse."

"If there is such a thing as sin it is certainly not commonness. As for coarseness—I will try to refrain from belching with too much enthusiasm."

It was two days before the first dinner and Fanny and Louise were building to minor panic. "George has procured a fat hog from a ranch on the Nebraska side of the border and Julia is bringing apples to make applesauce. Is that too fancy?" Fanny spoke with some sarcasm.

McGillycuddy rolled his eyes. "As long as the hog is not too fat."

"Your portion will be particularly lean." She was harried but took the time to smile.

McGillycuddy too had been feeling the pressure of

entertaining the secretary of the interior but understood how hard Fanny was trying. His hat was already on his head but when he saw the tired smile he went back to Fanny and pushed a damp lock of hair from her face. He was not an openly affectionate man and besides, Louise was working in the pantry. But he did remain standing close. "And how is Mrs. McGillycuddy feeling?"

"I'm worn out, Valentine. About this time every day I can hardly move. I just want to lie down."

He looked into her eyes and his expression went from caring husband to appraising doctor. The look had begun with affection but now went deep—first her left eye and then the right. "If you are tired and feel like lying down then you probably should lie down." His voice was distant and she could tell that he was thinking about what he was seeing in her eyes.

"I'm all right."

"Umm," he said absently. He had exhausted Flavin's book on human diseases over the winter. He was on his own now. "You should stretch out for an hour."

"There is too much to do."

"Nonsense, an hour will not be missed." He nodded toward the pantry. "Louise seems to have her job well in hand." She started to object but McGillycuddy raised a finger to her nose. "Doctor's orders." They both smiled. "Doctor's orders" was a long-standing joke between them. It brought back memories of passionate days and Fanny's face reddened. *Recollection fresh enough for her to cause a blush. A distant memory for me.*

He kissed her on the forehead. "Go on now." He took a hold of her shoulders and turned her gently. The shoulders resisted for an instant but then relaxed thankfully and let themselves be guided toward the door.

When she was gone McGillycuddy stepped into the pantry. "Louise, could you prepare a cup of tea for Mrs. McGillycuddy?"

The thin, walnut face looked up with a smile. McGillycuddy did not often speak with her. "Of course, sir."

"Make it stout. Add three full teaspoons of sugar."

"Mrs. McGillycuddy don't take sugar."

"Three full spoons," McGillycuddy said. "Tell her it's doctor's orders." *But is it the right thing?*

When Louise nodded and he was sure that she understood, he stepped through the backdoor and nearly collided with Julia Blanchard. It had been a year and a half since he first met her and it struck him hard that she was no longer a child. She was not yet a woman but the promise of that incredible metamorphosis was everywhere. By holding his gaze rigidly on her very blue eyes he tried not to give away the fact that he had begun to notice the filling lips, hips, and breasts. He did his best to appraise her passively, nodding to her smile of greeting, commenting automatically on the bag of apples she held aloft, pointing to the kitchen table as if he knew where they should be put. She breezed past with an innocent and happy toss of her yellow hair and McGillycuddy caught the smell of her and felt the urge to grasp the porch rail. *For crying out loud.* He refused to take the railing and walked unassisted down the steps. Then, with measured pace, he moved on to the administration building.

The first of the Schurz dinners was planned as the more casual and private of the two. It did, after all, include strong supporters of McGillycuddy and no business was conducted. The Blanchards and the Young Man Afraids were old friends and had done business with each other for years before the Oglalas were settled on Pine Ridge. They had known each other since Young Man Afraid's band had surrendered. The men liked each other and the wives too liked each other. O'Donald had come to know both these men and, true to his character, served as a catalyst to bring them out in conversation and to include the secretary. The predinner chatter was quite lively when McGillycuddy came into the kitchen to re-fill whiskey glasses, he nodded to Louise and gave Fanny a kiss on the forehead. This was uncharacteristic of McGillycuddy and Louise pretended not to see the kiss or Fanny's response—which was to push him away as if the kiss were not appreciated. "Lovely party," McGillycuddy said.

Fanny was bustling back and forth. "This is the easy one. Everyone here likes each other."

"Practice," McGillycuddy said.

"Practice indeed." Fanny was still hustling about. She opened the oven and the smell of roast pork filled the kitchen in a fog. "George at least supplied us with quality food. No telling what Cowgill will come up with."

Three days later they discovered what Cowgill thought appropriate for a dinner with Secretary Schurz and Chief Red Cloud. The day before the dinner a group of Oglalas showed up at Fanny's door with a twelve-pound buffalo hump roast. It was one of the last of the Republican River herd, an area off-limits to the Sioux. It was illegally killed just three days before and rushed to Fanny's kitchen. Of all the thorny guests that were invited to this business dinner the buffalo hump roast appeared to Fanny to be the thorniest. She sent Johnny Provost riding hard to Young Man Afraid's lodge with a plea that Yellow Moccasin come to help prepare the meat.

It was a dicey operation to have a wife of the competing—some would say usurping—chief as chef for what could be viewed as a state dinner. But Yellow Moccasin was a wise "first lady" and instantly recognized the position in which Fanny had been placed. She appraised the hump roast and smiled. She nodded to Fanny as if to say that it was a good piece of meat and that all would turn out all right.

But when Fanny pointed to the woodstove and shrugged to ask if that was the proper way to cook such a chunk of meat, Yellow Moccasin shook her head and pointed to the back door. "Fire," she said.

Fanny pointed too. "Outdoors?"

"Peta kin ile ya yelyo."

Fanny looked to Louise. "Have you ever cooked out of doors?"

"Some. But never a roast like this." She pointed to the buffalo as if it were a tyrannosaurus roast.

Fanny looked from the mulatto girl to the dark-skinned Indian woman and thought how important the dinner was. For political reasons Yellow Moccasin would have to be long gone from the house when the other guests arrived. She could help, and seemed quite excited about the prospect, but for those last critical hours it would be only Fanny and Louise. What if they spoiled the meat? O'Donald and Schurz might not know the difference. The Cowgills may or may not know what good buffalo tasted like. But the most important diners would know. The Red Clouds would know. And Valentine would know.

Fanny longed for an alternative plan, for a menu she was comfortable with. But it was too late. She nodded to Yellow Moccasin. "Can you help in the morning?"

The handsome woman squinted her eyes, trying to guess Fanny's meaning. "Ah . . ." Fanny thought. "Hihani?"

Yellow Moccasin smiled broadly. She pointed to herself. "Han hihani kin wau kte."

"I will see that you have help when you arrive," Fanny said.

And so by eight o'clock the next morning the two young helpers Fanny had recruited had collected green ash logs from the river bottom, cleared a place for a fire pit just outside the back door of the McGillycuddy house, and had built a fire. The fire was hot by the time Yellow Moccasin appeared with rawhide bundles carried by two of her young daughters. The girls chattered back and forth and glanced and giggled at the boys tending the fire. But at the command of their mother, they settled to the ground and began unpacking the bundles. Behind them came three more boys carrying river rocks from White Clay Creek. They brought the rocks in leather slings that hung from their shoulders, dumped them into the fire, and turned, jostling each other with good-natured shoulder bumps, and ran back toward the creek for more. On a piece of tanned elk hide the girls laid out an array of wild onions, turnips, buffalo berries, plums, and gooseberries. They continued to tease each other and laughed as they trimmed and sliced the fruits and vegetables with trade knives as sharp as broken glass.

Their mother went to the kitchen door that had been left open since the nights were now cold enough to kill the flies. She knocked lightly on the jamb and Louise came close enough to peer out, nervous and wary of working with Indians. But Fanny came right behind

Louise and welcomed Yellow Moccasin with a hand on her shoulder. "Come in, come in."

The two women smiled at each other, feeling the pressure of a lack of language. But as soon as Yellow Moccasin saw the buffalo hump laid out on the wooden table her face went determined and confident. She moved to the table and felt the buffalo like a person massaging the back of another. She nodded and said something in Lakota that neither Fanny nor Louise understood. Yet they knew what Yellow Moccasin meant. It was a good piece of meat.

Then Yellow Moccasin took charge. From the leather bag she had brought with her she produced a knife and laid it beside the meat. After rolling the huge roast in her hands to find the grain of the meat, she took a small bottle from the leather bag and began rubbing the meat with the contents. It smelled like vinegar and Yellow Moccasin continued to add the liquid as she made incisions through the roast at intervals of less than an inch. She worked deftly as the other women watched. But after the slits were made and Yellow Moccasin had gone to the door and called something to her girls, she shooed Fanny and Louise away with a shy smile and a tiny wave of one hand. Louise went back to grinding the corn supplied by Cowgill for the bread and Fanny continued cleaning the beautiful, crisp, green beans that one of the Indian farmers of White Clay Creek had brought in early that morning. She worked with trepidation because this was certainly the most important dinner party she had ever hosted. There would be intense feelings all around the table and she was sure that vital business would be transacted. She wanted everything to be perfect and so she couldn't help worrying about the main course.

Yellow Moccasin's girls came to the kitchen door. They stood tittering to each other and peering into the house. It occurred to Fanny that they had likely never been inside a house and had been told to come no farther than the back steps. Her instinct was to stop her work and invite them in, but that would be interference with Yellow Moccasin's instructions to her family so she only nodded a hello to the girls and made a mental note to invite them another day. Fanny could not help admiring the caramel-skinned girls as they stood patiently with aprons full of what Fanny suspected were sliced wild onions and Indian turnips. She had seen children digging on the south-facing hillside above the agency the day before.

Yellow Moccasin went to the door and the girls emptied their loads of the tiny hard vegetables into their mother's apron and waited while she transferred them to the table beside the roast. "Wakalapi?" she asked of Louise.

Her tone was kind and shy but still, Louise froze as if frightened. Fanny stepped up beside Louise. "Wakalapi?" Yellow Moccasin asked. Automatically she turned toward the door and found Johnny standing there. Fanny was glad she had sent one of the boys to retrieve him.

"Coffee," Johnny said.

"Oh, wakalapi." Fanny laughed and turned to the canister on the shelf.

"Coffee."

"Cega?"

"She needs a pot too," Johnny said.

"Of course."

Louise took the enamel coffeepot down from the cupboard and handed it to Yellow Moccasin, who took it cheerfully, went to the water bucket and filled it nearly full. Then she came to Fanny who still held the coffee canister. She removed the lid and dipped out two large handfuls into the pot. She handed the pot to the girls who disappeared with it.

Fanny assumed that Yellow Moccasin wanted a cup of coffee but, if that was the case, she certainly liked her coffee strong. She returned the coffee canister to its place and moved past the table where Yellow Moccasin had gone back to work on the buffalo hump roast. She was assiduously stuffing the knife-slit holes with the onions and turnips that had been diced to cubes no more than a quarter of an inch square. Fanny casually picked up a piece of onion and a piece of turnip and popped them into her mouth. When the flavor bit her tongue she turned so that Yellow Moccasin would not see her spit them back into her hand.

By the time Yellow Moccasin had carried the roast to the fire the coals were red hot and the coffeepot boiled wildly. Beside the fire the children had hung a water-filled skin from three poles and as their mother approached with the roast draped over both hands, the boys, using two sticks, picked a rock from the fire and dropped it into the suspended hide. To Fanny it seemed a horrible mistake or a childish prank. When the nearly red-hot rock hit the water there was almost an explosion. Steam shot into the air and everyone jumped back except Yellow Moccasin. She smiled broadly and proceeded to the hide with the dinner's main course in her hands. She stood above the suspended hide for an instant before she dropped the meat into the steaming water. Then she motioned for the boys to add another rock. One of the girls removed the boiling coffeepot from the fire and handed it to her mother as she was instructing one of the boys to continue adding logs to the fire. And, as Fanny and Louise watched from the kitchen door, Yellow Moccasin dumped the entire pot of thick boiling coffee, grounds and all, into the leather cauldron.

14

The rest of the day was difficult for Fanny. She went on preparing the meal: cutting sweet corn from cobs, slicing apples for pie, rolling out crust, peeling potatoes, but all the time she worried about the meat. It was, after all, the main dish and she had let control of it slip away. Though she liked Yellow Moccasin very much, now she had to fight thinking of her as a simple savage. This made her ashamed and it complicated the day even more.

She and Louise labored until afternoon and all the time Yellow Moccasin and her daughters moved around the fire in the backyard, urging the boys to bring more wood and feeding it steadily onto the already hot fire. It was indeed a large roast and it would take a great deal of heat to cook. But, as Fanny stood by the backdoor watching the Young Man Afraid women and the steaming hide, she could not help feeling that the fire was much too hot and that the broth in which the meat simmered was much too strong. Several times Louise caught her watching the Oglala cooks and fretting over the fate of her dinner. When their eyes met Fanny tried to smile but, as the day wore on, she became too tired to smile. By two o'clock her face was as crestfallen as the dark-eyed mulatto girl's. Finally, as she had become accustomed to doing, Fanny retired to her bedroom to nap. Louise knew what tasks remained and Fanny told herself that she had done all she could. But as she lay on her bed she felt sick to think that she had let her husband down at such an important time and, worse yet, that she had neither the strength nor the resources to put it right. Finally, as sleep began to wash over her, she reverted to a practice from her youth. She prayed that she would be forgiven for a ruined meal and that Valentine would forgive her weakness.

She awoke at five o'clock, not rested but well enough to dress and go to the kitchen for last-minute preparations. Louise had her extra-sweet tea ready and, as she drank, she told herself that she felt stronger. The guests would be arriving in one hour and she resolved to bull ahead. She would make the best of what had been given her and she threw herself into the task of hosting a dinner for the secretary of the interior and the chief of the Oglala nation.

As was his custom, McGillycuddy put in a complete day and arrived home at five thirty. He smelled the buffalo roasting in the backyard and came around to see what was happening. He took the time to chat with Yellow Moccasin, conscious that this was the wife of the chief he hoped to install soon as the head of the reservation. He spoke to the children and came into the house through the backdoor and cheerfully lifted lids and sniffed the contents. He was not oblivious to the tension in the kitchen but assumed it had to do with normal predinner party anxiety. He was too cheerful to suit Fanny but she said nothing until he had gone upstairs.

"He has no idea," Fanny said to herself. But Louise

overheard and nodded her head as she removed a pie from the oven.

Brownie O'Donald arrived early but his considerate good humor was welcomed. The Young Man Afraid women had just left and Fanny suspected that Brownie had met them as they stole away. But, if he did, he said nothing of Fanny's daring. He only grinned and asked if there was anything he could do so Fanny put him to work setting the table and was pleasantly surprised to find that he knew how it was done. "My dear old mother taught me," O'Donald replied when he was asked about his skill. "Must have known I'd never attract a mate."

"Come now, Brownie. I'll bet you've attracted plenty of women."

He smiled as he straightened a knife. "I like to think so, but all of that attraction dynamic is quite mysterious to me."

"To us all."

"To you and Valentine?"

"Particularly to Valentine and me."

"It doesn't seem mysterious. It seems to make perfect sense." He was watching Fanny closely but it did not make her nervous.

"Nothing mysterious at the beginning. We were quite the couple." Fanny laughed as she placed a centerpiece of willow branches laced with wild sunflowers on the table.

"The mystery came later?" O'Donald laughed with her.

"It's been mostly a mystery." Fanny was surprised that this man had gotten her to think of anything but the coming dinner. "Nothing is quite what you expect."

O'Donald reached out and touched a tiny flower petal. "Well, thank the good Lord for that. I was never one to expect much."

"Nonsense. Your future with the Department of the Interior is very bright. You should be expecting a great deal." She was moving back to the kitchen and her mind was racing back to the buffalo roast baking in thickening coffee.

"Now there," O'Donald laughed, "is where I believe in mystery."

Fanny was almost to the kitchen when McGillycuddy stepped from their bedroom dressed in a light brown suit with a brocaded vest. He was smiling and clearly anxious for the dinner to come. Fanny looked him up and down. "You look nice."

"So do you. And the meal smells wonderful."

Fanny was instantly upset. She looked to him to be sure that he wasn't teasing her but she found no undue sparkle in his blue eyes and she was overcome by a need to tell him about the roast. But just as she started to open her mouth there was a knock on the door.

O'Donald was at the window and looked out. "Secretary Schurz," he said and looked to McGillycuddy for permission to greet his guest.

McGillycuddy motioned to open the door and Fanny, though she had met Schurz two nights before and had liked him very much, turned and scurried to the kitchen.

When the door came open the secretary was facing out toward the road where a long line of Indian freight wagons happened to be passing. The creak of axles and the shouts of mule skinners filled the air. Schurz was studying the teams as they passed and seemed not to hear the door open, and McGillycuddy and O'Donald stepped out onto the porch behind him. He stood transfixed as ten, fifteen, twenty heavy freight wagons passed. Then, still not acknowledging the two men, he began talking. "It's quite a sight," he said. "When I en-

tered upon my duties with regard to the Indian problem
I was told that we would never be able to do anything
with the Lakotas until they had received another thor-
ough whipping. And now I find these freight wagons on
the roads, hundreds since I arrived, with young warriors
on the boxes. It has the smell of self-sufficiency, Dr.
McGillycuddy."

"We have not arrived at that point but it is our goal."

Now Schurz turned to McGillycuddy and O'Donald.
"As you know, I was out in the countryside yesterday. I
found chiefs out in the fields with their people making
hay and cultivating the fields for fall planting. I noticed
several families building houses. I am quite impressed."
The line of freight wagons was still passing behind him.
The squeak and strain of harness so natural that it
might have been the earth turning.

"We are making progress, sir."

"You certainly are McGillycuddy." He grinned. "And
without the aid of the Holy Roman Church."

McGillycuddy smiled and O'Donald raised a hand to
indicate the last of the freight wagons. "I don't believe
those drovers are churchgoers."

They all looked again to the road, the dust rising with
the movement of hoof and wheel, and observed the
building sunset behind the cedar ridge. The light slanted
at a magic angle and the long shadows of trees and
buttes were framed in gold. The last wagon passed on
and revealed Red Cloud and his wife waiting to cross
the road. They stood in the dust and even after the
wagon had long passed, did not move. When much of
the dust had settled they came toward McGillycuddy's
house and the chief raised a hand in greeting, and his
wife lowered her eyes in respect.

*   *   *

By the time greetings were exchanged and the guests made their way into the house Fanny had laid out the bowls of potatoes, creamed corn, and green beans. Cowgill arrived with a bottle of whiskey, which McGillycuddy put aside for later. Fanny filled the wine glasses with red wine that Schurz had sent the day before. The only thing missing from the table was the roast buffalo meat, which was being transferred by Louise from the blackened hide to a platter on the kitchen table. Fanny had taken a quick look at the roast. When Johnny had brought it into the kitchen it was crusted with a rind of oily coffee grease that so disheartened Fanny that she could not even oversee its arrangement on the platter. She refused to face the impending disaster and settled herself at the table to encourage the guests to sit and begin passing the side dishes.

Red Cloud had come into the house in a cheerful mood but had gone right to vocalizing his complaints. He began with a protest over the treatment of Father McCarthy. "I want Black Robes to teach my children," Johnny translated in a deferential voice.

"Tell him," Schurz said, "that the issue has been decided. The Episcopalians will teach the children." Schurz was dismissive and clearly wanted to change the course of conversation and move on to the meal. He sat down next to Fanny and complimented her on the table. The others followed suit but Red Cloud would not leave the subject.

"The Episcopals speak Lakota," Johnny said from his chair set away from the table. "Red Cloud wants English for the children." He was translating quickly because Red Cloud was rambling on at a good clip. "You want my children to be ignorant and my warriors to become women." Red Cloud was pointing his finger and his voice was heating up as if this were a council of war.

Everyone was seated now and Schurz, who was normally a very patient man, looked up from his conversation with Fanny with obvious irritation in his eyes. "We want no such thing," he said. "We don't want your children ignorant, we want them educated. We don't want your warriors to become women, we want them to become farmers." He stopped to load his plate with mashed potatoes but there was still disdain in his eyes. McGillycuddy too was busy passing the food and, though interested to see this fire in his boss, wanted Red Cloud to simply shut up. "Honestly," Schurz went on, "I find your desires to be contradictory and simply argumentative."

Johnny began whispering the translation to Red Cloud just as Louise came into the room carrying the buffalo roast. Fanny closed her eyes. First an argument between the honored guests and now the ruined main course. When she opened her eyes they fell on Cowgill, the donator of the meat, and saw that he was shocked at the sight of the roast. Johnny was finishing the translation, having trouble with the concepts of contradictory and argumentative but only Red Cloud was listening. All the whites were looking at the coffee-flavored mass on the platter and showing amazement on their faces.

Red Cloud's face scowled with building darkness until his eyes fell onto the buffalo. When he saw what he was meant to eat the scowl dissolved and, his face lit up. "Tatanka?"

Fanny knew the answer to this question. "Hau, tatanka." She said it with some hesitation but could see that Red Cloud was very pleased with the answer. The chief elbowed his wife, Pretty Owl, who had been sitting beside him in sullen silence. "Tatanka." He repeated for her sake.

"Tatanka," Pretty Owl said and reached for the platter to serve her husband.

Look at the old boy. The warrior-diplomat defers to his stomach.

There was a lull in the conversation as Pretty Owl cut through the bitter crust to reveal rich, steaming meat. Red Cloud's smile broadened as the slices were piled higher on his plate. He sat back with knife and fork at the ready but did not begin eating. He waited as the meat was passed from guest to guest and Fanny grimaced as she saw Valentine lean and look closely at the slab of buffalo nestled between the potatoes and the beans. He had spoken many times about his earliest days on the plains, when buffalo were common. He told her that he liked no food better than buffalo. But he had never mentioned anything about coffee or an entire afternoon boiling over an open fire. She watched him as he squinted at the meat. It was very unlike him to scrutinize his food this closely and it was not until he began to flex his nostrils unnaturally that she realized that he had noticed her watching him and was teasing.

O'Donald was the first to cut into the meat and when Red Cloud saw the white man begin, he started slicing and eating as if he had not eaten in years. In fact, he had not eaten much buffalo for years and he expressed his pleasure in a series of sighs and moans that needed no translation. After an initial minute of awkwardness the entire table followed suit and the room was consumed in something of an orgy of eating.

Nothing but the sound of knives and forks against the plates and the purrs and titters of the guests issued from all quarters. No one spoke until Schurz, ever the gentleman, extended his compliments to the cook. He took up his wine glass and raised it to Fanny. "To the chef," he said.

As Fanny raised her glass, she caught the eye of McGillycuddy who was smiling so hard that his usually drooping mustache was only a horizontal line below his nose. She was a success as the entertainer for her husband and it struck her, just then, that she could do even better. She did not sip from her glass until she had swung it slightly toward Red Cloud. "And to the chief," she said.

Even before the dessert was served McGillycuddy could see that Fanny was getting very tired. When she started to rise, he reached under the table and touched her hand. "I'd be happy to help Louise," he said. But Fanny would not hear of it. She rose and brought the apple pie to each guest with Louise following with vanilla ice cream. In turn, the guests sighed in gratitude and Cowgill, who was particularly delighted because of his part in supplying the now famous buffalo roast, laughed and encouraged Louise to pile his dish to overflowing.

When the gentlemen retired to the porch to smoke their cigars, Fanny was left with Pretty Owl. Since Pretty Owl did not speak English and Johnny had gone to the porch to translate for Red Cloud, the women's coffee time was awkward, to say the least.

Pretty Owl was old now but had clearly been worthy of her name. She had no doubt been an alluring maiden and there were several rumors about her and her relationship to Red Cloud. The most notable thing about their relationship was that it was monogamous. One of the traditions that McGillycuddy was trying to discourage was the practice of multiple wives and, in that respect Red Cloud was already civilized. But the rumor was that his lifestyle was not exactly chosen freely. It was said that as a young man he had intended to take a second wife immediately after marrying Pretty Owl. The woman's name was Pine Leaf and she had been in love with Red Cloud even before he developed an interest in Pretty Owl. During the marriage ceremony of Red Cloud and Pretty Owl, Pine Leaf, who had not been told of Red Cloud's intention to marry her, too, had committed suicide in grief over losing Red Cloud. Some said the event had made a huge impression on Red Cloud and that was the reason he chose the matrimonial style of white men. But others said he had tried to marry younger women and Pretty Owl had discouraged all such interlopers by threatening to kill them.

They commented in single words and sign language about the china that Fanny had brought from Detroit. The silverware was engraved with the initials of her grandparents and Pretty Owl seemed awestruck by simply holding a fork and tracing the letters with her fingers. The women wondered about the traditions of the other. What could it mean to be the wife of a chief?

When the elementary conversation turned to children Fanny did her best to hold up her end but the fatigue of the day settled on her hard. The Red Clouds had a son. His name was Jack and he was a leader in his own right. It was said that he had helped to kill Custer. When Pretty Owl looked at Fanny to explain where her children were she was answered with a wan smile and Fanny was relieved to hear McGillycuddy call from the front door that Brownie O'Donald was leaving and would Fanny like to come say good night.

There was a round of handshaking and farewells on the porch as the guests took their leave in the pleasant cool of the September night. O'Donald flattered Fanny gallantly and sauntered off with a freshly lit cigar in his mouth. Cowgill followed suit. But the Red Clouds and Schurz lingered; the men still engaged in a conversation that Fanny could tell was contentious by the stern look on her husband's face.

In an effort to silence Red Cloud, McGillycuddy sent Johnny home to his cabin built on the edge of agency buildings. Without his interpreter Red Cloud went silent long enough for Schurz to tell Fanny in glowing terms what a fine evening it had been. He seemed relieved to be disengaged from Red Cloud and took Fanny's hand. "The most superb hospitality since I left Washington, D.C." Then, as if Fanny had written his lines, "You are a credit to your fine husband." He even winked—a departure from his noble bearing. "He's a lucky man."

And for Fanny that ended the night. She too took her leave and held herself erect long enough to put one hand on the door. She nearly made it into the house before staggering and being held up by McGillycuddy. This embarrassed her and she tried to smile as if it were nothing. But McGillycuddy had her arm and Schurz urged him to take her to bed. "She must be exhausted after such a big day. You take care of her, Valentine. We're done here."

So Fanny let herself be led into the house and into the bedroom. But she would not let McGillycuddy help her undress. "I can manage," she said. "Please see that Louise is finished in the kitchen. Let her go to bed in any case. Then come to bed with me."

McGillycuddy was very close to her and looked down with great love. "You were wonderful," he said, and kissed her on the forehead.

He stepped out into the darkened house and looked about with a sad pride. Red Cloud had been impossible but, personally, the evening had been a stunning success. The Secretary of the Interior was very pleased with him and what he had been doing at Pine Ridge. There was a great deal to be thankful for and, though he was worried about Fanny, he believed that she would improve now that things were running so smoothly. He walked to the kitchen and found that Louise had gone to her room and everything was in good order. The house was still and solid. *A lucky man.*

A lamp burned in the parlor and as McGillycuddy moved to extinguish it he thought of Fanny just through the door of their bedroom. He thought of her naked and slipping between the clean sheets and he needed to be there with her. The yellow light on the walls faded with the twist of the wick and gradually the room went to black. He turned to the bedroom but was distracted by voices on the porch. He stepped to the front door and recognized Red Cloud's exercised voice. "A bad man," he said. "Dangerous." *The old fraud knows enough English to be admitted to college.* "Tell the Great White Father. Tell him I want him gone."

Then he heard Schurz speak with exasperation. "The Great Father is a wise man, Red Cloud. He knows everything. If there is anything wrong with your agent he will know it before either you or I know it." There was silence. Then, "Go home, Red Cloud. Good night."

McGillycuddy stood by the door until the sound of footfalls was gone. Then he went to his bedroom in hopes of sharing a few moments with his wife. He felt at once robust and weak. It was a time when he needed his woman. He wanted to hold her and talk with her and make love to her. But he found her asleep and so he undressed and slipped into bed and lay awake thinking of what Schurz had said. He was angry at Red Cloud for forcing Schurz to say what he had said, and he knew he would have to deal with that soon. There was nothing truly wrong with the words Schurz had chosen— certainly Red Cloud had them coming. But in the dark of his own bedroom the condescending tone struck McGillycuddy as cruel.

Part Five

Outbreak

FALL 1882

15

Just as McGillycuddy's innovations for the Pine Ridge Reservation were beginning to show results for the Oglala people, the dark-horse candidate, James Garfield, was elected president. He had been a lay preacher in an Ohio congregation called the Disciples of Christ and was not supported by former President Ulysses S. Grant. Both these facts made McGillycuddy suspicious, but Garfield was a Republican and was known for his belief in the spoils system. So, when he was inaugurated in March 1881, all Republican appointees, like McGillycuddy, felt secure in their jobs, no matter how successful their service.

But Garfield's disdain for civil service reform proved to be his downfall when he was gunned down by a Republican jobseeker named Charles Guiteau. Guiteau had assumed Garfield was so corrupt that Republican credentials were all that was needed to ensure a job in the administration. The president died in September of his first year in office, just as the third harvest of the Pine Ridge Reservation was being gathered. The harvest was exceptional because of a wet spring and summer, and fresh vegetables and grains were abundant. Most other supplies for the reservation were being hauled in

from depots in Nebraska and on the Missouri River by
Lakota teams and drivers. In short, the Indians were
showing signs of progress along "the white man's
road," and McGillycuddy's aspirations for the reservation were developing as planned. McGillycuddy felt in-
debted in part to the luck of good weather for his
success. In fact the unusually productive growing season
might well have been the reason for his confidence in
keeping his job when the reform-minded Chester Arthur
took over the presidency.

During Garfield's brief tenure as president, both Hayt
and Schurz had resigned to move forward in their political lives. A man named Price replaced Hayt and S. J.
Kirkwood replaced Schurz. On a brief visit to the capital, McGillycuddy met them both and came away believing that though he did not have the rapport with
them that he had had with their predecessors, he could
work with them.

This belief was put almost immediately to the test
when Red Cloud sent the new president a letter asking
that McGillycuddy be removed as agent. He complained of several small disappointments concerning ox
teams and wagons that had been promised and not delivered, but particularly that McGillycuddy had insisted
that the residents of the reservation be counted. Here he
was referring to the annual census required to establish
proper distribution of food. The letter went through
Kirkwood's office and a copy was sent directly back to
McGillycuddy asking for an explanation.

Had the letter not come as such a shock and had it
not been sure to elicit a governmental investigation of
the agency, McGillycuddy would have read it with perfect contempt. Particularly troubling was the allegation
that it had been signed by ninety-six chiefs of the

Lakota nation. *Ninety-six. Do we have that many chiefs?*

He read the petition three times, his rage building with each reading. He was quite sure that his job was secure because great progress was being shown on the reservation and because by assigning his best man, Brownie O'Donald, to the books of the reservation, he had ensured that all accounting was perfect. But, if the signatures were real, he was very hurt. If the signatures were fraudulent, he was extremely angry.

From the beginning McGillycuddy was convinced that Red Cloud had neither the power to influence the chiefs that were represented on the petition nor the acumen to write such a document. He calmed himself and read the petition one more time. Certainly the progress of the common Indians was leading to independence, which threatened Red Cloud. There was no question that the old chief wanted McGillycuddy gone. But Red Cloud was a warrior, not a petty whiner. No, the letter had the earmarks of another hand.

There were many who stood to profit by McGillycuddy's dismissal. They were almost all whites or part whites who were on the government dole by virtue of marriage to Lakota women: people who wanted McGillycuddy out of the way so they could cheat the government through illicit contracting or by illegally bringing alcohol to the reservation.

There had been many incidents of Lakotas trading their food rations, ponies, and even women for cheap illegal liquor brought onto the reservation. Eight people had been killed as a result of drunkenness in the first year of McGillycuddy's tenure. So the agent had cracked down on the illegal trade. Men like Johnny Provost's brother, Charlie, found that their incomes crashed. For this they blamed McGillycuddy. Defrauding of the government was also rampant in all phases of the intersection between agencies and private enterprise. To a large extent it was winked at and perceived as benign. Of course corruption only cheated the taxpayers and the client Indians. But only on Pine Ridge, where the clients were still a formidable fighting force, could the consequences of mishandling the Indians result in open conflict, war, and carnage.

As he reread this poison petition once again, it settled darkly on him that few whites took the threat of a violent Oglala revolt seriously. To many it was fanciful, romantic, or even humorous. As he sat in his office trying to decipher who was behind this attempted usurpation beside Red Cloud, it occurred to him that perhaps it was only he and a few army officers who understood the volatility of the situation. Then he wondered if perhaps he was overly cautious, even paranoid. He had been accused of being too serious about some issues and perhaps this was one of those times. It flashed in his mind that he might be less than brave. *No, you have proved that false many times. And you are not mad either; there is something unwholesome and unsettled in the air.*

He spent the afternoon alone in his office with the copy of the petition. The smart thing would have been to concede. His salary was $2,250 a year. It was assumed that agents would skim off the top and end up with a good wage. But McGillycuddy would not skim and could certainly make more money in private business. It was his refusal to play by the corrupt rules of the game that had made him a target and Red Cloud, trying to hold onto the traditions of his people, was using the situation to his advantage. All that day McGillycuddy

was first disheartened and then angry. But finally he resolved to fight for his vision of what the Oglalas must
become in order to survive. Sometimes he believed that
he loved the old ways as much as Red Cloud. After all,
it was that freedom and integration with the sweep of
landscape that he had fallen for. But those days were
ended. He loved the Lakotas he had met when he had
come to the plains as a very young man but the buffalo
were gone and so were the buffalo hunters. If the culture was to survive at all it would be integrated into the
lives of white farmers and herdsmen.

By the end of the day he had calmed and sent for his
two most trusted assistants. When Brownie O'Donald
and Johnny Provost entered his office, they were handed
the copy of the petition. "Tell me what you think,"
McGillycuddy said and walked to the window to give
each man the time and privacy to analyze the petition.
The document began, "We as a people have lost faith in
our Agent." It went on to accuse McGillycuddy of:

> *unjust treatment of us in many cases. He says we
> have no rights on our reservation when we differ
> from his opinion. He has tried to depose our head
> chief Red Cloud which the nation does not want
> and we believe he steals our goods and we know
> he lies to us.*

After reading the petition, Johnny lowered his dark
eyes in a predictable way and waited for one of the
white men to speak first. O'Donald read quickly then
looked back to the top of the page. "*Lost* faith in their
Agent? When the hell did Red Cloud *have* faith in anything except perhaps in ability to obstruct progress."

"So you believe it's Red Cloud that's behind this?"

"Red Cloud and his *gaboons*."

"And what of all those cosignatories?"

O'Donald looked at the list of names on the original. "If these men's marks appeared on this letter, most were forged."

"And you, Johnny? You are closest to the Oglalas. What are they saying? Is there widespread discontent with my administration of this reservation?" McGilly-cuddy could hear his own voice rising. He did not want to frighten Johnny out of an honest response and so took an instant to let his anger drain. "In your opinion, Johnny, who is behind this?"

Johnny had been looking toward the floor as McGillycuddy spoke and when he looked up it struck the agent that he was in many ways like a woman. His brother, Charlie, also lived on Pine Ridge but was very different from Johnny. He had inherited more of their Sioux mother's culture. It was difficult to tell Charlie from any of the other Indians except for the fact that, like Johnny, he could speak his father's language. But where Johnny used his ability with English to promote understanding, Charlie joined ranks with the squaw men. He occasionally made fun of his brother's small stature, smooth skin, and large eyes inherited from their French father. Even Johnny's hands were small and he moved them gracefully as he spoke. "Red Cloud wants you gone because you threaten him. The squaw men want you gone because you threaten the money they make off the Indians. They have become allies."

"The half-breeds want the illegal commerce of these captive people," O'Donald said.

McGillycuddy nodded. "And what does Red Cloud want?"

"He's a spoiler," O'Donald said. "He doesn't want

anyone to progress and is trying to get rid of you so his half-breed friends can make a killing off the government and the Indians."

"Johnny?"

"What Mr. O'Donald says is true but there is more."

"Go on."

"Red Cloud believes the old ways are best and that he is the old way."

"And what of the other signatories?"

"Some may be true. Most are false."

"Precisely," O'Donald said. "Fraudulent and perpetrated by whites and part whites for economic gain."

"Who?" McGillycuddy had left the window and now moved to his desk. "Do you have a guess Johnny?" McGillycuddy sat in his chair and placed his long hands on the desk. His time of indecision was finished. "What's your guess, Johnny? I want to see if it is the same as mine." *Look at him twist his hands. He's such a kind man. Concerned about the feelings of rattlesnakes.*

O'Donald was excited and could not wait for Johnny. "It's Nick Chappell, for one."

McGillycuddy agreed with O'Donald but waited for Johnny's nod. "Okay," McGillycuddy said. "The illustrious brother-in-law of the chief is the ringleader. Who else?"

"All the men who have married the Oglalas. Many are not officially married." There was a hint of resentment in Johnny's eyes as he spoke of the whites that had followed in his father's footsteps but without honor.

"Of the signatures, which do you think were forged, Johnny?"

Johnny looked over the list of chiefs carefully.

"Do you believe Young Man Afraid signed as the letter says?"

"No."

"I don't either," McGillycuddy said.

"And neither do I," O'Donald chimed in. He was still quite upset. "Let me go get him. He was at Blanchard's earlier."

"Do that, Brownie."

While O'Donald was gone McGillycuddy and Johnny went over the other names on the list. By the time Young Man Afraid came into the office followed closely by O'Donald walking officiously as an aide-de-camp, they had identified dozens of suspect names. "But we only need the one to begin with," McGillycuddy said as he stood to meet Young Man Afraid.

The chief was dressed for his day at the traders and wore a canvas coat covering a corduroy vest. His hair was only medium length and a silk bandana was tied in a square knot around his neck. He was much younger than Red Cloud, handsome with dark eyes and a pleasant smile. But Young Man Afraid's smile faded as he saw McGillycuddy's face. He understood that McGillycuddy was angry but showed no sign of preknowledge as to what was on his mind. They shook hands over the desk. "I have two simple questions for you, Young Man Afraid." Johnny translated. McGillycuddy slid the copy of the petition across the desk. "Have you ever seen this letter and did you sign it."

Johnny translated McGillycuddy's words then began putting the letter into Lakota. But before Johnny had gotten through the first sentence the chief's face was contorting in confusion. "No," he said. "No, no."

McGillycuddy pointed to the petition still in Johnny's hands. "You did not put your mark to this paper."

"No," Young Man Afraid said firmly.

McGillycuddy nodded and took the petition from

Johnny. "I didn't think that such a progressive man would be party to any such thing. Please sit." He motioned toward a chair and bade the other two men to sit also.

Once they were all seated McGillycuddy took a moment to collect his thoughts. "I've been considering this for some time," he said. Young Man Afraid nodded. He only looked to Johnny when he needed clarification of his understanding of the English words. "I've been thinking that Red Cloud is detrimental to the progress of your people along the white man's road. He seems bent on rekindling war between our people and to humor him is to hasten that war. He represents the old savage ways and you, that is we, need a new leader." Here Young Man Afraid turned to Johnny to be sure he was hearing McGillycuddy properly. "You are the hereditary chief of the Oglalas. Red Cloud is only a war chief, and there is no war. If I'm to be blamed for deposing a chief, that is exactly what I shall do." He pointed to Young Man Afraid's chest. "I want you to replace Red Cloud effective this very day. From this moment on Red Cloud is a common Indian and you are chief of all the Oglalas."

Young Man Afraid sat rigid in his chair. He showed no sign of emotion and nodded with a gravity that assured McGillycuddy. "It is good," Young Man Afraid said. "Red Cloud is not fit to be agency chief. He does not know how to do business."

McGillycuddy nodded. "Couldn't agree with you more," he said and smiled shallowly. "Now I'm going to ask Mr. O'Donald to take down my response to this treacherous petition and I want you to listen. Johnny will translate when needed but I want you to understand completely."

Young Man Afraid nodded with increased dignity.

"Brownie, please take this down for immediate transmission to Secretary Kirkwood with a copy to Commissioner Price.

Dear Mr. Secretary,

Regarding the alleged petition for my removal. I am sure that the petition will precipitate an investigation and rest assured that I will cooperate. Also rest assured that said petition is a complete fabrication of reservation whites and the egregious old fraud, Red Cloud—the deposed chief of the Oglalas. I have already taken steps to correct this situation and will take further steps to see that the influence of wicked white men is terminated on this reservation.

Sign it, V. T. McGillycuddy—Agent."

16

Red Cloud was enraged. For weeks rumors abounded of his imminent breakout to join Sitting Bull's hostiles in Canada. Riders galloped from one camp to another. Chiefs and headmen loyal to Red Cloud conferred with chiefs and headmen loyal to Young Man Afraid. Alliances shifted. Settlers for hundreds of miles shuttered their windows and kept their rifles close.

McGillycuddy refused to talk with Red Cloud. He referred to him only as "the former chief" and did all agency business with Young Man Afraid, who took to his new duties with a zeal and aptitude that pleased many Indians and many whites. But there were some whites who were not pleased and these were the whites McGillycuddy confronted. He put O'Donald and Captain Sword to the task of composing a list of illegitimate squaw men, known whiskey- and gunrunners and livestock thieves. The men on the list were deemed persona non grata and the list was posted around the reservation with a clear threat of imprisonment for those who remained. From Pine Ridge all the way to New York City editorials claimed McGillycuddy's actions were illegal and pugnacious. But there were many more who felt that the agent was well within his rights and deserved

praise for gaining control of the reservation. Red
Cloud's response was to wire T. A. Bland and ask his
friend to collect money from Indian welfare groups and
permission from the Bureau of Indian Affairs, for him
to travel to Washington, D.C., to discuss "problems on
the reservation." Bland was effective and very soon
telegraphed that Red Cloud should come and bring
whomever he wanted to accompany him—to a limit of
twelve people.

Again, McGillycuddy intercepted the communication
and determined that whites were behind it. Indications
pointed to Nick Chappell. Both Price and Kirkwood assured McGillycuddy that they supported his manage-
ment of the reservation and that Red Cloud would be
little more than humored, but he still seethed that Chappell would even be granted permission to travel.

Night after night Fanny watched him pace back and
forth in front of her rocker as she knit. An inspector was
scheduled to arrive about the time Red Cloud left for
Washington and though McGillycuddy felt that he had
acted well within his mandate as agent for the reservation, he worried that he had not seen a way to act more
diplomatically. He was aware of his tendency to act
rashly and tortured himself thinking that he had done
so at the expense of the common Indians. Fanny hated
to watch him twist with self-recrimination and worry.
He was drawn and pale and she wondered that the pres-
sures of his job might be too much. And when she
thought like that she feared that she had not been as
much help as she might have been. After all, wasn't it a
wife's duty to ease a husband's strain? Wasn't it unnat-
ural for a wife to fail to respond to her husband's needs?

She knew Valentine McGillycuddy and even though
some thought him compulsive and prone to fits of

anger, he kept most of his rage inside and he was capable of decisive action powered by that rage. "I have to find a way to bring these people to civilization," he said and drove his fist into his hand.

"You are being opposed from all sides," Fanny offered.

"That hardly matters. A man up to the task would find a way."

"You are finding a way. This reservation has made huge strides."

"Yet we are constantly on the brink of war. Does no one understand that? Does no one see the danger here?"

"You have handled every issue with wisdom."

"I have been difficult. Too self-assured."

"Sometimes the job calls for strength. A firm hand."

He paced more. Back and forth a half dozen more times. "A firm hand," he said. "I believe in a firm hand." More pacing. Then, "Why does he oppose me so? Why can't we do this noble thing together?" At times like this Fanny knew not to answer. He was thinking out loud, testing propositions, searching for solutions.

"The Smithsonian Institution is sending delegates out to observe the Sun Dance." He spoke as if Fanny did not already know this. "It may well be the last Sun Dance in the history of the world. They are coming to document pagan rites of torture and to assess my progress in discouraging those rites. Is my work to be judged by how Red Cloud acts? Will I be forced to have him thrown in jail in the presence of the finest anthropologists in the country?"

She caught his hand as he passed the thousandth time. "Doctor." She knew he considered the title a sign of respect and held the hand tight until she was sure that he would stay stopped. "Things will be all right." He started to complain. "No, Valentine. Things will be all right." She squeezed harder. "They will." She shook the hand. "They will."

Finally he smiled. "You are a hopeless optimist. In that way as hopeless as old Clearance Looking Dog."

"He's a fine old man and you should listen to him and to your wife. This crisis will pass and you should not let your worry and anger get the best of you." He nodded his head but would not look her in the eye.

McGillycuddy knew that she was right but he was not good at repressing worry and anger. He tried to bury himself in his work but just when he thought he had succeeded in relegating the issue of Red Cloud to the dustbin of his mind something would happen to bring it back full blown into his consciousness.

Two days before Red Cloud was to leave for Washington and a week before the Bureau of Indian Affairs inspector was to arrive to question McGillycuddy, the agent happened to look out of his office window just as Nick Chappell walked past. McGillycuddy had recently been provided with a list of Red Cloud's entourage for the Washington trip. Reviewing the list infuriated him because Red Cloud's permission to travel came from Commissioner Price, and he had no authority to limit or alter the list. If Nick Chappell was not legally married to Red Cloud's sister he would have been first on the list of men banned from the reservation. The fact that he was first on the list of those allowed to visit Washington brought McGillycuddy to a rage. But that had been days before and in the afternoon, before he saw Chappell passing his window, he was of the belief that he had gotten over the outrage of the little white man's obvious negative influence on his reservation. But when he looked out the window and caught the sight of Chappell's sauntering, cocky gait, his anger flared and he was on his feet and at the door with clenched jaw.

By the time McGillycuddy stepped outdoors Chappell was thirty yards down the path toward Red Cloud's camp and though he knew he should let it go, McGillycuddy was off his porch and striding after him before he could think. He moved much faster than the shorter man and had nearly caught up when Chappell entered the trees along White Clay Creek. The path was dusty and made no sound when walked upon. It occurred to McGillycuddy that he could be within reach of Chappell before he knew he was being followed. As the willows and cottonwoods thickened a strange feeling came over McGillycuddy: first, that he could kill Chappell and be rid of one of his main problems, then, as he fought that feeling, he began to think that Chappell might kill him. *Small but mean and deceptive. Certainly he carries a knife or two. I am without a weapon. Without a weapon.*

Chappell had fought on the Sioux side against the United States Army. He had seen battle and no doubt killed men. As McGillycuddy narrowed the distance between them he knew he should be more cautious. But he had fought in battles too and besides, the look of the greasy, long, black hair, braided in the Oglala way, disgusted him. No matter how he dressed or wore his hair, Chappell was an outcast who preyed on the plight of the Indians.

"I want you to know," McGillycuddy said calmly when he was three feet behind Chappell, "that I am watching you."   .

He had hoped to startle Chappell but his words seemed to make no impression. The buckskin-clad Frenchman did not jump, stop, slow, or even look around. "So, it is you, McGillycuddy," Chappell said without altering his pace. "I wondered who would be so foolish as to follow me down into these trees."

"I'm your man, Nick. I'll be behind you from here on out. Think of this walk as a metaphor."

"Metaphor." He continued to walk with McGillycuddy a single stride behind.

"Metaphor, Nick. A thing that represents other things. Like you representing all that's wrong with white men and their relation to the Sioux."

Chappell swung quickly with the intent of frightening McGillycuddy, but the agent stood his ground and the little man came close enough for McGillycuddy to smell his breath. "It is not me McGillycuddy. I have accepted Sioux ways. I am married to a Sioux. I am the father of Sioux children. It is you. You with your need to see all men alike." His eyes were a startling blue. "You are a fool to follow me into these woods."

"I am not afraid of you, Nick. Though perhaps I should be. You have proved that you are treacherous. You take unfair advantage at every opportunity. But I am not afraid of you. I suspect that you are a coward." McGillycuddy leaned over to challenge Chappell to attack him. They stood only inches apart, staring into each other's eyes, until the Frenchman's eyes flickered and he moved a step back.

"You go to hell, McGillycuddy. It is where you belong." But the fire was out of his eyes.

"I'll be watching you Nick. I'll throw you off this reservation at my first opportunity."

Chappell swung his blanket over his shoulder. "To hell," he said and turned back to the path that ran along the creek bank.

McGillycuddy let him go and as soon as the little man

was out of sight among the willows, the agent reached out and steadied himself on the trunk of the closest cottonwood. *What, for the love of God, am I doing?* He felt faint—the way he had felt after combat, when all the cases of arrow, rifle, and battle-ax wounds had been treated. He needed to sit and settled on a log near the running water. During that time nothing much passed through his mind. It was a trick he had learned long before: he repeated the word "quiet" ever more slowly in his thoughts. *Quiet . . . quiet.* Letting himself go as heavy as the log he sat upon. *Quiet.* Until the trees and creek forgot he was there. *Quiet.* Until the birds began to scurry and twitter in the brush and the hum of tiny insects began to pulse like a heartbeat.

Nothing of Red Cloud, or Fanny, or T. A. Bland came into his mind. Time slipped on and he did not think of even himself. Once he thought that he might like to live in the old way with the Sioux—as Chappell was pretending to do. *Quiet . . . quiet now.* Then nothing until he heard the sound of voices and was brought back to find that an hour had passed since he had followed Nick Chappell into the woods.

The voices were young people. A mix of English and Lakota and McGillycuddy was pulled by them along the creek and deeper into the woods. He made no noise and moved slowly. Still in his trance of relaxation, he imagined that he was nearly impossible to see, like a coyote, a mink, the breeze itself. He moved behind a tree trunk and slipped partway around to see five young women bathing in a pool no deeper than their knees. Four of the women were the color of finely tanned leather. They stood giggling, willowy and lithe with sable braids and only a hint of black where their legs met. The fifth was facing away from McGillycuddy and her alabaster whiteness stilled his breathing. Her blonde curls tumbled from her shoulders and, as she turned, her breasts were surprisingly ample with large rose-colored nipples. McGillycuddy could see the sunshine sparkling in her pubic hair and felt himself swelling with the sight.

Even before he raised his eyes to her face he knew it was Julia Blanchard. When their eyes met he no longer felt invisible. She did not shy from his gaze or fumble to cover herself. She was no more afraid of McGillycuddy than he had been of Nick Chappell. There was no embarrassment or shame in her expression and for the instant before McGillycuddy's own embarrassment came crashing down, he felt himself swelling even more. But suddenly he was exposed and caught the eyes of one of the other women. She covered herself but did not call out. She knelt into the pool and looked at McGillycuddy, then back at Julia who made no pretense at modesty. As McGillycuddy turned, now with some haste, she took Julia by the hand and pulled her gently down into the water.

The investigation that McGillycuddy had at once feared and welcomed never materialized. The fact that Red Cloud was given an audience in Washington with Commissioner Price and Secretary Kirkland while McGillycuddy was given little opportunity to defend himself assaulted the agent's sense of fairness. While Red Cloud's delegation was in Washington he fired off repeated telegrams asking to be investigated, demanding a chance to explain his actions. But he was answered with little more than patronizing from his superiors. He feared his credibility had suffered and he could not control his urge to be heard.

Sitting Bull had recently come down from Canada

and surrendered. He was temporarily safe in military prison but there were still many of his warriors wandering Dakota and were perhaps even more dangerous than when they were hidden in Canada. Some were filtering onto Pine Ridge and McGillycuddy could feel their unsettling effect. As time for the Sun Dance approached he appealed for guidance concerning this influx of Lakota fighting men openly hostile to the United States. But he had perhaps spent his political capital because his requests were nearly ignored by Washington. *Do they not know what it means to have northern warriors here for the most fanatical religious ceremony on the Lakota calendar?* All he received was a list of dignitaries from eastern institutions who would soon be arriving to observe the Sun Dance. Congress was moving to outlaw the ceremony on grounds that it was a rite of torture, unchristian, and antithetical to the goals of civilization. This Sun Dance would be the last and suddenly anthropologists, religious leaders, and well-connected curiosity seekers were acutely interested. He also learned that Red Cloud had been received very well in Washington and New York by the press and Indian reform groups—particularly T. A. Bland's National Indian Defense Association. Red Cloud would be arriving home something of a hero. And just in time for the last Sun Dance.

McGillycuddy had attended several Lakota Sun Dances and felt they were akin to other religious ceremonies. He considered all such ceremonies as little more than superstitious rites that exploited common people and contributed to their helplessness and backward thinking. As far as he was concerned the Sun Dance should be stopped—but he felt the same way about Christian baptism, communion, and pious worship in general. He was more concerned about the practical matter of controlling the Lakotas when many thousands of reservation Indians with additional hostiles would be encamped together for the four days of torture and sun worship. The ceremony always served to work the Indians into a frenzy of longing for days of freedom and war.

McGillycuddy would have liked to confront Red Cloud when he came back to the reservation in the middle of June but he refrained for two reasons. First, he did not want to honor him with such a confrontation and second, eastern ladies and gentlemen had begun arriving to witness the Sun Dance of the Lakotas. Instead of creating the impression that Red Cloud was still an important personage, he directed the Sun Dance visitors to the camp of Young Man Afraid. There were many visitors to the reservation and McGillycuddy insisted on checking the papers and interviewing each person. They were a mixed group: some violently opposed to what they called the "Torture Dance" for its non-Christian character and some who revered the Lakota religion, believing it pure, benign, and somehow strongly related to Christianity. McGillycuddy tried his best to deny visitation to those whites he thought might disturb the relative calm of the reservation but it was a daunting task. To his way of thinking, no one had any business gawking at the pagan rites of these people and should be stopped from creating a public safety risk by condemning or aggrandizing this crudest of religious observances.

Almost all who showed up to observe the Sun Dance carried letters of introduction from some highly placed government official and McGillycuddy was able to turn very few back. He assigned white reservation workers or congenial Lakotas to small groups of visitors and divorced himself of all visitors except two whom he agreed to host personally. A fiery Methodist minister named Leroy Stubbs had arrived at the reservation in the company of a Miss Fletcher, an ethnologist from the Peabody Institute in Boston. They both carried important letters of recommendation from Secretary Kirkwood.

The pair did not seem to be great friends but rather two people thrown together by circumstance. In fact, after the initial luncheon, hosted by Fanny on the porch of their home, McGillycuddy concluded that they were of nearly opposite camps with regard to their reverence for the pagan ritual they had traveled so far to see. The central feature of the Sun Dance of course was the piercing of the flesh of the participants. Rev. Stubbs and Miss Fletcher talked excitedly and with some knowledge about the manner and severity of the cuts to be made on the dancers. Miss Fletcher seemed to understand at least part of the reasons the participants would submit to having their chests and backs slashed and wooden stakes threaded through the slits to be eventually ripped loose. She saw the dance as a physical substitution for Christian sacraments and claimed that most religions were similar in that sense. Such talk drove Rev. Stubbs nearly to an apoplectic rage. As she went on about the sacrificial qualities of the dance and likened it to the agony of Christ, Rev. Stubbs seethed with indignation that the government had not stopped the practice years before. Fanny remained cheerful throughout the discussions and kept a close eye on her husband. He had witnessed Sun Dances and if she saw a certain hue on his face, an indication that he was ready to jump into the conversation, she interrupted and offered the guests more iced tea or homemade ice cream.

The Sun Dance was a four-day affair but bands of

Lakotas began arriving a full two weeks before. There had been great debate and argument between Little Wound, Red Dog, High Wolf, Red Cloud, Young Man Afraid, and a myriad of medicine men as to where the ceremony would be held. For prestige's sake each chief wanted the Sun Dance to be held near his own camp and the medicine men lobbied for the camp of their favorite chief or in accordance with a dream they might have had. Finally, McGillycuddy and Young Man Afraid selected a neutral site just over the Nebraska line.

O'Donald estimated that there were ten thousand Indians camped in the area of the Sun Dance grounds. That meant that several thousand Lakotas from other reservations had somehow filtered onto Pine Ridge and McGillycuddy, Captain Sword, and O'Donald concerned themselves with trying to find out just who the visitors were. The majority were likely Spotted Tail's people from the Rosebud Reservation but some were no doubt Sitting Bull's newly surrendered renegades from Standing Rock on the Missouri River. These were highly excitable warriors who needed to be watched. Sword deployed his spies with orders to report any talk of local raiding inspired by the heightened religious fervor and the Indian police force was sent out among the camps on scheduled rounds.

On the first day of the celebration McGillycuddy dutifully loaded his charges and Johnny Provost into a three-seated depot wagon rented from Ott Means and pulled by four bay geldings. They took the trail that dipped through White Clay Creek and up onto the ridge the agency was named for. There, two miles beyond the agency buildings they met the dignified old Clearance Looking Dog, who was dressed in fine, white buckskins with eagle feathers tucked neatly into his elegant black braids. The old man greeted them with the cheerfulness he was known for. He was a chief and a holy man of sorts and his everyday friendliness was now augmented by excitement over the impending Sun Dance. McGillycuddy had arranged for Clearance Looking Dog to accompany them every day of the Sun Dance beginning with this day—the procurement of the sacred tree.

The old man grinned and raised his eyebrows in sheer joy to be riding with the honored white guests. Even before he was seated he began chattering with Stubbs and Miss Fletcher in his broken English and listened intently to decipher Miss Fletcher's noble attempts to speak Lakota. When he realized that Stubbs was a Methodist minister he laughed. "Me," he said, patting his chest. "I am a minister too."

Word had come to McGillycuddy that a tree suitable to be used as the Sun Dance Tree had been located near a spring southeast of the agency. He urged the horses into a trot in an effort to be there when the holy men arrived to bless the tree and prepare it to be cut down and carried to the sacred circle. A hundred people were already at the site when they arrived but they were in time to watch the young virgin girls symbolically strike the tree with axes. Miss Fletcher was excited and intensely interested to witness everything she could. She climbed down from the wagon and encouraged Clearance Looking Dog to take her into the crowd of worshipers who pushed in toward the tree. Knowing that she would have difficult questions, McGillycuddy waved Johnny to go along. He indicated with a nod that he would see to Rev. Stubbs who had not yet ventured from the wagon seat.

McGillycuddy picketed the horses and walked back

to stand beside the reverend. "They've selected a tree that suits them—one that will stand the pressure of a dozen men pulling on it," he said.

"That's the tree they will be tethered to?"

"Yes. Leather lariats are tied to wooden pegs or eagle claws forced through a series of slits in the chests and backs of the dancers."

"And the other end of the lariats tied to the top of that tree?"

McGillycuddy nodded and looked up to gauge the reverend's expression. He was incensed. "That's right. Lots of blood and ecstasy." *Gently. No sense tipping him over. It will come.*

"Disgusting."

"Terrible."

By then the men who had pledged to dance and be tortured were chopping at the tree with double-bit axes. "But they don't dance here?" Stubbs still had not come down from the wagon seat.

"No, no. More than a mile from here. They'll fell the tree, trim it up, and carry it to be replanted in the Sacred Circle."

"Sacred Circle, my foot."

McGillycuddy couldn't help himself. He pretended not to hear this last comment. "It's a sanctuary."

"Sanctuary?"

"Of sorts."

Now Stubbs was coming down off the wagon. "For the love of Pete."

"Come along, Reverend, they are purifying the tree with sweetgrass and sage. Incense."

Stubbs followed close behind McGillycuddy and they pushed in to where they could see the medicine men, bleeding already from multiple, self-inflicted knife wounds as they walked slowly around the fifty-foot-tall tree. The warriors, stripped to nothing but breech cloths, chopped steadily at the tree. Miss Fletcher, beside herself with interest, came trotting to their side. "They've been doing this since time immemorial," she said.

"Exactly," McGillycuddy said. *Except for the iron in the axes and the woven cloth covering their privates.*

Over the next two days McGillycuddy dutifully showed his guests dozens of young men ensconced in remote areas surrounded by stakes flagged with multicolored cloth. "They will," he explained, "remain sequestered without food or water until their vision comes."

"And they will see their future," Miss Fletcher said with awe.

"Simple exhaustion." Stubbs snorted.

"Exhaustion, to be sure," McGillycuddy said. "But not simple. They believe it is a sort of prophecy. They live by it."

Occasionally, as they walked about the camps and sacred grounds they saw young, bleeding children run screeching from the brush where the crude piercing of ears was taking place. Once they came across an old man sitting on a rock with a knife in one hand and a leather awl in the other. With the awl he would pluck the skin of his leg and raise it up to be neatly sliced off with the knife. Clearance Looking Dog talked with him and turned back to say that the old man was too old to dance but he wanted to suffer to spare the suffering of his family. He had already sliced twenty pea-sized pieces of flesh from his leg and was still slicing when Rev. Stubbs and Miss Fletcher turned away.

They watched the nearly naked dancers as they entered the Sweat Lodges early in the morning of each day.

It was a purification rite that Miss Fletcher wanted very much to see up close. She beseeched McGillycuddy to use his influence but all the agent would do was turn her over to Clearance Looking Dog whose pleasant expression dissolved as he came to understand what the woman was asking. But Miss Fletcher was a persistent anthropologist and assured the old man that her interest was strictly in the interest of science. Finally, Clearance Looking Dog went to one of the medicine men who was in charge of one of the Sweat Lodges and for five minutes talked earnestly to the man. At last he turned to Miss Fletcher and waved her to come over. Without fanfare, the medicine man pulled back the flap of the hide wickiup and Miss Fletcher peered inside. When her head reappeared, her hair was moist and the curl had disappeared. But she was smiling and dug into the leather bag for her pencil and pad.

The fourth and final day of the Sun Dance was the culmination of the celebration. It was the day of piercing, overt sun worship, and a time for all the bands to gather at the sacred circle to support all who were sacrificing for the people. To that point McGillycuddy had traveled many miles through thousands of people and managed to avoid coming in contact with Red Cloud. Nothing could have pleased him more. The last thing he wanted was to confront Red Cloud while the reservation teemed with visitors. But the old chief seldom missed an opportunity to impress outsiders and McGillycuddy knew that on the last and most important day of the Sun Dance, the chances of Red Cloud making an appearance were great.

The Sacred Circle was a flat area two hundred feet across and surrounded by a crude shade hut made of branches cut from the nearby cedar trees. The Sweat

Lodges and an array of small tents for the dancers and
holy men were set up behind the shade shelters and
buzzed with activity. But inside the Sacred Circle no one
moved except the occasional medicine man, making
final arrangements for the day-long ceremony to come.
The Indian police had built a small set of bleachers for
the visitors and, as McGillycuddy and his personal
guests arrived, the officers tipped their hats to the agent
to let him know that they were strategically stationed
around the grounds. Fanny had felt well enough to attend and McGillycuddy was glad to have her on his arm
as he and Rev. Stubbs walked the grounds.

It was still very early on a pleasant summer day and
McGillycuddy was taken back to the early days of his
attraction to Fanny. In those days he was more capable
of expressing the beauty he saw in such a day and he
tried to find that buoyancy again. He knew that outside
the Sacred Circle, and for a mile distant, tepees of the
gathered bands were pitched in groups. He saw them in
his mind as riding the gradual hills like seagulls on the
ocean. And from those tepees came thousands of
brightly dressed and excited sun worshipers. From
above, the Sacred Circle would have appeared like the
nucleus of a cell, and around that nucleus pulsed the
functions of life. But, though McGillycuddy imagined
the scene in that way, he did not consider expressing it
that way.

"This is where the cutting takes place," he said.
Fanny tugged at his arm, smiling. He waved his hand
toward the Sacred Circle where the Sacred Tree now
stood decorated with sage, chokecherry branches, and
more colored cloth. The leather lariats that the dancers
would be attached to hung almost to the ground.

"Indeed," Miss Fletcher said. She was again writing

in her notebook and nudged Clearance Looking Dog who was now acting as her personal assistant and guide. "What is that?" She pointed to two black flags and a buffalo skull.

"Etay," Clearance Looking Dog said.

George Sword had approached to speak to McGilly-cuddy. He had just whispered into his ear that Red Cloud had arrived and when he heard Miss Fletcher's question, he spoke to her before Johnny could translate, "It is like your altar."

McGillycuddy nodded and stepped out into the Sacred Circle. He felt suddenly belligerent and, instead of denying it as he tried almost always to do, he yielded. He began pointing out the features of the Sacred Circle. "The skull is much like your altar, Reverend. You'll see the priest monkeying around up there on and off. It's stuffed with sagebrush and the flags behind it are black for the direction west." He pointed in the other three directions. "White for the south; yellow, east; red, north. A little like the Stations of the Cross, I guess." Fanny made to move toward him but did not want to enter the Sacred Circle.

Miss Fletcher was nodding and jotting in her notebook. Rev. Stubbs was disgusted. McGillycuddy kept talking but was conscious of a disturbance on the other side of the Sacred Circle. "The drums and singers, the choir if you please, sit over there."

Now a swarm of Indians were moving on the other side of the Sacred Circle. It was not yet time for the entry of the dancers and McGillycuddy knew it was Red Cloud. "What's he up to?" he said half to Sword and half to himself. And then Red Cloud appeared rigged out in breechcloth, paint, and feathers. He was serving as some sort of "whipper in" for the dancers. He danced and spun in a combination of ecstasy and malice and behind him came his entourage including Red Leaf and Nick Chappell.

McGillycuddy cut right across the center of the Sacred Circle and was face to face with Red Cloud in an instant. Behind him, though it would have made no difference to McGillycuddy, was Captain Sword and, from nowhere, Young Man Afraid. "What is the meaning of this? I will stand for no inciting of these people." Red Cloud was still spinning like a dervish and the crowd jumped and spun in imitation of his movements. "Red Cloud!" McGillycuddy shouted and this brought the old chief from his trance.

He smiled and looked around to see that white visitors were collecting in to hear what he had to say. "I am a holy man for my poor people." Chappell was translating to the crowd. "I am here to dance for our sick and troubled."

McGillycuddy cut him off. "No one will listen to a man who has written lies to the president of the United States, Red Cloud," Sword translated.

Red Cloud glanced around with an affected expression of confusion as the translations were made. He held his hand up. "I wrote to the Great Father in hopes that he would keep us still."

"I will not be still. You accused me of lying and cheating the Oglala people. You forged signatures on your letter."

Sword stumbled over the translation of the word forged and Johnny Provost took over. McGillycuddy listened and nodded when he understood the Lakota word for stole. "Do you deny that you charged me with lying and cheating. Do you deny you stole other people's names?"

"I never said that you lied or cheated us. I want to go to Washington and get this straightened out."

"You have been to Washington quite enough." Now McGillycuddy was pointing a finger into the chief's face. "This thing comes down to who has lied. And I say it is you." At this Chappell stopped translating and the crowd stood awed. McGillycuddy's jaw was rigid and from the corner of his eyes he saw Chief Young Man Afraid. The followers of Red Cloud waited for him to act but when nothing happened they began to move and slowly the tension drained away. McGillycuddy turned to Young Man Afraid and with a studied smile he said in Lakota what was designed to deliver maximum humiliation to Red Cloud. "Ah, it is Young Man Afraid, chief of all the Oglalas."

17

The Sun Dancers had been awake since four o'clock. They had spent an hour praying in the Sweat Lodge and carried their sacred pipes around the Sacred Circle several times. Each time they prayed at the four directions. They were bare to the waist and wore red cloth skirts below. For three hours they had danced in place and now that the sun was high and the air was still, the temperature was practically unbearable. Still the dancers lifted their faces to the sun and shuffled their feet to the monotony of a single drum.

Thousands of people surrounded the Sacred Circle and pressed in to bear witness to the sacrifice of the dancers. The whites and many elders were privileged to sit in the shade of the cedar boughs. The throngs of common Indians stood in the sweltering sun and moved their feet in sympathy with their relatives inside the circle. McGillycuddy still felt an edge of irritation from his confrontation with Red Cloud. Now he sat with the white spectators and did his best to explain what was happening. "They dance to appease their God. They barter prayers and sacrifice for health and prosperity, just like us."

"Christian prayer," Rev. Stubbs began, then cleared

his throat. "Christian prayer does not operate on a quid pro quo basis."

Self-righteous and pedantic to boot. "It certainly does not," McGillycuddy said. He felt Fanny watching him from the corner of her eyes and he wanted to leave his comment at that. But he could not. "The question is whether or not it operates at all."

Stubbs snorted and Miss Fletcher giggled discreetly. The other whites in the bleachers stared straight ahead. "Look," Fanny said in the same tone that a parent uses to distract a child, "the medicine man is coming."

From the camp of the dancers came an old man carrying a metal bucket. The crowd that had been tittering with gossip quieted and pressed forward to watch the medicine man approach each dancer. Twelve times he lifted a dipper of water to the lips of the sweating men and twelve times the offer of a drink was refused. They opened their eyes to the sun and danced on until the signal was given to place the eagle-bone whistles in their mouths. A thin screech began to be emitted from each man with every step and the sound built until the entire landscape seemed to pulse with their dancing.

Miss Fletcher was sketching the scene in her notebook and McGillycuddy couldn't help noticing that her drawings were quite accurate. She looked up from her work, then back down, as busy as a brown thrasher in a hedgerow. In the margins of the page she wrote neat notes of explanation. The drawing that McGillycuddy noticed was of the Sacred Tree, now completely decked out with ribbons and leather lariats that stretched out tightly to pegs in the ground. She worked feverishly on the details at the top of the tree and McGillycuddy saw her squinting to understand the crude doll tied at the very top. McGillycuddy

could have explained the amulet but did not know
how to broach the subject. A small breeze rose and, in
addition to giving the dancers a breath of air gave
Miss Fletcher a better look at the doll as it blew clear
of the tree. It hung silhouetted against the sky for only
an instant and in that instant Miss Fletcher leaned forward and squinted with surprise. By the time the next
gust of wind lofted the doll into clear relief she had
dug a small pair of opera glasses from a canvas tote
bag. The wind died quickly, *Should have got a good
look that time,* and Miss Fletcher lowered the glasses
to reveal a furrowed brow. She leaned forward and
whispered into Clearance Looking Dog's ear. The old
man nodded to show that he understood her question.
Then he smiled and took a good hold of his crotch.
"Meta winchichala," he said.

Miss Fletcher sat back on her bench in deep thought.
A few last-minute spectators were filing in and Fanny
turned to greet them. McGillycuddy took the opportunity to lean in Miss Fletcher's direction and whisper,
"It's a man on horseback with an exaggerated member."

"A phallus?" Miss Fletcher was not embarrassed and
spoke normally.

"Indeed." Rev. Stubbs had caught the drift and
turned away from the new people sliding to their seats.

"Fertility?" Miss Fletcher asked.

"I would imagine," McGillycuddy said.

"Disgusting," Stubbs said.

"Fascinating," said Miss Fletcher.

When McGillycuddy looked up to the newcomers his
eyes met those of Julia Blanchard. They were exactly as
they had appeared on that day when she stood naked
before him. "Heathen," Rev. Stubbs was saying. "To
celebrate lust is purely the work of the devil." Julia

smiled with complete innocence and McGillycuddy tipped his hat.

"I don't think I could agree, Reverend." Miss Fletcher was sketching with one hand and periodically glancing into her opera glasses. "This is universal. This is very important and the Peabody would be very interested in obtaining that artifact for our collection. Might that be possible Mr. McGillycuddy?"

McGillycuddy was shaking hands with George Blanchard. "The doll?" he asked. "You want the doll?"

"It would be priceless."

The agent nodded. He was as dizzy as the dancers. "Why, yes," he said. "I will see what I can do."

The sun was at its highest and the breeze had died to nothing when the first of the dancers lay down on the buffalo robe beneath the Sacred Tree. He was an old man with long hair streaked with gray and Clearance Looking Dog said his daughter was having trouble with a pregnancy and he was dancing for her. The drums stopped and the old man was given a small bundle of sage to bite down upon as the medicine man knelt to thrust the wooden pegs through the skin on each side of his chest. The white women winced and looked away and the men grimaced but leaned forward. A titter of approval washed through the Lakota people and the old man stood up as blood trickled down his bare chest. He raised his face to the sun.

A lesser medicine man tied leather thongs around the ends of the sticks protruding from the old man's skin as the second dancer stood with his arms extended and eyes staring straight ahead. He was pierced standing upright and led to the end of the twenty-foot-long lariat to be tied to the Sacred Tree as the old man before him.

The third man suffered eagle claws to be threaded into his back and was tied with leather ropes to a huge buffalo skull that lay upside down on the ground near the tree. The cavity of the skull was stuffed with sage.

As the dancers were pierced the drums remained silent. Had any dancer cried out it would have been heard easily by any of the thousands gathered to watch. But no man whimpered. Their blood mixed with sweat, but not with tears and they stood motionless until all were pierced and the music began again. As the drumbeats commenced the dozen men tied to buffalo skulls walked to the Sacred Tree four times. Each time they touched the Tree with outstretched hands and raised their faces to the sky. Those tied to the tree did the same. One man was tied tightly to the tree with skewers in his back and chest, and he stood on the back of a kneeling old man at the base of the tree. He had only to reach out to touch the tree. "He had a sad vision," Clearance Looking Dog said with starry eyes. "He sacrifices for those who will never hunt the buffalo."

Once all the dancers had touched the tree they began to blow on their eagle-bone whistles in what started off as a random cacophony but soon became the familiar, high pitched, communal throbbing. Even though McGillycuddy had seen this all before he could not take his eyes off the dancers as they began to shuffle their feet and pull back on the thongs that tied them to the Sacred Tree and buffalo skulls. The old man who supported the dancer tied by his chest and back rolled out from under him and left him hanging in the midday sun from stretched and bleeding skin. The monotony of the eagle-bone whistles and the drumbeat dulled McGillycuddy's mind but despite being exposed to battle and medical procedures of the grossest sort, his heart re-

fused to be calm. It beat hard and rose in his throat to
the extent that he was forced to think it back to calm-
ness. Once he was in control, he looked about him at
the white visitors. Fanny hid her head and covered her
eyes. George Blanchard's jaw muscles pulsed with the
beat of the drums. Julia wept into the sleeve of her father's cotton shirt. Miss Fletcher could not look away
but her face had gone lowly and her complexion was
white. Rev. Stubbs would have been outraged if he
could have controlled his animal fear.

The dancers flung themselves against the lariats that
held them. The horns of the buffalo skulls dug into the
dirt and jerked the men who pulled them backward.
Human skin and meat stretched to extraordinary
lengths and, in the center, the man who had dreamed of
the life after the buffalo were gone, hung with head and
arms back, prostrate to the sun. The crowd chanted and
Clearance Looking Dog gazed out upon the scene with
sad but ecstatic eyes. He breathed quick and deep and
held his head high as his left hand trembled with a palsy
McGillycuddy had never noticed before.

When the first dancer broke free he crumpled to the
ground and was helped by family members who stepped
forth. George Blanchard stood up with Julia under his
arm. "Probably had enough, for a bit." He petted Julia's
head. "We'll take a little walk." McGillycuddy swung
his bony knees to let them pass from the bleachers and
as they passed he looked at Julia who was trying to be
brave and not show that she was crying. Her hand
passed within inches of his and he felt heat coming from
it as surely as if it were a woodstove. The sensation of
heat brought his eyes to the hand and he watched it as
she passed. When he looked up Fanny was looking out
at him from behind fingers held to shield her from the

sight of the Sun Dance. She saw what he had felt and though McGillycuddy was instantly defensive, there was no need. She smiled a wan smile snuggled close to him. "I don't know why we came to watch this," she said.

McGillycuddy pressed her face against his shoulder. "Genetic memory," he said. "I suspect it wasn't many generations ago that our ancestors too were out there dancing for salvation." *Leaving that behind is what the last two thousand years was all about.* "Think of it as anthropology."

Fanny shook her head with eyes closed. "Tell me when it is over."

A dancer broke pace with the drum and whistles. He ran across the Sacred Circle and leaped back against the lariat that held him fast to the tree. The force tore him loose and his father and mother rushed into the circle to help him to his feet. They comforted him only with encouragement to continue dancing. And dance he did, with blood streaked down over his stomach and dirt from the Sacred Circle rubbed into the wounds by the medicine man.

One by one the dancers pulled themselves free. They continued to dance to the drums that had not ceased now for more than three hours and though McGillycuddy noticed signs of severe exhaustion in their pace, he marveled at their stamina. No one had lost enough blood to be in shock but certainly their hallucinations were vivid. They moved around the circle blowing into their whistles and jerking with the adrenaline of fatigue and excitement. *Snake charmers, faith healers, Baptists, and priests.*

Only the trial of the man who hung from the Sacred Tree remained. He had hung lifeless now for a very long time and it was whispered among the whites that he might be dead. But as the sun continued its fall into the west and the dancers danced on, he would occasionally twist himself in an effort to tear the flesh. There was a period of time when the whites who had been so outraged by the ceremony seemed to forget that there was still one man calling his people's pain down onto himself. The whites became comfortable enough to discuss their reactions. Predictably, Miss Fletcher was fascinated and Rev. Stubbs was disgusted. Fanny took it as an exercise in tolerance of the beliefs of others. George Blanchard had returned with a revitalized Julia and simply shrugged. McGillycuddy, as was common for him, was not sure what to think. But he did not let on. He was about to make a devilishly caustic comment that he thought might tantalize Miss Fletcher and incense Rev. Stubbs, when there was a commotion in the Sacred Circle.

When they looked they saw a young woman fighting her way past the medicine men. She was strong and lithe but it was clear that the medicine men were not trying with all their power to stop her. "Che ke," Clearance Looking Dog said with the first smile he had shown all day.

"She is his lover," Johnny translated.

The woman did not scream but chanted in time with the drums that did not cease. By the time she reached the young man swinging from the Sacred Tree the crowd had begun to lend her their voice. They keened as she took the man's arms and tugged back on them. The drums increased and the crowd pulsed to give the girl their strength. Clearance Looking Dog stood up and nodded with pride. The girl continued to pull and call to her lover. The whites stood speechless as the man's skin stretched six, eight inches but did not break. Finally the girl wrapped her arms around her man and added her weight to his. It was enough to tear him loose and when they came to the ground she held him in her lap and fought the other dancers who came to help.

"Barbaric," Stubbs said.

The only Christian thing to happen today, and he missed it.

"Capital," Miss Fletcher said.

In the aftermath of the Sun Dance McGillycuddy walked the grounds of the Sacred Circle. The whites and many Indians still stood around the bleachers recounting the day but McGillycuddy had had enough of the asinine questions of the whites, the solicitous smiles of the progressives, and the pugnacious stares of Red Cloud's people. He had walked to the shadow of the Sacred Tree to be away from them all.

Around the grounds, camps were being torn down and people were beginning to move back to the farming communities. *Their only real salvation.* Now the Sacred Circle reminded McGillycuddy of a city park after the circus tents had been struck. A few medicine men gathered up their flags and symbols. The Sacred Tree stood forlorn in the center of what would soon become another corner of the prairie trying to regain its wildness.

"Now it is an archeological site," Miss Fletcher had come up behind the agent and watched him with bright eyes. She was shadowed by Clearance Looking Dog who, though he still smiled and nodded pleasantly, showed that the long day had been taxing for a man of his age.

"You have witnessed history, Miss Fletcher."

"Indeed." She held up her notebooks and shook them in a show of power.

McGillycuddy nodded and couldn't help smiling at

her energy. "It would surprise me if this rite lasts too many more years. Even in secret."

Miss Fletcher looked at him. "It is not the way of man to forsake his religion easily."

"It has not been easy."

"It is not forsaken."

McGillycuddy smiled. "We are apt at forsaking. Only another of earth's simple species."

Now Miss Fletcher laughed. "You are prone to taking your point a step too far, Mr. McGillycuddy. We may be one of earth's species, but there is nothing simple about us." She moved her hand to indicate the Sacred Circle. "What simple beast could conceive of this?"

McGillycuddy liked this wiry little woman and nodded his head with a shrug of good-natured resignation. "Your point is well taken." He smiled and nearly laughed. "Just to the limit, but not too far."

She beamed up at him through her thick glasses. "I was wondering," she said and looked up over McGillycuddy's shoulder to the top of the Sacred Tree. He followed her stare and found the leather horseman-doll with the giant penis swinging in the wind. "It seems to have been abandoned and the curators at the institute would be thrilled."

The doll did look abandoned. *Forsaken, and so well appointed!* "I think it could be arranged," McGillycuddy said. As he spoke his eyes were attracted to the group around the bleachers. It was a subtle thing. They were divided into conversational groups and one of the groups included Brownie O'Donald and Johnny Provost. McGillycuddy noticed Sword approach them and saw Sword whisper into Brownie's ear. Before Brownie even looked up, McGillycuddy knew they would be coming to him. "I'm sure it can be arranged."

He reached out and touched Miss Fletcher's shoulder and his touch silenced her as the men approached.

McGillycuddy stepped out to meet them and turned first to Johnny. "Could you help Miss Fletcher? She would like to have the horseman amulet at the top of the tree." He pointed over his shoulder without looking back and faced O'Donald. "What is it, Brownie?"

They moved away from the tree so that Miss Fletcher would not hear them talking and O'Donald frowned. "Red Cloud has been counciling with Sitting Bull's men, a bunch of breeds, and a man who claims to have connections in Washington. Sword's spies have been in on the meetings."

McGillycuddy turned to Sword. "And?"

"More meetings are planned."

"With the objective of what?"

Sword never betrayed his emotions. His mouth moved automatically and his eyes seldom blinked. "They want a new agent."

"I imagine they do. I imagine they would all be happier if this reservation was not administered by the United States government." *This is nonsense. It is not Sword's fault.* "And how do they propose getting this new agent? Violence?"

"There is talk," Sword said.

The three men stood in silence and McGillycuddy let his eyes shift from Brownie's face to Sword's and back again. Miss Fletcher interrupted them. "This won't do," she was saying.

McGillycuddy nodded to his men. "We will meet on this issue in the morning." Then he turned to Miss Fletcher.

"The man is mutilated," she said and handed the doll to McGillycuddy.

The doll was in two pieces. The beaded horse and rider lay in one of McGillycuddy's hands and the penis in the other. McGillycuddy looked at Johnny and knew instantly that his sense of propriety had not allowed him to hand the doll to a woman intact. *His white side has the upper hand today.* "I'll see that the figurine is repaired good as new," McGillycuddy said.

Miss Fletcher smiled broadly. "Thank you, Mr. McGillycuddy." She shrugged apologetically. "It is the point, don't you think?"

McGillycuddy looked at the rider in his hands and nodded. "Yes," he said. "It is the point. It certainly is the point."

18

Without permission from McGillycuddy, Red Cloud left the reservation accompanied by several lesser chiefs and a group of squaw men. Their destination was a ranch on the Nebraska side of the border owned by Louis Shangrau, one of the squaw men McGillycuddy had exiled from the reservation for selling liquor to the Oglalas. Sword's intelligence failed to forecast their illegal departure and so McGillycuddy passed a good portion of the day studying Flavin's medical book.

Fanny had been unable to leave her bed that morning and upon examination of her numb and tingling feet McGillycuddy had found sores. When questioned Fanny pretended to notice the sores for the first time. But it was obvious to him that these sores had become chronic. He was appalled that he hadn't noticed them before. McGillycuddy sat on the bed and studied her face as he massaged the feet. She had gained more weight but the face was still lovely. It was a kind and sturdy face. She smiled and reached to touch his hands. "It comes and goes," she said. "I will be fine this afternoon. I'm so sorry."

"Sorry? You're sick. I am the one who is sorry. I'm the doctor. Your health is my responsibility."

"And your life is my responsibility. I feel that I'm failing you. I know the stress you are under."

He rose from the bed and stroked her hair. "Perhaps you should drink less of Louise's sweet tea."

For these new symptoms, sweet tea seemed to be vilified in Flavin's book. But for her other symptoms sugar was recommended. *I simply do not know.*

Late that evening McGillycuddy was still scouring the pages of medical text in hopes of finding something definitive that he had not already read that would allow him to feel he had risen to the occasion of his wife's illness. But all he found was frustration. *Might as well be a shaman leaping in the moonlight.*

It was at the height of his self-doubt that Brownie O'Donald knocked gently on the door. A caller at such a late hour was unusual and something that McGillycuddy generally discouraged. But Brownie was always welcome and when he saw who it was, McGillycuddy opened the door and waved him in like a brother. Fellowship was one thing that McGillycuddy enjoyed though something in him seldom allowed it to show. Brownie O'Donald had given up a great deal to be McGillycuddy's second in command on Pine Ridge and McGillycuddy was thankful for several reasons. This night, after the frustration of coming up empty-handed in his research, Brownie was particularly welcome.

"Come in, Brownie. Whiskey?"

"Love one, Mac," he said as he removed his hat. "Sorry to say, I'm thinking we're both going to need one."

McGillycuddy tried to ignore the grave tone of Brownie's voice. He motioned toward a chair and went to the cupboard for the bottle. "Another crisis?"

"Potentially serious. Sword just got word that several of our Oglalas are off on a clandestine rendezvous."

McGillycuddy carried the bottle and two glasses. "Who and where?"

"We're not sure yet. Sword is checking as we speak. But one of the conspirators is Red Cloud and the meeting is being held at Shangrau's ranch."

"Off the reservation." The bottle paused in midair with a glint of amber liquor at the lip of the neck. O'Donald nodded and the liquor resumed its flow. "Some additional treachery no doubt."

"I'm afraid so, Mac. Initial report is that they are planning your removal."

"They?" McGillycuddy raised his glass.

"Red Cloud, his white hangers-on . . ."

"The usual suspects."

"With one addition."

"Pray tell."

"Don't have a name. Outsider that claims to be a friend of our boss. School chum of the new secretary of the interior." Kirkwood had been replaced suddenly and neither McGillycuddy nor O'Donald knew much about his replacement, Henry M. Teller.

"Meeting illegally with Red Cloud?" McGillycuddy asked.

"That's the scuttlebutt."

They drank in silence and poured themselves seconds.

"Well, son of a bitch," McGillycuddy finally said. "God-damned Democrat, I'm betting. They pay little attention to the law."

"No telling if he has any sway with the director or just knew him once."

"The director can't be in cahoots with such a scheme, though this character might gain his ear."

"We'll know more in the morning," Brownie said tentatively. He was expecting the agent to blow up any second.

"This is serious, Brownie."

"I know."

"But I'm not going to let it upset me now. Not until I have the facts. Let's talk of something else. How is Mr. Brownie O'Donald?"

"I'm fine."

"And how do you like this crazy job?"

O'Donald did not trust his casual tone. "I like it. Challenging. I really like the people. Love the country."

"Ah, the country. Seductive as John Barleycorn himself." He raised his glass and gazed at it with a squint. When he looked back to O'Donald he smiled and O'Donald smiled back.

"You seem relaxed tonight," O'Donald offered without bothering to hide his surprise.

"I'm not going to let any of it get to me. We're off duty. This should be our time to reflect on the glories and frailties of life." He poured them both another glass. "We'll fight Red Cloud in the morning. Tell me, Brownie, has there ever been a woman in your life?"

O'Donald accepted the whiskey and smelled it before he spoke. "Yes. Still is."

"Is that so?"

"She's the reason I took this job when you offered it." He sipped and thought. "She's actually a little like Mrs. McGillycuddy. She's from back east in Pennsylvania. Good family. Better than mine." *Aha, there is the rub.* "Haven't seen her for nearly two years, but we write often. I've been saving my wages."

"For marriage?"

"That's my hope."

"And the lucky lady?"

A rare, shy smile. "She seems to be planning on it. We

have plans." They raised their glasses but more in personal contemplation than in a toast.

"That's wonderful, Brownie. It is an enormous commitment."

"Of course."

"Oh, I don't mean it the way the preachers mean it. I mean she'll be expecting a lot of you."

"And I'll be ready to do what is needed."

But how can we know what to do? Sometimes . . . sometimes . . . McGillycuddy wanted to be clear but exactly what he wanted to say escaped him. "Sometimes it's hard to know."

"To know?"

"Ahh, life." He shook his head and smiled as if he were thinking back on a pleasant event. "Full of responsibilities." Then the smile broadened and he looked to O'Donald. "But we're up to it, aren't we now?"

They were both back thinking about Red Cloud. "Tomorrow we'll have Sword's report."

McGillycuddy got to his feet and held his glass up to O'Donald as he rose to leave. "They just keep coming."

"Sir?"

"Tomorrows," McGillycuddy said as he drained the glass. "They just keep coming."

O'Donald finished his drink. "This tomorrow will be a big day."

"Very big," McGillycuddy said as he ushered him toward the door. "The next few tomorrows promise to be large."

"Right you are," O'Donald said and uncharacteristically held out his hand to shake McGillycuddy's.

"Let it come." The door closed and McGillycuddy laid his forehead against the pine boards. *No way to*

*know which tomorrow will get you until you look it
level in the eyes.*

He was up before light and in the first grayness could
see the outline of Sword waiting on the steps to his office. Before the door was unlocked O'Donald too had
appeared from the darkness and the three men walked
inside. McGillycuddy lit the lamp without fumbling and
trimmed the wick until the room was awash in pure,
white light. He motioned the men to sit and took a pencil and paper from his desk drawer. When he was ready
he looked up to Sword. "All right, George. What do we
know?"

George Sword always looked the same. There was little chance that he had slept the night before. No way to
know how many miles he had ridden in the black of
night, how many lodges he had visited, how many men
he had collared to extract information. His uniform was
the same as always: neat to the point of appearing
pressed. His round face and Asian eyes showed absolutely no expression. "He left Shangrau's late last
night and is in his camp now."

"And who else left the reservation without permission?"

"He Dog, Woman's Dress, Cloud Shield, American
Horse."

"Take those names down, Brownie." McGillycuddy
turned to Sword with a question. "He Dog?"

"A Hunkpapa from Standing Rock."

"One of Sitting Bull's men."

"A chief."

"The same Woman's Dress who is a scout at Fort
Robinson?"

"Yes."

"Arrest him." McGillycuddy pointed to be sure his command was written down. "And what of the rumor about a white man?"

"Godfrey. A friend of the new secretary."

O'Donald spoke up. "A friend of Teller's."

"And do we know his business?"

Sword nodded. "He brought a letter for Red Cloud to sign."

"Another goddamned letter?"

Sword drew a folded piece of paper from a leather pouch hung around his neck and handed it to the agent. He did not read English and McGillycuddy could see that he had come to the part of his intelligence report where uncertainty began. "And where did you come by this?"

"Fort Robinson," Sword said. "They sent a copy to Major Sumner. He wrote it again and sent this to you."

"All the way to and from Fort Robinson in the night? My, my Captain, you have had a busy night." He unfolded the letter and began to read about "many acts of petty tyranny and insults we are daily compelled to endure from our Agent here." He read the last part of the letter aloud for the benefit of Sword and O'Donald.

If the incumbent U. S. Agent is not removed from this Agency within sixty days, or a proper person sent out in the meantime to fully investigate his gross misconduct here, we will upon the expiration of the above stated time take upon ourselves the responsibility of politely escorting him out of our country, and let the consequences be what they may.

McGillycuddy let the letter rest on his desk and looked up at O'Donald. "I'd say this constitutes a hostile act toward the United States government. I can't believe the old fool let himself be manipulated so."

"Perhaps he didn't know what he was signing." O'Donald was as dumbfounded as McGillycuddy. As they sat wondering if Red Cloud was aware of what he had committed himself to a knock came on the door.

Johnny Provost did not wait for the door to be opened. He did not stand quietly waiting to be recognized. "Red Cloud has threatened to kill the freighters." Now all three men were on their feet. "They were leaving this morning for the rail station at Thatcher. Now they are scared. They will not move."

McGillycuddy puffed out a lungful of air as if expelling his patience. This could not be tolerated. The Indian freighters were McGillycuddy's prime example of Indians accepting the ways of free enterprise. "Captain, position your men to protect the freighters. Tell them not to move but see that they are not harmed. Brownie, go wake up the telegraph operator. Clear the lines and wire Commissioner Price of this contemptuous letter and Red Cloud's threats. End it with these words." O'Donald scurried for another piece of paper. "Tell the commissioner this: It depends on your department whether I am to be agent or chief clerk for Red Cloud. Tell him we expect an answer today."

Slightly after noon of that day the answer was received. Commissioner Price assured McGillycuddy that he would be "sustained by this office as agent against the claims of Red Cloud."

Telegrams began to flood into the agency from concerned citizens around Dakota and Nebraska. Settlers were flocking into the nascent communities around the territory. Everyone wanted to know when war would break out. They suspected a general uprising and were clearly preparing for war. Both Commissioner Price and General George Crook telegraphed to ask about the rumors that Red Cloud was about to go on the warpath. McGillycuddy wired back to say that the situation was in hand. He was in contact with Major Sumner at Fort Robinson, who was ready to move as soon as he was given the word, but no troops would be needed as long as he was backed up as agent.

The next morning he called for Captain Sword. "This is the scenario we described when we initiated the Indian police force. We assured the common Indians that we would keep the army off this reservation. Despite Red Cloud's disregard for a possible slaughter of his own people, we must do all we can to deliver on our promise. Can we hold a lid on this, Captain?"

Sword nodded and handed a copy of his own telegram that he had already sent to Commissioner Price. "Most of the Indians want to live in peace and enjoy the prosperity which has come to them. Red Cloud has been trying hard to make trouble and I think that any foolish Indian who thinks he can make trouble should be locked up."

McGillycuddy grinned with pride and pushed the copy back to Sword because he knew the captain would want to keep it. "Lock 'em up, huh? Does that include Red Cloud?"

Sword did not have to think. He nodded. "Yes."

"That's good because I intend to wire for permission to arrest Red Cloud if it becomes necessary. I've also called a general meeting of the chiefs and headmen to find out what they propose to do about his threats to peace. The council is set for tomorrow afternoon. Have all your men ready."

*   *   *

Young Man Afraid and Little Wound took charge of the meeting. They were quite aware that Red Cloud was still in his camp and rallying his men against anyone who would defend the agent. Rumors flew that he had been reinforced by Sitting Bull's men, that he had a secret stash of rifles, that he was not only intent on intimidation but ready to do violence to anyone representing the present agent. The freighters took his threats very seriously and it took courage for the rest of the Oglalas to even meet.

To a large extent McGillycuddy left them alone to decide what to do about Red Cloud. The rankling went on all day but by nightfall the group had decided that Red Cloud's behavior should not be allowed on their reservation and that he should be reprimanded. Armed with this consensus McGillycuddy, responding to Commissioner Price's and General Crook's excited telegrams, wired them to say that the progressive chiefs had backed him and that no troops would be needed. He laid the blame for everything on Red Cloud and asserted that he would "always be a source of trouble and should be removed to Leavenworth, and the continual interference and counseling of white cutthroats prevented." He asked that he be given the authority to arrest Red Cloud if necessary. The next day permission came through and he wasted no time in pressing his advantage.

Sword was reporting that Red Cloud had gathered his young men, that they were armed and in a nasty mood. O'Donald advised caution and suggested that troops be reconsidered. But McGillycuddy did not flinch. He called the friendly chiefs together and demanded that they go to Red Cloud's camp and order him to come to hear Commissioner Price's telegram authorizing his arrest. A runner was sent to Red Cloud's camp and returned in short time with Red Cloud's answer. When McGillycuddy heard the response he turned to O'Donald. "A typical, flippant and condescending reply. I believe, under all his babble, that he might be a coward." Red Cloud's answer to the agent's demand was that he was glad to hear from the commissioner and that he hoped he was feeling well, but he could not come in to listen to his message because he was feeling tired.

"He is outrageous," O'Donald said.

"Toying with the safety of his people and ours will not be tolerated." McGillycuddy turned to Sword and Young Man Afraid who had been standing by. "Man Afraid, you must send him a message insisting that he come in. Sword, if he does not come in, you must be ready to go out and arrest him. I will see him in federal prison if his behavior does not change."

From a nearby hilltop McGillycuddy watched with field glasses as the message was delivered in Red Cloud's camp. Immediately there was a great deal of excitement. Women began to tear down tepees, boys gathered the horses from their pastures, and young men rode back and forth in a frenzy of speed. It was a scene from the Sioux Wars of years before and McGillycuddy trembled to think of those heady days. O'Donald stood nearby as McGillycuddy watched the scene. *No doubt Brownie believes I am making a mistake.* He swiveled the binoculars one hundred eighty degrees without lowering them. There was also tremendous activity at the agency. White families were packing their belongings and loading wagons for the trip to fortified communities in Nebraska. McGillycuddy did not let on that he felt

O'Donald's eyes as he swiveled the binoculars to study. the action at his agency. *Maybe I am making a mistake.* The field glasses fell on the wagon of George Blanchard. Three children were in the back along with a black-and-white-spotted dog. George carried a rifle but leaned it against a wagon wheel to help his wife up onto the seat. It was clear to see that George planned to stay but he wanted his family safe. At the edge of McGillycuddy's vision Julia came into view. She was nearly as tall as her father and had traded her usual cotton dress for men's overalls. She moved up beside her father and reached up to comfort her mother. She too was staying and along with George urged her mother and younger siblings to make haste.

The scene gave McGillycuddy heart. "Brownie," he said after he had lowered the binoculars but before he turned. "The police have been issued rifles?"

"Yes, sir."

"How many more rifles do we have?"

"Over fifty, Mac."

"Issue them to any whites who want one and the rest to friendly Indians starting with Young Man Afraid's people."

"Shouldn't we wait, sir?"

"Wait for what?"

"Red Cloud's answer."

"No, Brownie. The issue of arms will help Red Cloud to think clearly about his answer."

"And troops?"

"No troops. We gave them our promise."

They walked down the hill and McGillycuddy took command of his forces. An hour later he stood at the head of a hundred well-armed men and waited to hear from Red Cloud. They expected a runner from Red

Cloud's camp, but just in case, Sword had his informants who would warn them of an attack or of Red Cloud making a run for the north. McGillycuddy took the time to go to his house and make sure that Fanny and Louise were protected. He left Johnny Provost and four friendly Indians with the women and went back to his men. There was nothing more to do but wait. He concentrated on remaining calm and setting an example for his men. But he did not have to keep up the facade for long. A messenger arrived saying that Red Cloud would come in to hear what Commissioner Price had to say.

But Red Cloud still did not come in and the delay sent McGillycuddy into a temper that was hard to keep from the common men. He called all the other chiefs together and asked them what they intended to do. *Inaction on your part makes you no better than Red Cloud.* The chiefs realized that McGillycuddy was at the end of his patience and went into serious council. They decided to give the old chief one more chance and gave this message to McGillycuddy:

> *Tell him that we make one last call. That to prevent bloodshed, if he does not come at once, we will turn our young men and police in with the troops and disarm and dismount Red Cloud's band. Or, if you say so, we will give you our young men to help the police and bring him away.*

It was an incredible show of support for the agent but neither McGillycuddy nor O'Donald was sure what effect it would have on Red Cloud. "It'll bring him in," O'Donald said.

"Or loose the hounds of war."

"What is your choice?"

"I have none. Send him this last summons. He will either come in meek or riding a gust from hell."

The messenger went out and the armed men settled in to wait.

It was an hour before the first intelligence came in. The reports insisted that Red Cloud was coming to council. He had said that before and so no one left his post or eased his grip on his weapon. McGillycuddy sat calmly with a cold Colt .45 thrust into his waistband. Other riders came from Red Cloud's camp and they continued to say that Red Cloud was coming. Still there was no real sign of Red Cloud. *He's counciling all right. Counciling with his war chief for an attack.* Suddenly McGillycuddy was crushed with doubt that the delay was a ploy to gain military advantage. He had been sitting on the steps of the council building but now jumped to his feet. "Sword," he called to his captain who was standing close at hand. "Mount your men."

But no sooner had the captain saluted him and turned toward his men than a murmur went through the crowd. When McGillycuddy looked up he saw that Red Cloud was indeed coming. He rode a thin old horse with no feathers or paint. No other chiefs rode with him. He was trailed by a few ragged boys and rode with the humble appearance of Christ himself.

The minute McGillycuddy caught sight of him he knew that he had won. This was no bellicose warrior but a defeated politician. *Defeated or crafty. Hell, I'm too tired to care.*

Red Cloud was led into the council room and remained standing as the other headmen pressed in to hear what the agent would say. Rifles were stacked at the door and though every man carried a knife or ax, the fight had gone out of everyone. McGillycuddy read the letter giving him permission to arrest Red Cloud if necessary. He would allow the chief to remain at large but would hold the other chiefs responsible for Red Cloud's good behavior. Should any Indian ever again threaten any official of the reservation they would be arrested and sent to Leavenworth. The United States government would not be trifled with and as if to rub the humiliation into the old chief, McGillycuddy closed the meeting without allowing a single Indian to speak. Red Cloud was sent back to his camp on the same poor horse he had ridden into the agency but the horse carried a heavier load than when he arrived.

He found Fanny close to sleep, exhausted as usual. He rubbed her swollen feet. *The church bell is ringing and the flag of the United States still floats.* He wanted the tension to seep out of him and he wanted to talk to her about his doubts. He rubbed the feet and felt the particular heat he associated with the feminine. *The mother-goddess. A refuge stronger than any walled fortress.* Something inside him wriggled like a reptile and he found that the touch of Fanny's skin had aroused him in a way he had nearly forgotten. He let his hands wander to her calves and then to her thighs just above the knee. He imagined that her own hands and perhaps even her lips would be sparked into the old passion.

But as his hands reached the smoothness of her inner thighs he found no electricity and knew that Fanny had succumbed to her fatigue and fallen asleep. He continued to rub her legs but slid gradually back down to the swollen feet. He wondered briefly what he could do to help her. He tried for a different interpretation of Flavin's book on human diseases but the day had been

far too difficult. Instead, he let himself slump to lie quietly beside Fanny and shut his eyes. It was the first night
that he dreamed of Red Cloud.

The dream began in a familiar way, with Julia Blanchard's eyes and skin and nipples blended into a smooth
syrup that flowed and mixed with the air along the river
where he had seen her bathing. It focused on her face
but slowly the white face blurred to a soft brown and
went dark as the deepest shadows along White Clay
Creek. It was the face of Julia's Indian friend who pulled
her down into the water. In the dream McGillycuddy
warmed with embarrassment but the face turned again
and then he felt fear and shame. Now the face was
darker yet, with high cheekbones and skin that sagged
with worry and time. The braids were salted with gray
and a single eagle feather projected skyward from a
leather headband. Red Cloud watched him like a disappointed father.

Part Six

Ghost Dance

1884–1889

19

In November 1884 Grover Cleveland was elected president of the United States and the anti-McGillycuddy forces rejoiced. In the ongoing parade of public servants, John Atkins replaced Commissioner Price and the new secretary of the interior was L. Q. C. Lamar—both Democrats and both prone to support liberal Indian policy. Dr. Bland's *The Council Fire* was filled with hope for their radical view that Indian policy reform should come only from the Indian's own initiative. They touted Red Cloud as the symbol of a chief fighting the bureaucracy of the United States government and McGillycuddy as the representative of that bureaucracy. This time it was personal. In June of that year McGillycuddy received the news that Dr. Bland himself had arrived at Valentine, Nebraska, and was waiting for Red Cloud to meet him and bring him to Pine Ridge.

"Can't happen, Brownie."

"They tell me he will be here this afternoon."

"The last time I checked, I was still Indian agent on this reservation and Indian agents can still control visitation on the reservation."

"Bland does have powerful friends."

"He is a troublemaker. Here to create disturbance.

Things are moving along quite nicely. The Oglalas are becoming independent farmers and freighters. This bleeding heart in our midst is capable of setting us back further than a Sun Dance and two or three barrels of whiskey." O'Donald smiled and squirmed. *Ease up now. You've made him uncomfortable.* "It is in everyone's best interest that this privileged man of the east does not get the chance to fill our people with idealism."

"I couldn't agree more," O'Donald said. But McGillycuddy could tell that he was nervous about Bland's political connections. O'Donald was still saving for that hoped-for marriage and was worried about his job. McGillycuddy understood this and was ready to ease his fears with a shot of whiskey and gentle conversation when a knock came on the office door.

It was Sword with news that Bland had just checked into the agency hotel. Red Cloud had gone to meet him and brought him to the reservation. Sword reported that Red Cloud intended to let the publisher rest and then bring him to meet with the agent in the afternoon. McGillycuddy slowly rose from his chair as he listened to Sword. By the time the captain had finished he was standing with both hands on the desk and his nostrils flared. "Is that so," he said. "Is that so?"

He stood for an instant gathering his thoughts. "Captain. Take two additional men, go to the hotel, and bring Dr. Bland to me." Sword nodded. "Don't let him pull any monkey business on you. If he resists, bring him to me in chains."

For ten minutes, McGillycuddy paced. "Don't move," he told O'Donald. "I want you here as a witness. This man is treacherous. He has told unnumbered lies to promote his ill-informed view of the Indian problem. He's done more harm with his utopian views than half the wars prosecuted on these people. He is quite capable of lying about anything that might happen to him on this reservation." O'Donald nodded, but it was a tentative nod.

By the time Bland arrived McGillycuddy had calmed himself. But when the knock came he rose to his feet and met Bland at the door. He did not offer the little man his hand but did wave him into the office. He motioned for Sword to wait. "We may be needing you, Captain."

Bland had expected a civil, if cool, greeting and now stood inside the door with an envelope in his hand. "You cannot stay on this reservation," McGillycuddy said as he moved to his desk and sat down with his head artificially high.

The aggressive comment took Bland slightly off guard. He had already removed his hat and now he pushed his wire-rimmed glasses back up onto his nose. He wore a mustache and goatee similar to McGillycuddy's and held himself in a dignified way. The dark eyes flicked back and forth as he formulated his response. After assessing the situation he stepped up to the desk. "I think you should look at this letter," he said.

McGillycuddy took the proffered letter calmly and read it aloud for O'Donald's benefit. It was a straightforward letter of permission from Secretary of the Interior Teller. It was quite clear in its intent. The secretary had given Bland carte blanche to visit Pine Ridge. After checking the letter for authenticity, McGillycuddy handed it to O'Donald. "Make an official copy of this, if you please."

O'Donald took the letter and disappeared into the next room to make the copy. After they were left alone, McGillycuddy looked up to Bland. "Ordinarily, I take great pleasure in observing the orders of the secretary, but in this case I shall not. You will leave the reservation this afternoon."

Bland had been standing but now took a chair. He looked kindly at McGillycuddy. "Are you sure you want to do this?"

"Quite. We have no need of someone of your persuasion on this reservation. You, sir, are a troublemaker. We have enough troublemakers here."

"You refer to Red Cloud."

"He is the heart of the matter."

"He is the chief of these people."

"The ex-chief."

"Your calling him the ex-chief does not make it so. He has led these people through war and peacetime. You cannot change that."

"I'm quite aware of the ex-chief's résumé."

"But you seem to have forgotten a few items. He has pled his case in front of the president of the United States. He has spoken to large gatherings of prominent citizens. He has made his case eloquently for the autonomy of these people."

McGillycuddy hated himself for hesitating. "Eloquent when translated in your publication."

"I'm proud of that little newsletter." Bland smiled with obvious pleasure.

"A subversive rag."

"Because it is at odds with your views?"

"That and the fact that my views are working to bring these people into the modern age."

"Your view toward assimilation? Your view that European Christianity is the only proof of worth? Your views that their culture is inferior to our cruel and acquisitive culture?"

Even before he said it, McGillycuddy knew he was avoiding Bland's point. "Their culture is plenty cruel. I know it firsthand."

"We've robbed these people."

We have. "That is a matter of opinion."

"First we promised that they could have the Powder River country. We took it back. Then we promised they could keep all of the western Dakotas. We allowed homesteaders into the best of that land. Now we are taking the Black Hills for its gold."

"Nomadic ways are gone!" *Damn, damn.* "I've seen the old ways." *I loved those old ways.* "But they are gone. These people are being treated like tens of thousands of homesteaders."

"Indeed they are. Lied to. Misled. And swindled." Bland let that sink in. The pitch of his voice had risen slightly but now was steady. "You know it is a lie that this land can be farmed."

It was true that the last years had been wet and that the reservation farms were only barely making it. McGillycuddy had seen the land without rain and knew it would come again. "We are moving to the most modern methods."

Bland's arms were serene in his lap. "Well, Doctor. I too am a believer in science. But this land was never meant to accept the plow and the Sioux were not meant to walk behind the plow." When they could hear O'Donald moving in the other room, Bland looked up earnestly to McGillycuddy. "I believe that you know the old ways are the only way."

"The people cannot last by following the old ways."

"Then let them perish. But don't force them into our greedy mold."

Jesus, Jesus. "I love these United States."

"And I love the best parts of them."

O'Donald was standing at the door with the copy of Teller's letter in his hand. McGillycuddy felt exposed and, for an instant, scurried to gather his thoughts. Finally he gave up. "Humbug," he said. "You are a threat to the civil peace on this reservation." He turned to O'Donald. "Return Dr. Bland's letter to him and call Captain Sword."

McGillycuddy stared directly into Bland's eyes until Sword was standing beside his desk. "Take the good doctor to his room. Load his belongings into a carriage and take him to Nebraska. If he refuses to get into the carriage, throw his troublemaking ass aboard and give the horse a sharp slap."

At that, Bland rose to his feet. He turned to go, then hesitated and looked back. "You are at heart a good man, McGillycuddy. But one day your pride and temper will hang you."

"Get him out of here, Captain. Load him up and don't let him incite any of our good citizens in the process. I'll be down to see him off."

"Don't bother," Bland said.

"No bother, sir. Part of my job of keeping the peace."

After Bland left the office McGillycuddy and O'Donald sat in silence. *He thinks I'm mad.* "Do you think I was too strident?"

O'Donald thought for a second. "Perhaps," he said. "You are right to think that he is wrong."

"But is he right to think that I am wrong?"

Now O'Donald smiled. "I don't know, Mac. He's a dangerous man. He should not have come here and he must go."

Again they sat in silence until McGillycuddy placed both hands on the desk in front of him. "Well," he said, "shall we follow through and see that he goes without incident?"

O'Donald stood up. "I'm sure that Captain Sword has him loaded up by now."

"Should have done." McGillycuddy took his straw hat from the rack and picked up the fashionable ebony cane he had begun to sport on his evening walks. It was a gift sent from Washington by an admirer of his policies at Pine Ridge. "Shall we?"

They stepped out onto the porch of the agency office building and hesitated to look down what had become a proper main street. People passed in front of them on their way to the trader's stores, the livery, the clinic, the feed mill, the hotel. Whites and Indians alike nodded to the administrators and McGillycuddy touched the brim of his hat. They walked along as any two men might walk along the streets of any frontier town and the warm afternoon sun mixed with the dust from the freight wagons in a way that mellowed them both.

Sword had a buckboard pulled up in front of the hotel and Bland's luggage was already loaded. The captain and two of his men were mounted and waiting for Bland to say his goodbyes to the proprietor of the hotel, a swarthy German who glared at McGillycuddy over Bland's shoulder. When Bland followed the man's glance he jumped at the sight of McGillycuddy. He shook the German's hand quickly and climbed up onto the buckboard beside the third of Sword's policemen. No one spoke. McGillycuddy and O'Donald stood in the shade of a cottonwood and McGillycuddy made a simple nod to Sword. The heavy reins came down on the horses' rumps with a snap, the tugs went tight, and the wagon began to move toward the edge of the reservation. Bland sat rigid on the seat and would not give McGillycuddy the satisfaction of a glance.

"He'll cause us trouble," O'Donald said.

"Absolutely," McGillycuddy said. He wanted to go on to say something about how he appreciated O'Donald's support. He wanted to apologize for jeopardizing O'Donald's job and future but he was distracted by Julia Blanchard coming from her father's store. She wore a yellow dress that moved like ripe grass when she walked and swayed out of her way to smile at the Lakotas she passed on the boardwalk. Both men froze as she came their way. She carried a basket, the handle draped over her arm and her hands folded neatly in front. McGillycuddy removed his hat and she smiled.

"Good afternoon, Doctor. Mr. O'Donald." She stopped and the men leaned in toward her but at the same time drew closer to each other. McGillycuddy could not take his eyes off of her but was embarrassed not to. He heard O'Donald making small talk and riders on the road to their right. The clomp of the saddle horses passing pulled McGillycuddy's eyes from Julia's smile. When he looked up, Red Cloud was staring at him as he passed. He rode with several other men and moved steadily past without a word or a sign. But in his eyes McGillycuddy felt an accusation. It was as if the old man knew his heart, and in response, McGillycuddy did not look back to Julia but kept his eyes on the riders. They rode easily in the flimsy saddles and McGillycuddy was reminded of the way they rode in battle. He watched them pull the horses up and dismount at the hotel's hitching rail.

"And you gentlemen are out for a stroll?" She tilted her head and smiled. "A little early for you isn't it Dr. McGillycuddy? You seem to avoid the sun."

He had been watching the Indians entering the hotel but was drawn back by Julia's comment. "Why no, I do usually take my walk in the evening."

"I know," she said. "I watch you." She nodded toward the cane. "I like your walking stick. Very stylish." Suddenly the cane embarrassed McGillycuddy and he moved it alongside his leg to make it less conspicuous. O'Donald laughed. *He too has wanted to comment on the cane.*

A sudden and horrible wail erupted from the hotel and when they looked the Indians burst from the hotel. Red Cloud held his head and released another wail of extreme sorrow. The little black-haired German man was walking beside him with arms outstretched. He implored Red Cloud to be calm but the old chief slumped to the ground and tore at his hair. The other Lakotas stood off from their chief and hung their heads like children.

"Good grief," O'Donald said.

"Good grief indeed!" McGillycuddy was already striding toward Red Cloud, his cane kicking out with every step. As he approached, the German and Red Cloud's entourage stepped away from the prostrate chief.

"Kola waye kin yakte yelo."

McGillycuddy understood him perfectly but could not believe what he heard. "Nonsense. No one has killed your friend. I just sent the lout packing." Now McGillycuddy was standing over Red Cloud and was surprised to see that he was actually crying. "Kola waye kin yakte yelo."

"Poppycock."

"Bring me his body," Red Cloud sobbed.

"Oh, for the love of God. Stop with your theatrics. No one has killed your Galahad." Now McGillycuddy was fuming. He looked to the sky. "For God's sake, man. Get a grip. Stop with the cheap theatrics." When he looked down, Red Cloud was no longer sobbing, though his cheeks were streaked with tears. McGilly-cuddy looked away and saw that old Clearance Look-ing Dog was standing nearby with a look of pure pain. But Red Cloud's eyes were still on him and they pulled him back. They looked at each other and Red Cloud took control. He waited a long time before he spoke. "I know what is inside you, McGillycuddy. I know."

The agent was caught for a breath. Then, "Bullshit, you know. Bullshit." He spun away and as he passed Clearance Looking Dog, the old man spoke.

"It will be all right," he said. "It will be all right."

That night McGillycuddy rubbed Fanny's feet and told her over and over that he loved her. He had heard from Sword that Bland arrived safely in Valentine and was booked on a train the next morning. That news should have put his mind at ease but as the lantern light twisted down from white to yellow he laid his head on Fanny's stomach and moved to encourage her to stroke his hair. "I love you," he said. "I really do."

"Of course you do."

"I do," he said and fell asleep like that: with his head tight against her swollen stomach and her fingers light in his hair. He should have felt at peace but soon he was dreaming of Red Cloud.

"I know what is inside you," the sad old eyes said. "You killed my friend and I know your heart."

In the summer of 1885 Charlie Provost was accused of stealing a horse from a visiting Brulé Sioux and McGillycuddy was forced to confront him. Charlie was Johnny's full brother but different in almost every way.

Johnny had adopted the ways of his father. He spoke English and kept his hair short. He tried to look other men in the eye when he addressed them. Charlie rejected white ways and looked and acted Indian. He dressed like his mother's people and spoke only Lakota. But though Charlie could pass for a Sioux warrior he knew enough of the white culture to be dangerous on the reservation.

McGillycuddy had information that Charlie was responsible for a tragic event that took place on the reservation a few months before he took over as agent. A full keg of whiskey had been smuggled to one of the Lakota camps where liquor was absolutely illegal. From sad experience the Bureau of Indian Affairs had learned that Indians were not capable of resisting or handling alcohol. It was said that because their cultures had never developed alcohol that their systems had never had the opportunity to evolve a tolerance to it. McGillycuddy did not know if he believed that but he did know that the keg of whiskey Charlie brought onto the reservation had caused havoc. Charlie offered it to a group of fifteen young warriors. The first drinks were free but when the young men had gotten enough to want more Charlie began to charge: first a few coins per drink, then a knife or bauble. Soon the cost of a glass of whiskey had risen to a horse or a wife. After three days of debauchery and swindle Charlie slipped away. By then the young warriors had turned mean and, in the end, three lay dead with the rest impoverished, humiliated, and sick.

Similar events had taken place since McGillycuddy took over as agent but at a decreasing rate and he was never able to trace them to Charlie. This suited McGillycuddy because he did not want to punish Johnny's brother. But the theft of the Brulé horse was clearly

Charlie's doing and McGillycuddy was given no choice but to either bring Charlie in and dress him down with Johnny as interpreter or send him through the white justice system. To subject a half-breed who showed only his Lakota side to white courts was perhaps too stern a punishment so McGillycuddy determined to bring him into his office and rail at him in an attempt to shame and frighten him into changing his ways.

The horse had already been returned to the Brulé man and Charlie had spent a sullen week in the guardhouse. McGillycuddy had no trouble working himself into a rage. As McGillycuddy paced, and Johnny translated, Charlie wrapped his blanket tighter and slumped even more. McGillycuddy lectured Charlie about honesty and particularly the concept of private property. *As foreign as Latin.* Johnny interpreted with great effort but at the end of the interview McGillycuddy felt he had made his point. Charlie seemed properly ashamed of himself and left the office without a word.

An hour later McGillycuddy was walking the agency grounds when a shot was heard in the area of the livery. McGillycuddy raced toward the sound and halfway there met Ott Means running to meet him. "Charlie Provost took a gun from me and shot himself in the lot beside the barn." Ott was gasping for breath and shaken by what he had seen. But McGillycuddy did not break stride.

He found Charlie crumpled in the corral, his blanket covering his head and soaked with blood. *For the love of Jesus.* He had just gone to his knees and pulled the blanket back when another shot sounded. He was moving toward the noise before he had released the corner of Charlie's blanket. As he ran McGillycuddy knew that the second shot was related to the first. He feared

Johnny had heard of his brother's death and taken his own life for his part in Charlie's humiliation.

But McGillycuddy was wrong. When he came around the corner of the administration building he found a group of men surrounding his faithful translator. At Johnny's feet the body of a man he hardly knew, Clementi Bernard, squirmed feebly. Here too was a widening pool of blood and it seemed to repel the men who pressed cautiously in toward Johnny, who stood bewildered with a pistol still in his hand.

"Johnny?" McGillycuddy approached slowly. "Johnny. Give me the gun."

The young half-breed looked at McGillycuddy, then down to Clementi Bernard, who had ceased writhing. He looked at the pistol and the men who surrounded him held their ground. McGillycuddy stepped into the circle and stood with the soles of his boots soaking up Clementi's blood. "Hand me the gun, Johnny."

Johnny looked around with wide eyes and McGillycuddy reached out. "The gun," he said softly.

One of the men swore and McGillycuddy raised a hand to silence him. "The gun, Johnny. Just hand it to me."

Their eyes met. "Johnny, for the love of this land."

Johnny's eyes narrowed but his head began to nod. McGillycuddy moved a step closer, reached out, and eased the pistol away. He wanted to stop the men from seizing Johnny roughly but it took a moment for him to regain his equilibrium. It made no sense to any white man but, to the Sioux side of Johnny, what he had done was reasonable. In that culture everyone needed someone to travel with to the next world. To the Sioux, the killing of Clementi Bernard was a kindness to Johnny's brother. But Johnny lived in the white man's world and so the men pushed him to the ground and held him firm while McGillycuddy arrested him for murder.

The next week the agent personally took his friend to the city of Deadwood to be held over for trial. They drove in a buggy and in the two days of travel did not speak more than a few dozen words. When Johnny was asked why he reverted to the ways of his mother's people he could answer only that his mind had whirled. *His mind had whirled. Simple. His mind had whirled.*

Days later, on the lonely ride back from Deadwood, McGillycuddy marveled at how quickly the boundaries of reason can shift, how tenuous life can be, how dangerous it all is, how a veneer of civilization can evaporate with the whirling of a mind. All of it made him heavy with sadness.

20

McGillycuddy had told Red Cloud, Dr. Bland was not dead. He was, in fact, very alive and as soon as he returned to Washington he dedicated that life to destroying McGillycuddy. His newsletter carried editorial after editorial describing and embellishing his treatment on Pine Ridge. He portrayed Red Cloud as the noble savage and McGillycuddy as the ignoble savage. Some of his facts were true, some exaggerations, and some wholly fabricated. McGillycuddy found the accusations of financial impropriety the most disheartening and for the first time he began to wonder if his tenure as Indian agent (he was now the longest serving agent in the history of the department) was worth the fight.

By the fall of 1885, McGillycuddy knew that the Cleveland administration was angling to get rid of him. But he also knew that because they had run on a platform that included a strong stand against the spoils system he was nearly impossible to fire. For that reason, when Department of the Interior inspectors came to the reservation to look into Bland's charges, McGillycuddy gave them no assistance. "What you are doing here is a farce," he told the inspectors. "My books are, of course,

open to you. But this is the last interview you will get
with me."

Brownie O'Donald saw to it that the inspectors got
what they needed and though the final reports included
negative appraisals of McGillycuddy's personality, no
evidence of financial misconduct was found.

During the extended time of the inquiries McGillycuddy spent an inordinate amount of time touring the
reservation communities and talking with the progressive Lakota leaders. The last year had been drier than the
previous three and the crops had suffered. Though the
Lakotas were still moving toward self-sufficiency they
were also still dependent on the beef issue and other government programs for their survival. As he moved from
one farming area to the next McGillycuddy could not
help being disappointed in the overall progress of his
people. He had hoped that the government could one
day move away from the subsidies they had promised in
treaties. The agreement had been that, in return for their
land, the Lakotas would be given food, schools, and the
necessities of life. But no one had thought the obligation
was open-ended. Always it was assumed that the Lakotas would become independent sooner or later. McGillycuddy had been a proponent of sooner rather than later.
But in that dry year of 1885, as he drove his surrey from
one settlement to the next and saw the stunted ears of
corn and the grasshopper-chewed tomatoes, he wondered if he had been too optimistic.

Perhaps the naysayers were correct. The United States
Geological Survey, the agency that had first brought
him to the Great Plains, had a new director who was
proposing that all lands beyond the one-hundredth
meridian were unfit for dryland farming. Pine Ridge
was well west of that point so according to John Wesley

Powell, too dry to support the kind of community McGillycuddy had been advocating. His detractors were beginning to use Powell's writing to bolster their claims that the reservation system was cruel and misguided. But if Powell was correct in his assessment, then 90 percent of all homesteading was equally misguided and cruel. McGillycuddy snorted when he thought of it. No. *It's not some arbitrary line on a map. It's patience and industry that make the difference!*

In his efforts to avoid the inspectors he found himself spending more time at home with Fanny. He had determined years earlier through studying Flavin's book on the diseases of man that her malady had something to do with the relationship between sugars and carbohydrates and their effect on the body, but Flavin was not clear on the subject and McGillycuddy had to admit his helplessness. *A clear failure of my responsibility as a doctor. Let alone a husband.*

He continued to rub her feet but he did not bother her with his own self-doubt. They talked instead of the politics of the proposed new state of South Dakota and the fact that the territorial officials had asked that he be a signatory on the new state constitution. Fanny was very proud and teased him about becoming a politician. But McGillycuddy was more interested in the booming mining towns of the Black Hills. They had traveled several times to Deadwood and Rapid City and though they loved Pine Ridge, the hustle and bustle of growing commerce and community was seductive and they found themselves talking about the wonderful times they had had in Washington, D.C. In Fanny's voice McGillycuddy heard a note of longing, but as he had done when they had fallen so in love with the nation's capital he did his best to steer the conversation back to the plains, the Lakotas, and their calling to serve.

They passed the months of federal inspection in very close proximity and enjoyed each other's company more than they had in years. Louise smiled to see them taking their meals together again and Fanny seemed to feel better for the pleasant times. But the inspection loomed over them and when the inspectors left to make their reports to the new commissioner of Indian affairs, John Atkins, McGillycuddy confided in Fanny that he had a bad feeling about what was to come. While it was true that Cleveland had campaigned for civil service reform and would be attacked in the national press if he fired an agent for political reasons, McGillycuddy sensed that the forces against him were marshaling their power. It made him angry and he fumed indignantly when Brownie O'Donald reported that the inspectors had found no financial abnormalities. "Of course they found no irregularities. But they're up to something."

"They cannot discharge you," O'Donald said.

"Perhaps not," McGillycuddy said, "but they will do something." He said the same thing to Fanny. "They will do something. I have a premonition."

"You don't believe in premonitions. You scoff at mystery."

"That's true," he smiled. "It must be something scientific."

"You and your science. You stretch it every which way."

"Just because we haven't found the reason for a phenomenon doesn't mean that reason is magical."

"Since when is rhetoric a scientific tool?" She smiled at her own cleverness.

"A scientist uses the tools at hand."

"And is capable of grasping at straws."

*   *   *

There was no word from Washington and the winter of 1885–1886 passed without incident. In the daytime McGillycuddy and O'Donald worked on plans for expanding agriculture and building more housing and at night the McGillycuddys sat by their potbellied stove and read Charles Dickens and the Brontë sisters to each other. It was not until the spring, when the rains did not come and planting of the crops was delayed that McGillycuddy received a telegram from the Department of the Interior saying that yet another inspector would be arriving soon. McGillycuddy read the telegram to Brownie, who had already read it. For Brownie's sake he read the telegram with an air of contempt but inside he knew what the message meant. *They've found a way to get me.* "It's more of their posturing," he told O'Donald. "We have nothing to worry about."

"He will be here in two weeks."

"Yes," McGillycuddy said. He affected indifference. "A Mr. E. D. Bannister. No doubt a pencil neck that will want to look over the books once again. But I may well be gone when he comes."

"Oh yes. Johnny's trial."

"Johnny's trial." The thought of poor Johnny penned in the jail at Deadwood silenced them both. He'd been there nine months waiting to be tried.

"Not much doubt that he did it."

"No. I'm going as a character witness. Plead for him. Try to tell the judge it is not as clear cut as he no doubt will imagine it to be."

"No idea what he might imagine, but it certainly is not clear cut."

McGillycuddy shook his head. "No, but he will be convicted. It is only a matter of what the sentence will be."

"Your being there will help with the judge and jury."

McGillycuddy smiled. "It is amazing how my popularity increases with people who have something to lose from an Indian uprising."

"How your popularity improves with people who have a sense of the situation."

"People outside the pale of eastern sentimentalism, you mean."

O'Donald smiled and nodded. "You could say that."

"So you take care of Mr. Bannister until I return."

"Rest assured. And I know you'll do your best for Johnny."

McGillycuddy nodded. He would do his best. He would advocate in the courtroom and he would try his best to speak with the judge and the jury out of the courtroom. But an Indian who killed a man would never be set free. *Any sentence short of freedom was likely a sentence of death.*

McGillycuddy was checked into the Homestake Hotel in Deadwood when E. D. Bannister arrived at the reservation. The Homestake was only a series of canvas tents, much like most of the town of Deadwood. But there was a telegraph at the land assayer's office, and when he received the message that Bannister was upset that McGillycuddy had not been there to greet him, the agent did not hesitate to wire back to tell the inspector that he was involved in important business and he would return to Pine Ridge when he was finished. In fact, the trial was nearly over. Johnny sat quiet and cowed as a leg-trapped coyote during the entire trial. He spoke only once in answer to the judge's question: "Why did you do it?"

"My brain whirled," was all he could say.

But the judge listened to what McGillycuddy told him

about Johnny and in the end, in his instruction to the jury, he spoke of mercy and of Johnny's service to the U. S. Army and to the agent at Pine Ridge. Johnny was given five years in the Detroit House of Corrections. It was an incredibly mild sentence but as soon as McGillycuddy saw Johnny in his cell after the trial he knew even five years was much too long. Johnny sat on the floor in the corner of his cell with his knees up and his chin set hard against them. His skin was pale and his eyes as dull as an ox's.

McGillycuddy sat on the edge of the bunk and leaned forward so that his bony elbows rested on his legs. He felt like lowering his head into his hands but he could not let himself do it. "It wasn't too bad," he said. "Five years is not as long as it seems. You'll be free before you know it." He knew he was babbling. *Inane.* "They have some training in those places."

And when Johnny still did not answer, McGillycuddy stood up and looked down on his friend of ten years. "You're a good man, Johnny Provost. Good by any standard." He reached out and touched the dark black hair. "You're just a little wedged between cultures." *Like us all.* "It is a shitty deal."

On his way back to the reservation McGillycuddy rode his sorrel horse down Whitewood Valley and turned south at the edge of the Black Hills. He rode alone along the foothills for most of the morning but passed many other riders and wagons hauling goods to the gold fields from Rapid City, the fast-growing hub for most of the activity in the northern hills. He let his horse rest on Elk Creek and counted the wagons that passed on the road while he ate jerky and bread in the shade of an enormous cottonwood. In the hour he took to rest ten freighters and fifteen horsemen passed. When

he had first come to the Black Hills with a survey crew
more than ten years before, they had seen no one for
nearly a month. The increase in activity saddened him
but excited him too. He had planned to ride through the
night and arrive at Pine Ridge in the morning. But
though something in him wanted to ride on into the
night like he had in those years gone by, something else
wanted to take a good look at the town of Rapid City.

It was midafternoon when the first buildings came
into sight. The traffic on the road to Deadwood had
steadily increased and by the time the grain mill and
brick hotel came into view he had pushed the fate of his
half-breed friend in the damp cell in Deadwood to the
rear of his mind. For three hours he rode the busy streets
of Rapid City. He had been there many times before but
this time he noticed how it had grown. He saw the
names of acquaintances hanging from storefronts. Attor-
neys, merchants, doctors. Many men who had written
letters of support to him over the years. He stopped in a
saloon and once he was recognized he had a half dozen
beers in front of him purchased by admirers.

He drank only two of the beers before he went back
out to the sorrel and swung up onto his back. It was
nearly dark when he rode to the south edge of town. It
would now be midday before he arrived in Pine Ridge to
face Bannister's music. He let the sorrel meander among
the newly constructed houses of the townspeople of
Rapid City and thought how happy they seemed. At the
very end of town there was a large house with children
playing a game of hide-and-seek among the newly
planted trees of the spacious yard. McGillycuddy sat still
on the sorrel for a long time. He watched the children
running and laughing until it was too dark to see.

He rode into the night knowing that he was still sixteen hours from Pine Ridge. It would make a thirty-six-hour day of it but he was not concerned. There was something in the fatigue he felt and the even greater fatigue that would come that excited him. It reminded him of the Sioux Wars when he'd ridden against honorable men like Crazy Horse. The fatigue reminded him of when he had helped survey this land and when he had marched with General Crook to secure it for settlement. The sorrel was a good horse, better and better fed than the ones he had ridden in those days, and they moved easily along the east flank of the Black Hills. Drainage by drainage they passed on to the south. Rapid Creek, Spring Creek, French Creek, Battle Creek, Lame Johnny Creek.

The moon rose when they were nearly to Buffalo Gap, where the great herds had once funneled from the open prairie and onto the high pastures of the Black Hills. A community had begun at the place where buffalo hunters had made their gruesome camps and McGillycuddy swung wide enough so that the dogs of the settlers would not be aroused. The country was always alert for Indian attack—with good reason. Before the settlers and before the buffalo hunters, the Lakotas had used this same campsite for generations. *It must rankle every Indian who rides this way to have to skirt those squalid huts and smell their whiteness.*

He turned east on Beaver Creek and in the moonlight picked out one of the trails that had led the buffalo and the hunters to that magic gateway into the Black Hills. He had ridden the trail many times, as had many people. He had seen the herds drifting along his route, but not for years. The slaughter had been that complete. From hundreds of thousands, to none. It was a hard reality that his plows and the plows of the settlers had replaced the buffalo. He knew it was a poor bargain but he also knew it was the only bargain.

The trail wound along Beaver Creek until it found the main artery of the Black Hills. He paused on the bluff above the Cheyenne River and in the moonlight below he saw the milky ribbon that nearly surrounded the Black Hills. The sight of it was otherworldly with the moonlit badlands beyond and he felt dizzy as he began his descent to the valley below.

Once beyond the crest, McGillycuddy had the sense that he was descending not into the Cheyenne River Valley but toward the River Styx. Perhaps that is why he did not pull the sorrel up or even stare when, to his right, the image of an enormous shaggy beast appeared from the lacey cottonwoods and began its slow upward trudge toward the distant, sacred hills.

O'Donald was there to meet him at the agency office porch but McGillycuddy walked the tired sorrel on to the livery to be sure it was taken care of before he faced what Bannister had to say. O'Donald followed him to the livery. He was clearly excited but knew enough to wait until the agent had given detailed instruction on how the sorrel should be cared for.

"He hasn't inspected a thing," O'Donald said when he got his chance. "He only wants to talk to you." McGillycuddy nodded and stretched the kink from his back. "He has an order for you but he won't tell me what it is."

"Where is he?"

"At the hotel. You don't suppose he's here to relieve you?"

"No. The settlers and many others would raise too much of a row. Bad politics. Tell him I'll be in my office."

"Don't you want to rest?"

"No. Let's see what sort of bite this snake has. I'll stop in to see Fanny and be at the office in fifteen minutes."

He wanted to tell his wife about Johnny, what he had seen in Deadwood and Rapid City, about the lone buffalo. He wanted to tell her how the people had respected him and how the land had changed since he had first seen it. He wanted to touch on the subjects and leave her waiting for the whole story, the way he had done when they were younger and he had returned from the West. But when he entered the house only Louise was in the kitchen and her nod told McGillycuddy that Fanny was in the bedroom. When he peeked in, he found her sleeping and so he only slipped into the room and stroked her hair as he stood above her. *It is my fault. I should be a better doctor—a better man.*

O'Donald and Bannister were waiting for him when he entered the office. Bannister held out his hand but McGillycuddy did not take it. He only moved to his desk and sat down with his fingertips lightly on the mahogany top. "I understand that you have an order for me from the Indian bureau. Or is it from higher up? Do you bring orders from the Secretary of the Interior? Perhaps even the president? Do they trust you, Mr. Bannister, with orders from that high up?"

"My message to you might come from farther up the chain of command but I take my orders from Commissioner Atkins."

"A Democratic hack."

"There is no need to be insulting."

"Yet you insult me."

"I have a simple order for you, sir."

"One that you are hoping I will refuse." A smile crept

onto McGillycuddy's face as he saw Bannister squirm. "I'm betting you have the authority to relieve me for insubordination if I refuse."

Bannister cleared his throat and took a piece of paper from his breast pocket. He fumbled for his glasses. "Come now, you weasel." McGillycuddy leaned toward him. "Don't tell me you need glasses to read what you have long since memorized."

Bannister gave up the search for the glasses and did not bother to look at the official order in his hand. "You are hereby ordered by Indian Commissioner Atkins to relieve Mr. Brownie O'Donald of his position with the Indian bureau."

The two men stared at each other. "I refuse," McGillycuddy said.

"Mac."

"Quiet, Brownie. I refuse, Bannister."

"You refuse a direct order from Commissioner Atkins?"

"I do."

"Then you are guilty of insubordination and, acting under orders from the secretary of the interior and approved by President Cleveland, I hereby relieve you of your duties as Indian agent of the Red Cloud Agency."

"Pine Ridge. How long do I have to leave?"

"Captain James Bell of the Seventh Cavalry will arrive tomorrow to take over as temporary agent."

"Until someone Cleveland owes a favor to asks for the job."

Bannister rose to leave. "The office should be cleaned out by tomorrow. Your residence in a week."

"You and your cohorts will be responsible for what happens here." It was O'Donald. He too was standing.

"You have no idea how volatile this reservation is. You have no idea what this man has done to keep the peace." He pointed to McGillycuddy who sat in his chair smiling sadly. Old Brownie. *He's a good man. Worth losing my job for.*

21

McGillycuddy received many offers for employment and investment. They could have gone back to Detroit to join a survey and consulting firm doing business in the West. There were jobs in government and an offer to join a medical practice in Saint Paul, Minnesota. But neither McGillycuddy nor Fanny wanted to leave the soon-to-be state of South Dakota and so, when the position of president of the new Dakota School of Mines was offered to him, McGillycuddy did not hesitate.

As soon as they were settled in a rented house on the east side of Rapid City McGillycuddy put his foot down. To that point Fanny had stubbornly refused to see any doctor besides her husband. He realized that there were questions of privacy and modesty, but Fanny's health had been declining for years. Now they were in a city where there was a young well-trained doctor. So, tough as it would be for both of them, McGillycuddy arranged for Dr. James Gaylord to make a house call even before he consulted Fanny. She raised only a token resistance and McGillycuddy knew that he had done the right thing.

Gaylord was strikingly young and it gave McGillycuddy pause to think that he no longer enjoyed the recognition of being the boy doctor. Gaylord was gentle in his questions and in his manner during the physical examination. There was nothing unusual in his procedure. He listened to Fanny's heart, pressed her skin with manicured fingers, and looked deep into her eyes. McGillycuddy watched carefully and saw nothing that he had not done. Gaylord jotted notes in a black leather notebook and kept up an easy chatter of questions about their years at Pine Ridge. In the end he won Fanny over and when the two doctors stepped out onto the porch, McGillycuddy was impressed with Gaylord's professional bearing.

"I'd like to see her on a weekly basis," Gaylord said. "She is chemically out of balance."

McGillycuddy nodded. "I've tried to monitor her temperature, heart rate, et cetera. They have varied for years but nothing I could identify as a cause." He felt he was being defensive. "Perhaps a sugar imbalance."

"You might be right, Doctor. But if that is so, the question is: too much, or too little?" He shook his head. "As you know, our understanding of such things is meager. It's believed to be affected by a hormone but that hormone has not been isolated."

"A hormone?"

"Probably secreted by one of the body's organs."

A hormone. "I see." *But I don't see.*

Gaylord smiled. "Of course we both know this is all highly speculative."

McGillycuddy nodded. "Of course."

"We may be at a place where we can only treat her symptoms. I will do my best."

McGillycuddy took Gaylord's hand. "Thank you," he said.

"It is my pleasure. I have always wanted to meet you, sir. I admire your work greatly."

McGillycuddy nodded as the young doctor descended the steps. His mind was blank when Gaylord turned. "Don't let her become housebound. Get her out and about. Give her something to live for."

To LIVE for? "Certainly. Certainly. Thank you doctor."

Within a week McGillycuddy had contracted to build a new home on a hill to the south of Rapid City's burgeoning downtown. From the very beginning of their residency in Rapid City, they were in social demand and now McGillycuddy began accepting offers of luncheons and dinner parties. Fanny did her very best to get out and meet the prominent families of the area and McGillycuddy found himself forever in speculative business meetings that he shared with Fanny. Over the years of his working as surveyor, doctor, and agent they had saved a reasonable nest egg and, once in the booming Black Hills, the opportunities to invest in mining and development projects were abundant.

He included Fanny in all these discussions and took her with him every chance they had.

The change seemed to do Fanny some good. She accompanied McGillycuddy in the evenings when he drove the buggy up to the construction site of their new house and she walked the grounds, planning the lawn and garden while McGillycuddy checked the work that had been done that day. In those early days of their new life, the building site was remote and it reminded them both of their home on the reservation. By that first fall, the agency house was occupied by H. D. Gallagher: a sixty-year-old Civil War veteran and well-connected Democrat.

McGillycuddy learned this from a group of businessmen he had begun meeting for breakfast at a local café. He could not get over his habit of waking early and, since he wanted to let Fanny sleep, he found himself haunting the Sweet Grass Grill. The food was good and the conversation civilized. It was a routine that McGillycuddy fell into easily and that surprised him. Of course, the other patrons of the Sweet Grass were strong supporters of him and his policies. *Perhaps we are all fools for flattery.* "Gallagher is a garden variety, political plum picker," one of McGillycuddy's admirers said. "He'll collect his money and whatever else he can scam off those redskins. Just hope the whole thing don't go up in smoke and us with it."

As the McGillycuddys wandered through the beginning of their new home they were engulfed in memories of that other life that neither had been able to forget. Fanny recalled the closeness of the community and McGillycuddy recalled, over and over, his last meeting with Red Cloud. He had gone to his office early the day after his termination to remove his personal belongings. He had learned from Brownie O'Donald that Bannister had guaranteed that he would retain his job as assistant at the agency. That had not surprised McGillycuddy, but Brownie was so conflicted over whether he should stay on or not that he too had shown up early that next day. "It was a rotten business," Brownie said.

"Rotten as old cheese," McGillycuddy said. "But quite predictable. You are in the realm of politics."

"I don't feel that I should stay."

"Nonsense. Don't take any of it personally. Besides, you need the job if you are ever going to get that young woman to marry you." McGillycuddy smiled and winked. "Not only that, Brownie, but I'm not going to disappear. I'll be interested to know what is happening down here. I'll need an inside man." Another wink.

"That you will always have, Mac." Brownie made an awkward move to stand in front of McGillycuddy and when McGillycuddy looked up, he was surprised to see emotion in his friend's eyes. "I've always believed in you, you know."

He looked as if he might cry and to spare them both the embarrassment McGillycuddy grinned. "Always?" He clapped Brownie on the shoulder.

"Nearly always."

"I thank you for that. Now you better get out of here before Bannister sees you cavorting with the enemy." Brownie started to say something more but McGillycuddy shook his head. "Go on now. You haven't heard the last of me."

Brownie nodded and looked up to the door. When McGillycuddy followed his stare he found Red Cloud filling the doorway. "Go on now, Brownie. It looks like the chief has come to gloat."

"I'll stay, Mac."

"No need. Go on now. Go."

Red Cloud stepped aside and Brownie passed into the street, and every evening as McGillycuddy inspected first the foundation of his new house, then the framing, roof, plaster, and paint, he recalled the odd look in the old man's eyes. *What was that look? What crack in that granite exterior?*

"You look like you've lost your best friend. Or is it your best enemy?" Red Cloud did not understand the joke and continued his stare. *Hate? Contempt?*

"It is very hard," Red Cloud said.

"You'll survive."

"Hard for us both."

McGillycuddy was making a show of packing a wooden box with the contents of his desk. "What is it that's hard for us?" The odd look on the chief's face was still the same. *Sorrow?*

"What our people expect of us."

McGillycuddy inspected the fine carpentry work of the railing around the new porch and tried to be engrossed by the craftsmanship. But he could still hear those last words of Red Cloud and he could still see the expression. *Fear.*

When their wagons were finally packed it was midafternoon and any other man would have waited for an early start the next morning. But McGillycuddy was used to traveling at night and Fanny seemed ready to move on to their new life. Fanny was up on the first wagon and beside her with reins in hand was one of Young Man Afraid's men. Around her, offering her their best wishes gathered the Blanchards and Cowgill. The second wagon carried Louise and a second of Young Man Afraid's teamsters. McGillycuddy had purchased from Ott Means a green-broke bay, saddle horse that danced sideways with the approach of every well-wisher. Only twice did the horse stand still when people came to greet McGillycuddy.

The first to charm the horse was Clearance Looking Dog who appeared from the crowd of onlookers and walked straight to where the bay stood shaking its head against the bit and raising his front end to beat his hooves down repeatedly in the same dusty spot. The old man was wrapped in his usual yellow blanket and wore his characteristic single heron feather in his graying hair. The horse snorted when he saw that the man would come all the way to them but Clearance held his hand out and the stomping ceased. The bay stretched his nose out to the old man's hand. He accepted a caress between the eyes and even nickered to hear the halting English. "For now you go, McGillycuddy."

"Yes, old man. Now I go."

Clearance Looking Dog nodded. "It will be all right. God will protect us all."

McGillycuddy leaned to stroke the nervous horse. *So comforting to believe.* "We will be protected."

Clearance Looking Dog nodded and smiled while he rubbed the horse's head. "Go then, McGillycuddy. I will see you again."

I hope so. "Good-bye old man."

After Clearance Looking Dog left, the horse stood still and was standing calm when Julia Blanchard walked to McGillycuddy's side. He looked down into her blue eyes and they shared a smile. It was as if they needed no conversation but after a moment Julia spoke clearly. "I'll be leaving this reservation for education."

"That's a good thing."

"I think our paths will cross again."

I hope they do. "We shall see," McGillycuddy said. "It is hard to know the future."

"Except to say that it will be a surprise."

"Except to say that it will be a surprise."

And then the first wagon began to roll and the horse leaped sideways with enough force that most men would have reached for the horn. But McGillycuddy floated with the animal and tipped his hat in the process. In an instant he took the lead and led his family through a throng of Indians and off into the prairie. They crossed the Cheyenne River at the same place McGillycuddy had crossed only days before. It was dark as they rose out of the valley on the west side. But there was no moon and no one saw any sign of buffalo.

*   *   *

The breakfast eaters at the Sweet Grass Grill had much to talk about during the summer and autumn months of 1889. There was a great movement afoot for Dakota to become several states and everyone, save perhaps McGillycuddy who was flattered to be looked upon as a new state leader but generally silent on the issue, was strongly in favor of statehood. The men around the table clapped the new president of the Dakota School of Mines on the back and said loudly that administration of the reservation had gone straight to hell after he resigned. They noted that the crops had failed that spring and that the new commission sent from Washington to press for the privatization of most of the reservation was meeting strong resistance. "But they'll get 'er hammered through," a dapper little barber said. "It's only right the reservations should be broken up."

"Imagine," a dry-goods merchant said, "paying those Indians a buck fifty an acre!"

McGillycuddy could not remain silent. "That's what the land is worth."

"A family needs five hundred acres to survive," the owner of an overland freight company put in, to agree with McGillycuddy. "Takes about fifteen hundred working days to buy a farm. Five years of labor to pay for a homestead. That's the same as anywhere."

The barber was scrambling to keep up with the math. "Well," he said, "one thing is sure, the commission will be successful and half the reservations will soon belong to the new state of South Dakota." This was always a safe toast at the Sweet Grass Grill and he raised his coffee cup but failed to notice that McGillycuddy was no longer paying attention.

"Hear, hear to statehood. But what of the reports of

cutting of the Lakota rations?" It was the dry-goods salesman. "I've got lady customers that think it's a scandal. They say there is starvation on at Pine Ridge. They don't like it."

Whenever Pine Ridge was brought up every face turned to McGillycuddy. They all approved of the way he had run the reservation. Their attention brought him back from his reverie. "They recounted the Indians and came up with a much smaller figure," McGillycuddy said.

"That's what my customers say. Cut the beef and flour issue to match the new population numbers. My customers say people are hungry. Say the new numbers are bogus."

"It is hard to say," McGillycuddy said as he rose to go to his college office.

"They ought to send you back there, Mr. President. Before them savage bastards get desperate enough to break out."

"Let them break out," the barber said. "There's enough army in the territory now to handle them once and for all."

"No!" McGillycuddy said and took an angry, impulsive step toward the barber. *Easy.* He caught himself and straightened his posture. "No," he said. Then he couldn't resist leaning over into the barber's face. "You've never seen war have you?" He waited a beat. Until it was clear that his hunch had been right. "No," he said once more as he straightened again. "We don't want troops on the reservation. It would be to our eternal shame if we drove those helpless people to war."

The breakfast club liked it when McGillycuddy talked with authority. "What did I tell you, by God. McGillycuddy should be the governor." They raised their coffee cups again and all was forgotten.

Everywhere he went he received that kind of respect and everywhere he went people were talking about the deteriorating situation on the reservation. And always compassion was tempered with a giddy joy over the acquisition of half the reservation and the surety of statehood and compounding wealth. The possibility of wealth from the gold fields and from the commerce that fed them and the crush of homesteaders lining up to take over the soon-to-be-opened parts of the reservation was like a fever. McGillycuddy and Fanny felt it. In addition to the presidency of the college, the McGillycuddys invested in gold mines and a power plant for the town. When they moved into their new house it made the newspaper. It was the finest house in Rapid City and was referred to as a mansion.

But neither McGillycuddy nor Fanny took as much pride in their new life as they expected they would. From their porch they could look out over the scurrying community of Rapid City as it pulled itself into being from among the cottonwoods of Rapid Creek. Beyond that slender ribbon of trees and shiplap buildings was a prairie immense enough to dwarf the plans of all the settlers. Beyond that, fifty miles off but well within their vision were the badlands that stretched rough and bleak to the reservation.

They sat in separate rockers in the autumn evening and wrestled their respective serpents. Sometimes Fanny knitted in the failing light. She tried not to dwell on her poor health. Dr. Gaylord had been good for her. Though he admitted not being able to cure her, his positive attitude had been a blessing and she did her best to bring that attitude to her marriage. She asked McGillycuddy about his workday, showed him the knitting, and waited until he was ready to bring up the subject that was distracting him. "I saw Mrs. Calbrea at the mercantile," Fanny said. "She says her husband was hoping you'd run for mayor." *Run for mare. I'd like to. Haven't ridden more than a mile at a shot for months.*

Fanny was looking at him curiously. "What is going through that devilish mind of yours?"

"Nothing but blank pages tonight."

"Never blank pages. And certainly not tonight."

She had always been able to know when things were churning in his head. He wasn't sure he should share with her the telegram in his vest pocket. She, unlike almost any other concerned settler, might understand the import of the words that George Sword had sent to him that afternoon and he had learned that keeping turmoil inside had a dangerous effect on his mood. They rocked in the early evening light and watched the distant badlands light up like a prairie fire of apocalyptic proportions. He knew a little about the nature of light rays and that the sun setting behind them was sending that light from tens of thousands of miles, but it was hard for him to understand how such power could be invisible as it passed overhead. He looked up to the clear blue sky and saw nothing to cause the badland's brilliance. "I received a message from Captain Sword today."

"I thought he had been relieved of his duties."

"He will always be captain to me."

Fanny smiled. "For me too. What did he have to say?"

"It's a bit cryptic. Would seem out of context to most." McGillycuddy pulled the telegram from beneath his coat.

"The enigmatic Indian."

"Nonsense, George simply leaves out the small talk."

Fanny smiled to think of Sword's stony face. "A sweet man, really."

"Exceeded only by Clearance Looking Dog."

"Come on. Read it to me."

The paper was folded twice and McGillycuddy straightened it out as if it were an official writ. "It is only a few sentences." And before he began to read he looked out once more to the badlands and saw the clouds over Wyoming Territory were making themselves felt as shadows on the white barren land of Dakota. "The Oglalas have heard that the Son of God has come upon the earth in the west. They say that the Messiah is there, but he has come to help the Indians and not the whites." McGillycuddy studied the telegram and smiled. "He goes on to say the obvious. The Indians are happy to hear this."

After the telegram was read they rocked for a long time in silence. "What does Brownie say?" Fanny finally asked.

"I wired him late this afternoon. Had to be a bit secretive. Gallagher has been keeping a close eye on him. I'm sure his job is tenuous as usual. He'll let us know what the Oglalas are feeling as soon as he knows."

There was nothing more to say that night and they sat quietly until the sky was almost black. When the dark began to come down hard Fanny was surprised to feel McGillycuddy's hand seeking hers. It was not something he usually did and they both felt a warmth flowing back and forth along their arms. They rocked in unison and watched the prairie stars sparkle to life.

The messiah's name was Wovoka, a Paiute from beyond the Rocky Mountains. He had seen God in a vision and was told that if the Indians did what was asked of them that the old, happy, nomadic way would return. What God asked them to do was to dance, tirelessly, day and night, until he could see that the tribes were earnest in their desire for the return of the old life. As an added bonus, it was promised that if the dancers' faith was strong enough, their ancestors would be returned to life.

McGillycuddy was not the only person to note that the philosophy behind the Ghost Dance was similar to the Christianity that had been forced upon the plains tribes beginning nearly a century before. *A clear case of being bitten by your own dog.*

That winter the tribes of South Dakota sent emissaries to Wovoka and by the summer Ghost Dances were taking place on all the recently defined and reduced reservations. The government had finally lost patience with trying to get the Sioux to agree to the legislation that placed each sub-group on their own section of what was the great Sioux reservation set up in 1868. With the drive for statehood had come a summary reduction of half the Indian land. As a partial result, across the northern plains, the messianic craze exploded into life much as it was being practiced farther west by relatively peaceful, agricultural peoples. The significant difference, as McGillycuddy expressed it, was that now the cult of fanaticism was becoming embedded within tribes whose traditions were deeply warlike. He predicted that when the Brulé, Hunkpapa, and Oglala divisions of the Lakota people began to dance to frenzy and exhaustion the dance's focus would soon become the return of the buffalo and extermination of the white oppressors. "Desperate conditions," he wrote to O'Donald, "breed desperate action. Please inform Gallagher that this Ghost Dancing is a threat to the security and safety of *all* people on the plains."

O'Donald wired back to say that Gallagher did not consider the cult dangerous but promised to lecture those that he found engaging in the Ghost Dance. Word came to McGillycuddy that crops were being left uncared for. *Who prefers to hoe instead of dance?* But by the time the dancing reached the recently resettled people of Sitting Bull on the Missouri River and the entire Standing Rock Reservation followed that great chief in his antiwhite fanaticism, Gallagher had changed his mind. When two thousand Oglala dancers refused to disperse, Gallagher was shaken and, knowing that McGillycuddy would be immediately consulted, asked O'Donald for his advice. McGillycuddy's return message was simple. "Tell the fool to talk sense to the Indians, be stern with Red Cloud, and under no circumstances allow troops to enter the reservation."

There was hope that Gallagher would follow McGillycuddy's advice as relayed through O'Donald. But that hope died when the new administration of William Henry Harrison reshuffled the Indian bureau. Politicians who had been on the right side during the fight for statehood were rewarded for their service. The post of Indian agent at Pine Ridge was filled by D. F. Royer, who was described in the Rapid City daily newspaper as totaly ignorant of Indians and with nothing to qualify him to handle even Red Cloud, let alone the grave situation of the heathen Ghost Dance.

Across the Great Plains and on all the reservations of South Dakota the Ghost Dance gained popularity and the Lakotas danced it to the exclusion of all other pursuits. In Rapid City, McGillycuddy spent most of his time at home, waiting for reports from the reservations, conferring with other leaders, and watching his wife's health deteriorate. She had gained a great amount of weight and her complexion had gone from the fairest of the fair to ruddy. But her spirits were good and, in the afternoons, McGillycuddy sat at his desk and watched her preparing her garden for winter. *The strongest and best soul I have ever known.*

It was near the first of October when he found her collapsed in one of her flower beds. A small trowel was still clutched in her hand and she blinked up at the cool blue sky. "No, no," McGillycuddy said when her lips moved. "No talking. Relax. I'm here." He held her hand and called for Louise to run for Dr. Gaylord.

When she was in her bed Gaylord arrived. *A good doctor. A real doctor.* "Close your eyes, love. Rest." And McGillycuddy kissed her eyelids gently and stroked her forehead with his goatee the way she liked. "The doctor's here."

But again, there was nothing Gaylord could do but make Fanny comfortable.

The stroke left her paralyzed and without the faculty of speech. She remained in her bed for three weeks before she began to gain some strength. McGillycuddy sat beside her and, though no one else could understand her, she could communicate with him with the use of her eyes, a tiny tilt of her head. He attended to her every need, did not go to his office, and took only visitors who brought news of the Ghost Dance and the government's response to it.

By the end of November news had come to him that Royer had tried to stop the dancing by confronting the leaders at Pine Ridge and had been laughed at. His information claimed that Red Cloud too had appealed for the people to temper their dance and he too had been laughed at. McGillycuddy read the communications to Fanny as she lay in her bed or on her better afternoons sat up in the wicker chair on the front porch.

"Everyone is scared," he told his wife. His eyes were still on the written message and so he did not catch the movement of her eyes. "Fear brings on mistakes. Mistakes make for tragedy."

When he looked up he saw that she was trying to tell him something. The left side of her face had gained some movement and her lip quivered with effort. "What should be done? Is that what you're asking?" The eyes changed and he nodded. "I don't know for sure. I would have to be there to say for sure. But I think I'd let them dance. Winter is coming and that will dampen their step. By spring, when the messiah has failed to come, they will forget it and go back to farming."

He smiled. "I'm sure you didn't want that much information."

But the eyes told him that she did. "The worst thing," he went on, "is for the army to come in and frighten them. We are dangerous people you know." He wasn't sure but he thought he detected a hint of a nod.

Part Seven

Wounded Knee

22

When the weather turned too cold for Fanny to sit on the porch McGillycuddy arranged a chair beside the front window where she could watch the last of the cottonwood leaves quiver and let go, to skitter earthward and finally into drifts across their front yard. The news from the reservations was increasingly grim. Sitting Bull, one hundred fifty miles away on his Standing Rock Reservation, had embraced the Ghost Dance and gradually the implications of the dance had expanded to include not only a return of the buffalo and Indian dead, but also the death of all white soldiers. McGillycuddy knew it could easily slide into a religion of hate.

He had not been to the college in months, had not left Fanny's side since the stroke. He worked her hands and made her stand. He insisted that she try to walk. But mostly they sat and watched out the window and he talked of when they had met, his early days as a contract surgeon for the army, their time at Pine Ridge. Some days he talked about the Ghost Dance and occasionally she would make a sound that only he could comprehend. That was the way the courier carrying the telegram from the governor found them, seated in comfortable chairs looking out at the early sunset of November. He was a rough-looking, wiry little man who had obviously ridden hard to find the ex-agent, and he handed the entire leather pouch over to McGillycuddy. "Governor asks that you read this."

"What is it?"

"I'm sure I don't know, sir. But I'm guessing it has to do with the Indian troubles. Governor wants a reply."

McGillycuddy took the pouch, extracted the letter and handed the pouch back to the little man. Before he began to read he looked at Fanny. Her eyes were as bright as they had been since before the stroke. He grinned to her but his eyes snapped back to the letter and began to course the lines like a bird dog. When he was finished, he folded the telegram carefully. "Tell him that I am unavailable."

The little man was dumbstruck. "But they need you. Troops coming in, Indians going crazy."

"I thought you didn't know what the message was about. Send a wire and tell the governor that I must remain in my home. My wife is very sick. I don't plan . . ." But his voice trailed off when he felt Fanny's hand creeping slowly along his right sleeve. He looked at her with shock and reached for her hand with his left. The hand rolled slowly in his and accepted his desperate pressure. It gave that pressure back. When he looked up into the face he saw the lips laboring to move. Then, as clearly as ever before, Fanny said, "Go."

They looked at each other until they felt the courier fidget. Their hands were clenched so tightly that their pulses mixed. Without taking his eyes off his wife McGillycuddy spoke. "Tell the governor that I will be on Pine Ridge by morning."

*   *   *

After another all-night ride on the bay horse he'd purchased from Ott Means, McGillycuddy stepped down
in front of Royer's office as fresh as if rising from a
sound sleep. He was just in time for a council called by
General J. R. Brooke, who had made a forced march
from the railroad station in Nebraska with a thousand
men and arrived only the day before. When he saw
McGillycuddy he tipped his hat. They had never met
but had dozens of common friends. "I wish you weren't
here, General."

"So do I. But I'm here and my aim is to straighten out
this mess."

"Are troops headed for the other reservations?"

"Yes."

"Standing Rock? Are they going for Sitting Bull?"

"Especially Sitting Bull. He seems to be the only old
chief who's embraced this ghost nonsense."

"He's a combative man. Not a political hair on his
head."

"A rare case where politics might help."

At the door of the council building they found a well-
dressed, portly man with a balding head. It was Royer
and McGillycuddy shook his hand coolly. *You cowardly
little shit. If you were scared enough to call in troops,
you should be truly scared now that they are here.*

Red Cloud was not at the meeting. Young Man Afraid
was there but the younger men who believed that the
messiah had come to earth to save them drowned out his
voice. Neither Brooke nor Royer had experience con-
ducting such a meeting and in minutes it was out of their
control. The believers in Wovoka shouted down what
dissent there was and Little Wound, a young chief who
had recently risen to power, spoke to McGillycuddy. "If
the messiah is not coming, and his coming will not make

us a great people again, why are you afraid, why have the soldiers come to stop our dancing?"

McGillycuddy knew enough not to remain silent but he saved his comments for Royer and Brooke. "Were I agent here," he said in a strong voice behind the office door that was once his, "I would let the dancing continue." He paced before the seated general and agent. "You have these people frightened. Let them dance. Winter is here. Only whites are foolish enough to choose to fight in winter. Dancing in the snow will dissuade them."

Brooke was listening but Royer, obviously frightened, puffed himself up to speak. "There is a clear danger here, McGillycuddy."

"There certainly is. And it will explode if you treat these people like criminals. If the Seventh-Day Adventists prepare their ascension robes for the Second Coming of the Christ the army is not mobilized to stop them. Why shouldn't the Lakotas be given the same luxury?"

When McGillycuddy left the meeting it was snowing but he did not notice. It was only five o'clock but night was settling on the main street he had built. The stores were closed, many of the whites having fled to Nebraska for safety. McGillycuddy stood near the cottonwood that had so often given him shade in the summer months and felt as alone and solitary as that old tree. The inactivity and the hush of snow conspired to accentuate a prairie phenomenon that had forever fascinated McGillycuddy. He could hear the voices of children in a camp that he knew was a mile north of where he stood. A dog barked in the distance and when he stopped to concentrate he heard the sound of ghost dancers far off in the hills above the agency. The monotonous drumbeat pulsed in his ears like his own heartbeat and the drone of the dancers' chant filled the void between the thuds.

He was jolted from his reverie by the sound of Red Cloud's voice. "They have been dancing for eight days." McGillycuddy jumped and spun but the old chief stood perfectly calm. "They will dance until the savior comes or until they die."

McGillycuddy was not yet over his fright. "Good God, man." Then he saw the worry on Red Cloud's face. "There is no savior," he said.

Red Cloud nodded. The snowflakes were large and the wind no more than a breeze. The flakes settled on the wrinkled old face and melted against an expression that McGillycuddy had never seen. It was necessary to lean forward and squint to search Red Cloud's face. The sound of the distant Ghost Dancers drifted over them with the snow. "They have killed Sitting Bull," Red Cloud said.

McGillycuddy hardly knew what Red Cloud was talking about. Sitting Bull, Red Cloud's only real contemporary and equal, had been settled on his own reservation for years. "The soldiers came and shot him in his cabin."

"Nonsense. Why would they kill Sitting Bull?"

Red Cloud raised his chin in the direction of the dancing. "He believed."

Some kind of cockamamy vision. "There has been no word of trouble at Sitting Bull's agency. The telegraph wires have been quite silent."

Red Cloud shook his head slowly. "They have killed Sitting Bull. They will kill many more." He looked at McGillycuddy with rheumy eyes. Scared. "They will kill more."

*   *   *

What Red Cloud had known by seemingly supernatural means was confirmed by telegraph the next morning. On Sitting Bull's Standing Rock Reservation the Ghost Dance had reached a fever pitch and the Indian police, believing that Sitting Bull was behind the unrest, were sent out to arrest him. Sitting Bull, like thousands of dancers, had taken to wearing a long shirt painted with the likeness of celestial bodies in the belief that white bullets could not penetrate a ghost shirt. Forty-three policemen were sent out to Sitting Bull's cabin in the early morning of the fifteenth of December. A detachment of army troops was held in reserve at the agency in case they were needed. When the police arrived they found Sitting Bull's horses saddled and it was believed he was ready to ride for Pine Ridge where the Ghost Dancers were gathering from all over the plains.

A half dozen policemen crashed into the cabin and found the chief sleeping and unafraid. When they emerged with the old man in custody they found that one hundred fifty of Sitting Bull's supporters, dressed in ghost shirts and dancing to conjure up their savoir, had surrounded them. When the shooting began, the guards who held Sitting Bull in his own doorway, shot him without thought. The old chief, survivor of many battles died instantly of a head wound delivered from very close range. The Lakotas cut down the policeman who had fired the shot and, had it not been for the detachment of cavalry called into action, the slaughter would have been complete.

As the battle raged, Sitting Bull's people fled into the rough country of the Missouri River breaks. By nightfall perhaps a thousand Ghost Dancers were making their way through the badlands winter to the distant reservation of their last war chief, Red Cloud. The journey would be one hundred fifty miles and the Ghost Dancers were not only on foot but without supplies or shelter.

The first McGillycuddy knew of the new situation was when he emerged from the hotel to find two twelve-pound howitzers set up at the end of the street and pointed at the nearest Indian camp. Forgetting for a moment that he was there as an observer and was no longer agent, he strode up to the officer in charge and demanded an explanation. The officer was young and had no idea who McGillycuddy was. "I'm sure it's none of your business," he said. "Don't come any closer." His right hand moved to the sword handle at his hip.

"Good God, you pup, show some intelligence."

"You're the one who should show some brains. Step back."

The soldier meant what he said. *Step back. Forget the little bastard.* McGillycuddy sputtered and fought to hold his tongue but did not take his eyes off the soldier until he saw from the young man's demeanor that someone was coming up behind him. The officer took his hand off his sword and stood at attention.

It was General Brooke. "McGillycuddy, you're here for the governor. Might as well ride along with us. They're dancing on the White River. Come with us for a little reconnaissance." Now the general was standing between the young officer and McGillycuddy. He looked at the two men and shook his head. "Come along McGillycuddy. Carry on, Captain."

They rode for three hours toward the northeast. The general, Royer, and McGillycuddy stayed close and talked while an escort of thirty men rode fore and aft. "General Miles wants an assessment," Brooke said.

"Miles?" McGillycuddy was shocked that the famed Indian fighter seemed now to be in charge of what Brooke and Royer referred to as an outbreak.

"He's set up a command headquarters in Rapid City. Wants to know what the hell is going on down here. How many foreign dancers are here."

"A great number I'm afraid," Royer said as he bounced along behind them. "My reports say they cover the mountains along the White River."

Mountains along the White River? "You've never been on the White, have you, sir?"

Royer did not reply but when they finally arrived at the ridge above the camp where the Ghost Dance was taking place he rode to the front of the column and was the first to look down on the sight. For a mile McGillycuddy had, like the night before, felt the vibrations of the drums and when he rode up beside the clearly frightened Royer he too pulled his horse up abruptly. Below them were several hundred tepees and between the lodges and the ridge from where they observed was a circle of perhaps a thousand Indians. They were only a few hundred yards away and McGillycuddy was amazed that they had posted no guards until he recalled the belief that the ghost shirts they wore were impervious to bullets. He could see by the cut of the tepees that this Oglala band had been joined by Brulés from the Rosebud Reservation. He saw no sign of Hunkpapas from Standing Rock but he knew that this was only one dance camp of several on his old reservation and he had no doubt that Sitting Bull's people were slogging their way through the snows of the badlands to join this gasp of hope. McGillycuddy had been on such tortured winter marches and knew that there would be hundreds of frozen and bloody feet. They would try to find night shelter in the caves of the badlands but the subzero winds would search them out. He could imagine how the Ghost Dancers would seem to be their only hope. The dancers before them were men, women, and children. They shuffled their feet and raised their arms. They stretched out their fingers to their God.

"We should ride down there," McGillycuddy said.

"We've come only to observe," the general said.

"I think we've seen enough to know that they are on the verge of war," said Royer.

"Nonsense. They are praying." McGillycuddy touched his heels to his horse's flanks.

"Praying for our deaths," said Royer. "Don't go down there."

"We should go down. Talk."

Just then, the dancers sighted the column and though the dance did not stop, a few warriors moved out to be between the women and children and the troops. There were two puffs of smoke from the warriors and the bullets whizzed over the heads of the troopers. "That's enough," Brooke said. McGillycuddy was several yards down the hill. "Don't tempt fate McGillycuddy."

"I'm here as an assistant adjutant. Under orders from the governor." Another bullet sizzled over their heads and Royer retreated over the crest of the ridge.

"And I'm here under orders from the United States of America." The general's demeanor had changed. "Get your ass up here, Doctor. You are not in charge."

23

McGillycuddy filed his report to the governor knowing that his recommendation for calm would be lost in the frenzy of rumor. General Nelson A. Miles, famous for his relentless winter pursuit of the Sioux, sent more troops to patrol the frozen badlands where the terrified stragglers from Sitting Bull's reservation were suspected to be. The dispatches that came to McGillycuddy in his hotel room at Pine Ridge called the refugees reinforcements for the Ghost Dancers of Red Cloud.

But Red Cloud was taking no part in the Ghost Dance. In the nights that followed McGillycuddy paced the street outside the hotel. He could hear ghost drums from three distinct directions. The dancers' camps stayed alive day and night in the hope of conjuring up the dead. McGillycuddy could not sleep and walked to the livery stable and then to the edge of the settlement. He stood in the bone-cold stillness and listened. And when he ventured as far as Red Cloud's house he saw the old chief sitting with his wife on their frigid porch.

McGillycuddy watched them from a distance as they listened to the same incessant drumbeat that kept McGillycuddy awake. They sat close together and motionless, wrapped in blankets with a buffalo robe across their laps. Clouds of moonlit breath puffed from them as they exhaled. And once McGillycuddy knew they were there he could not keep away from the shadow of the cottonwood where he could see but not be seen. He listened to the drums and watched the old people throughout the week before Christmas, and on Christmas Eve the drums were joined by hymns from the Episcopal church where the whites, who were hardy enough to remain, celebrated the coming of their own Savior. Their songs were clear and sweet but the drums of the Indian messiah were more persistent and McGillycuddy listened to them into the morning of the twenty-sixth, long after the Christians were asleep.

Many groups of Ghost Dancers were moving in the badlands north of the reservation and troops of cavalry coursed those snowy hills with orders to arrest groups that had moved in from other reservations. Three days after McGillycuddy and Red Cloud had listened to the night filled with Ghost Dance drums and Christmas carols, Maj. Samuel Whiteside, commanding Custer's old outfit, the Seventh Cavalry, cut the trail of a large group of Ghost Dancers moving onto the reservation from the chaos of Sitting Bull's murder. The group was led by a Minneconjou chief named Big Foot and though Oglalas from Pine Ridge had joined it, most were foreigners, subject to arrest.

As soon as the ragged Indians saw the troops they raised a white flag. Of the three hundred fifty Indians, two hundred thirty were women and children. They were cold, mostly afoot, hungry, and very frightened. Whiteside, acting under orders, took the wanderers into custody, marched them to a campsite on Wounded Knee Creek, and sent a messenger into Pine Ridge with the news that a large group of dancers from Standing Rock were in custody and would be disarmed in the morning. McGillycuddy was standing at the cottonwood in the deep of night when the messenger rode past. He was overjoyed to be part of the troop that captured Big Foot's band and told McGillycuddy what had happened and what was to happen at first light. *Great God!* "And where are these people being held?"

"Wounded Knee Creek. Got them bedded down in the valley with a pair of Hotchkiss guns on the hills keeping an eye on them." The soldier laughed. "About enough firepower to blow them all to hell if they try something."

McGillycuddy knew the weapon. It shot explosive rounds at a rapid rate for distances up to two miles. He also knew Wounded Knee Creek: the place where the heart of Crazy Horse was buried. The stage was set for disaster but it seemed that only McGillycuddy was aware of it. It was possible that he was the only white man who knew the exact place. His first thought was to wire Miles in Rapid City. But even if he could convince Miles, there was no way that a message of caution could get to Whiteside before he began the process of disarming the dancers.

The night was bitter, clear, and the stars shown as icy pinholes in the black sky. The moon had not risen by twelve o'clock when he made his decision. He went to his hotel room and pulled out all his heaviest clothing, then made his way down the empty street to the livery stable. He banged on Ott Means's door until a lamp was lit inside. "What? What is it?"

"I need my horse, Ott."

It was long after midnight before McGillycuddy was saddled and ready to go. He and Ott stood at the barn door of the livery and listened to the distant drums. "It's been going for weeks," Ott said. "If the northern tribes join them there is going to be trouble."

McGillycuddy swung up on the horse and adjusted his buffalo-robe coat. "The northern tribes have arrived," he said and leaned forward. But Ott caught the bridle.

"You be careful, Doctor."

It was the first time Ott Means had ever called him doctor. "Thank you, Ott. I'm not so worried about myself, but thank you."

McGillycuddy put his horse into a trot. He would have to keep him moving at a good pace to reach the camp on Wounded Knee Creek by first light. The sound of the hooves on the snowy road blended with the sound of the ghost drums in a way that made McGillycuddy wonder at the relationship between the two sounds. He could have believed that there was only the sound of his horse had he not passed Red Cloud's house and seen the old couple leaning into the night. They were not listening to the rhythm of his horse and he could not tell if the raised hands were in greeting or disdain.

There was no direct road to Wounded Knee Creek, only a matrix of trails that was difficult to follow even after the moon was high. McGillycuddy pushed the bay as hard as he dared. He was sharp shod and willing but the snow and ice made it too dangerous to encourage him to lope. McGillycuddy was not sure what he would do when he reached the incarcerated Sioux and their captors. He wanted to help avoid a calamity but didn't know what his role might be. The only thing he knew for certain was that he would have no role if the bay slipped and fell on him. There might not be another

traveler for a day or more. A broken femur would mean
freezing to death on a forgotten trail in the center of the
Pine Ridge Reservation. *A man could do worse.* It had
been the choice of Crazy Horse, the wild Oglala that
McGillycuddy respected the most. No, the *man* that
McGillycuddy admired the most. And it occurred to
him that he was within a few miles of that sacred grave.
Had there been more time he would have visited his old
friend. But there was no time. He pushed his horse as
hard as he could but felt the vague blue light of dawn
long before he hoped he would.

He was not sure where he was until he saw the first
light of morning touching the top of Porcupine Butte.
The butte was northwest of his destination and he was
perhaps six miles straight south. *East, one drainage.*
Now, in spite of the danger, he kicked the bay into a
lope. The high ground received filtered light from the
rising sun but the lower trail was still black and
McGillycuddy gave his safety over to the bay. They
rocked steadily toward the top of the ridge that he believed separated them from the wide flat valley of where
the Sioux were camped. If he was right about where he
was he would top the hill a couple miles above the
camp. He scanned the ridges for sentries. *Whiteside has
certainly posted sentries.* But there were no sentries by
the time he reached the top of the hill and could look to
the next high country. He was one drainage off. The
camp was still a mile off and now he could see that there
were indeed soldiers on the next hill.

It was light enough that the army would begin to dis-
arm the Indians soon and the ride took on the feel of a
dream: the goal forever receding. Suddenly it was vital
that he at least get to within view of the camp on the far
side of the snowy valley. The bay was game and they

moved into a run. Down the hill and plunging into drifted snow at the bottom. They rode through a crystalline cloud and lunged up the other slope toward where the sentries stood looking down on the camp at Wounded Knee Creek. So engrossed were they with watching the scene in the camp below that they did not notice McGillycuddy charging up the rise at their backs. There were five artillerymen and McGillycuddy was among them before they were aware of him. The first thing he saw when he reached the top of the hill was the deadly Hotchkiss gun. It was chained in place like an attack dog and the long blue barrel was trained on the valley a quarter mile below.

With the added height of his heaving horse McGillycuddy could see that Whiteside had been reinforced in the night and the well-armed troopers had the Indian camp surrounded. *Sweet Mary and Jesus.*

When McGillycuddy saw that the disarming had begun the world slowed for him. The bay's deep breaths moved him like the motion of the sea. The Hotchkiss men jeered at him and in the camp below soldiers moved among the desolate Indians. Already a pile of knives and hatchets stood guarded at the edge of the camp and other weapons were being tossed on the heap. Only one old musket was hurled toward the pile and it turned slowly, end over end, as if the air were thick as water. The warriors were being ordered to remove their tattered blankets to be searched and when they did, they revealed their protective Ghost Shirts and even at the distance of several hundred yards, McGillycuddy could see the anger of this indignity.

McGillycuddy was already moving when the soldiers came to Black Coyote, a deaf Indian that McGillycuddy had known for years. When the Winchester came from under the blanket McGillycuddy was reaching hard with his riding crop. But the air was like syrup and he was still a hundred yards short when the first bullet hit Black Coyote. In an instant the world snapped back to real time. Then doubled.

The air went thin and lethal with hissing bullets. Indians and soldiers leaped for each other's throats. The Hotchkiss guns began to spit death over McGillycuddy's head and he knew that there was nothing he could do. *Perhaps there never was.*

The frozen unarmed warriors struggled with the soldiers and if they could wrench a weapon loose they used it with inspiration until a volley of rifle fire cut them to pieces. They fought with the strength of fathers, sons, and brothers. And at first they fought with the conviction that their shirts would protect them. But the point-blank rifle fire laid the warriors low and exposed the fleeing women and children. McGillycuddy could hear an officer call out for a cease-fire, but no one heeded his pleas. The rifle fire continued until dead and dying women and children cluttered the slope. The blood of the dead pooled in the snow and the trails of the fleeing wounded were wide and gruesome. As the survivors of the rifle volleys moved out of range of the soldiers the Hotchkiss guns began to bark from the hills. A woman was blown to pieces and her infant cartwheeled into the air.

The Seventh Cavalry pressed the attack and even as McGillycuddy found his senses and rode to the nearest wounded, the sound of sabers being drawn exploded a rage in him that only a supreme act of will could quell. *The wounded. The wounded. Your place is with the wounded.*

*   *   *

By noon the sinister popping of rifles in the surrounding hills had ceased and the temperature had begun to fall. McGillycuddy had commandeered a tent and taken command of the scant medical corps that rode with the Seventh. For five hours he triaged the wounded: the minor wounds bled into the snow at the side of the tent, he had sent a wagonload to the hospital at Pine Ridge, and there was another wagonload to go. The hopelessly grim were dying in the snow where they fell. He had stripped off his buffalo coat and covered a mother with a severed hand and dead toddler. He bound the stub with rawhide but did not even try to take the child from her arms. Her death song found the nucleus of every cell.

He worked into the freezing afternoon wearing only his white shirt and by the time the snow began to fall the front was soaked in blood. If even five minutes passed without replenishing that blood, the shirtfront froze stiff. But he did not feel the cold until all the survivors were headed for the hospital at the agency. Two officers had hovered near him all day. They did not dare confront him at first. Later, feeling his rage dissipate to bone-numbing sadness, they tried to apologize. But McGillycuddy would not listen. And when the officers and the corpsmen mounted their horses to escort the last wagonload of survivors they did not bother to ask him to come along with them. They left him in front of the tent and one of the enlisted men found his buffalo coat and hung it over his shoulders as he sat on an improvised bench of empty ammunition boxes. By then it was snowing with the huge twisting flakes that indicate that the temperature is below zero.

A few soldiers were left to guard the one hundred fifty bodies of the Indians that were strewn over the val-

ley, filling now with fluffy snow. They retreated to their
tents and McGillycuddy felt like the only living soul on
Wounded Knee Creek. He marveled at the quiet, the settling cold, the dark patches of blood, and the grisly
snow drifts that gathered behind the fallen warriors,
mothers, and children. There would be no drums that
night. The Ghost Dance was over.

Now there was nothing but ghosts. McGillycuddy
hunched in misery beneath the tent's canopy. Below
him, on the plain of Wounded Knee Creek, nothing
moved except the wind and the occasional shred of
cloth from the rags of the dead. The good bay horse
stood tied and hipshot behind the tent where he had left
him. A thoughtful corporal had unsaddled and fed the
horse. He stood with his rump to the snowy wind.
McGillycuddy stared out at the field of corpses and
tried to make sense out of what he saw. But there was
no sense to be found. From the hill where the guards
were camped came the sound of merriment. *A tapped
keg of whiskey. For all our shame.*
    He looked down at his hands and beneath the blood
of the wounded his skin was turning blue from the cold.
But he felt nothing. Memories and regrets pushed down
on him but he was not ready to reconstruct what had
happened, not ready to figure his part in any of it. Then
a nicker came from the bay tied at the back of the tent
and when he looked up there was another horse far out
on the field of death. Its rider dismounted and stood
stunned and confused in the field of fallen souls. It was
an Indian and dully McGillycuddy wondered if the soldiers camped above would shoot him too. But there had
been enough killing and the whiskey had their attention. The man was allowed to wander from corpse to

corpse, to bend and touch a familiar face, to straighten the blanket of a friend. McGillycuddy stared for a long time before he recognized that the Indian was Red Cloud.

The old man was wrapped in a blanket and his graying black hair was neither tied nor braided. It blew and mixed with the snowy breeze as he moved to kneel over each body in turn. He moved slowly, as if his arms and legs were sacks of grain. When McGillycuddy stood and began to walk toward the chief, he too felt heavy. The snow was six inches deep and fluffy from the terrible cold. McGillycuddy's feet dragged as he moved the hundred yards to the old, stooped-shouldered man.

The snow cushioned his footfalls and the wind masked the swish of his buffalo robe. He was beside Red Cloud before the old man knew he was coming. But when his old nemesis looked up, there was no surprise in his face. Just the deep wrinkles of age, the cold squinted eyes, and snow gathering in the wild hair. "McGillycuddy," was all he said.

Between them lay a body but the men looked at each other. Their eyes went deep into the other's and time ceased to matter. *Have I ever looked at this man before?* Wind. *Has he ever looked at me?* And when their eyes had had enough they looked down at the body between them. It was an old man, wrapped in a shabby blanket with a dirty shawl covering his gray hair. He was distorted in death, his legs twisted beneath him and his arm and fingers frozen into inhuman shapes. Red Cloud and McGillycuddy sank to their knees in the snow as they looked down at the old man. And when Red Cloud pulled the scarf away to reveal the face of Clearance Looking Dog, a ghastly wail rose and filled the field of death. The source of the wail was unknowable. It seemed to seep from the hills and trees that surrounded them. It oozed from the snow that was quickly covering the body of Clearance Looking Dog.

The terrible wail frightened McGillycuddy and his eyes searched for the source. But when he looked to Red Cloud, the old chief's lips were pursed and silent against the cold. *My God!* The wail increased in intensity and Red Cloud's eyes went wide and awestruck. *My God. It's me.*